"A perfect storm of great
storytelling, fast-moving plot,
and rich historical detail....
Chanel Cleeton's best yet!"
—KATE QUINN

The LAST TRAIN to
KEY WEST

A NOVEL

CHANEL CLEETON

New York Times Bestselling Author of *NEXT YEAR IN HAVANA*,
A REESE WITHERSPOON BOOK CLUB PICK

"A gorgeously atmospheric homage to a country and a past that vibrates with emotion on every page. Historic events, espionage, and a Kennedy-esque romance make this novel a rich read, but the addition of a formidable heroine truly makes it unputdownable. This is not just historical fiction, but also an unrequited love story for a country and a way of life, as well as a journey of self-discovery for a woman torn between love and the two countries she calls home."   —*New York Times* bestselling author Karen White

"Cleeton once again delivers a masterful tale of political intrigue tinged with personal heartbreak. Her ferocity and fearlessness can be found on every page, and Beatriz's story—one of vengeance, betrayal, and bravery—astonishes and thrills."
                                        —Fiona Davis, national bestselling author of *The Masterpiece*

"Scintillating. . . . An intriguing dive into the turbulent Cuban-American history of the 1960s, and the unorthodox choices made by a strong historical woman."
                        —Marie Benedict, *New York Times* bestselling author of
                                                            The Only Woman in the Room

"Atmospheric and evocative, *When We Left Cuba* captivates with its compelling portrayals of the glamorous Cuban exile community and powerful forbidden love set against the dangerous intrigue of the Cold War. Unforgettable and unputdownable!"
                        —Laura Kamoie, *New York Times* bestselling coauthor of
                                                                    My Dear Hamilton

"By turns a captivating historical novel, a sweeping love story, and a daring tale of espionage—I absolutely adored this gem of a novel."
                        —Jillian Cantor, author of *The Lost Letter* and *In Another Time*

"Oozing with atmosphere and intrigue, *When We Left Cuba* is an evocative, powerful, and beautifully written historical novel that had me completely captivated from the first page to the last. Take a bow, Chanel Cleeton!"

—Hazel Gaynor, *New York Times* bestselling author of
The Lighthouse Keeper's Daughter

"With a sure hand for historical detail, an impeccable eye for setting, and a heroine who grasps hold of your heart and never lets go, Chanel Cleeton has created another dazzlingly atmospheric and absorbing story of Cuba and its exiles. A beautiful and profoundly affecting novel from a writer whose work belongs on the shelves of every lover of historical fiction."

—Jennifer Robson, *USA Today* bestselling author of *The Gown*

"Powerful, emotional, and oh so real. One woman's fight to reclaim her own country, against all odds and no matter what the cost is intertwined with the real history of our lifetime and creates an unforgettable story."

—Rhys Bowen, *New York Times* bestselling author of
The Tuscan Child and the Royal Spyness Mysteries

"Rich in historic detail, *When We Left Cuba* has it all—the excitement of a page-turning thriller, the sizzle of a steamy romance, and the elegant prose of a master storyteller."

—Renée Rosen, author of *Park Avenue Summer*

"Cleeton draws you into the glamour, intrigue, and uncertainty of the Cuban exile community just after Castro's coup through a heroine who could give Mata Hari a run for her money. . . . You'll be rooting for Beatriz to change the course of history—and find her own hard-won happily ever after."

—Lauren Willig, *New York Times* bestselling author of *The English Wife*

"With a richly imagined setting and a heroine worth rooting for from the start, *When We Left Cuba* is thrilling and romantic, and timely to boot."

—Michelle Gable, *New York Times* bestselling author of *The Summer I Met Jack*

"A compelling, unputdownable story of love—for a man, for a country, for a past ripped away, and a future's tenuous promise. *When We Left Cuba* swept me away."

—Shelley Noble, *New York Times* bestselling author of *Lighthouse Beach*

"Electric and fierce. Beatriz Perez's romance with a handsome, important senator will sweep you away, but it's her profound loyalty to Cuba and her formidable determination to be her own woman despite life-and-death odds that will really hold you in thrall."

—Kerri Maher, author of *The Kennedy Debutante*

"In a tale as tempestuous as Cuba itself, *When We Left Cuba* is the revolutionary story of one woman's bold courage and her many sacrifices for her beloved country. An absolutely spectacular read!"

—Stephanie Marie Thornton, author of *American Princess*

"Beatriz Perez's brand of vintage-Havana glamour dazzles with equal parts intrigue, rebellion, and romance to make for an unforgettable story."   —Elise Hooper, author of *The Other Alcott*

"*When We Left Cuba* is a breathtaking book, and it captures what I love best about historical fiction."

—Camille Di Maio, author of *The Way of Beauty*

"A beautiful novel that's full of forbidden passions, family secrets, and a lot of courage and sacrifice." —Reese Witherspoon

"A sweeping love story and tale of courage and familial and patriotic legacy that spans generations." —*Entertainment Weekly*

"This Cuban-set historical novel is just what you need to get that ~extra-summery~ feeling." —Bustle

"The Ultimate Beach Read." —*Real Simple*

"*Next Year in Havana* reminds us that while love is complicated and occasionally heartbreaking, it's always worth the risk." —NPR

"A flat-out stunner of a book, at once a dual-timeline mystery, a passionate romance, and paean to the tragedy and beauty of war-torn Cuba. Simply wonderful!"
—Kate Quinn, *New York Times* bestselling author of *The Alice Network*

"Cleeton has penned an atmospheric, politically insightful, and highly hopeful homage to a lost world. Devour *Next Year in Havana* and you, too, will smell the perfumed groves, taste the ropa vieja, and feel the sun on your face."
—Stephanie Dray, *New York Times* bestselling coauthor of
America's First Daughter

"Don't miss this smart, moving, and romantic story."
—HelloGiggles

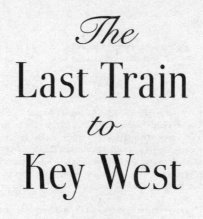

The Last Train *to* Key West

CHANEL CLEETON

BERKLEY
NEW YORK

BERKLEY
An imprint of Penguin Random House LLC
penguinrandomhouse.com

Copyright © 2020 by Chanel Cleeton
"Readers Guide" copyright © 2020 by Chanel Cleeton
Penguin Random House supports copyright. Copyright fuels creativity, encourages diverse
voices, promotes free speech, and creates a vibrant culture. Thank you for buying an authorized
edition of this book and for complying with copyright laws by not reproducing, scanning, or
distributing any part of it in any form without permission. You are supporting writers and
allowing Penguin Random House to continue to publish books for every reader.

BERKLEY is a registered trademark and the B colophon is a trademark of
Penguin Random House LLC.

Library of Congress Cataloging-in-Publication Data

Names: Cleeton, Chanel, author.
Title: The last train to Key West / Chanel Cleeton.
Description: First Edition. | New York: Berkley, 2020.
Identifiers: LCCN 2019051313 (print) | LCCN 2019051314 (ebook) |
ISBN 9780451490889 (trade paperback) | ISBN 9780451490896 (ebook)
Classification: LCC PS3603.L455445 L37 2020 (print) |
LCC PS3603.L455445 (ebook) | DDC 813/.6—dc23
LC record available at https://lccn.loc.gov/2019051313
LC ebook record available at https://lccn.loc.gov/2019051314

First Edition: June 2020

Printed in the United States of America
3   5   7   9   10   8   6   4

Cover art: image of model: Vogue 1952 © Henry Clarke/Condé Nast via Getty Images;
background image of Key West, Florida © Westend61/Getty Images
Cover design by Sarah Oberrender
Book design by Kristin del Rosario
Interior art: palm tree pattern by Nata Kuprova/Shutterstock.com

To my family, my heart

The Last Train to Key West

One

SATURDAY, AUGUST 31, 1935

Helen

I've imagined my husband's death a thousand times. It starts, always, on the boat. There are waves, and perhaps some wind, and then he's pitched over the edge, into the sea, the water carrying him away on a strong tide, his head bobbing in the churn of turquoise and aqua, the vessel swaying to and fro in the middle of the ocean without another soul nearby to come to its aid.

Sometimes the image assaults me as I go about my day, hanging the laundry on the clothesline, the white sheets flapping in the breeze, the scent of lye on the air. Sometimes I ease into it, my thoughts lulling me away as I daydream, when I'm frying the fish Tom catches when he goes out on the *Helen*, a vessel with whom I share two things in common: a name, and the fact that our glory days have long since passed.

Other times it comes to me in sleep, and I jolt awake, my breaths harsh and ragged, mixing with the sound of my husband snoring beside me, his hairy arm thrown over my waist, his breath hot on my neck, the scent of gin oozing from his pores.

This morning, it's the dream, and when I wake, no arm holds

me down; the space beside me is empty, an indent in the mattress from where my husband's body lay.

How could I have overslept?

I dress quickly, going through my morning ablutions efficiently in the water closet, hoping for the proper balance between looking pleasing and expediency. The tenor of our days is set in the mornings, in the early moments before Tom goes out to sea, the sun hours from showing its face.

If Tom is happy, if the weather is good, the fish plentiful, if I do as I am supposed to, it will be a passable day. If Tom isn't happy—

A wave of nausea hits me. Pain pulses at my abdomen, settling deep in my lower back, and I brace myself against the bedroom wall. The baby kicks, and I slide my hand down to catch the end of the movement.

These past few weeks, the baby has become more active, rolling and jabbing, pushing to make its way into the world now that the due date is near.

The nausea subsides, and I right myself, the pain passing as quickly as it came.

I walk from the bedroom to the main part of the cottage. Tom is seated at the table shoved into one corner of the open room that serves as our kitchen, living, and dining space.

When Tom first brought me here after our marriage nine years ago, it seemed the perfect place for us to start our life together—the home where we would grow our family. I scrubbed every inch of it until it shone, roamed the beaches when Tom was out to sea, and collected all sort of interesting things that had been cast ashore by boaters and smugglers, repurposing them as furniture we could ill afford to buy. The dining table where Tom's body looms was once a crate that likely carried contraband alcohol back in the day when doing so was a crime.

Where I once cleaned with pride for all of the possibility of what could be, I now see the loss of all we could have been, the house where I poured so many dreams just another promise left unfulfilled.

Floorboards are missing, paint peeling on the exterior, our living space shared with all manner of beasts and vermin that push their way inside all available nooks and crevices, the proximity to the water—not even fifty feet away—the only thing to recommend it.

Tom's boat is moored in the cove, within an easy distance. When Tom is at sea, the cottage is cozy, the mangroves surrounding us our protection from the outside world. When he is home, it is a pair of hands around my neck.

"Storm's coming," Tom rumbles, his back to me, the added weight from the baby making my footsteps heavier than usual, announcing my presence before I have steeled myself for the first moment of contact. His chair is positioned so he can gaze out the window at the ocean beyond. For a fisherman, the weather is everything.

"Rainstorm in the Bahamas," he adds, his voice gruff with sleep and an indescribable undertone that has developed through the years of our marriage. "It'll head this way eventually."

It was Tom's love of the sea that first drew me to him—the way the water clung to his skin, the faint taste of salt on his lips when he'd sneak a kiss, the wind in his hair, the sense of adventure when he would go out on his boat. I was younger then, just fifteen when we started dating, sixteen when we married, and I was drawn to things that seemed innocuous at the time—his big hands, the muscle and sinew in his tanned forearms, the broad shoulders built from days hauling boxes and crates of questionable origins. I thought he was a man who would keep me safe—another promise broken.

"Will the weather be bad?" I ask.

We get our fair share of storms down here in our little corner of the world. We've been fortunate we haven't had a strong one recently, but when I was just a girl, we had a nasty hurricane hit Key West. Luckily, no one died, but I still remember the wind blowing my parents' cottage around, the water threatening to engulf it. I was absolutely terrified.

"No one seems to think it's anything to worry about," Tom answers. "Heard on the radio that the Weather Bureau thinks it'll miss us."

"Will you go out on the water today?" I struggle to keep my tone light. I've learned not to press the issue of where he'll go or what he'll do. Times like these, a man will resort to all manner of things to put food on the table.

Tom grunts in acknowledgment.

I walk toward the countertop, careful to keep my body out of reach, my hip connecting with one of the knobs on the stove, my foot brushing against the icebox in the floor.

In a cramped cottage, in a cramped marriage, you learn to use the physical space around you as a buffer of sorts, to make yourself fluid and flexible, to bend to the will of another. But now, my body has changed, my stomach bloated, my limbs ungainly, and I've had to relearn the art of taking up as little physical space as possible— for me and the baby. It's difficult to be quick when you carry the extra weight of another.

I set Tom's breakfast in front of him.

He clamps down on my wrist, applying just the right pressure to make me wince, but not enough to make me fall to my knees. The state of our relationship isn't just evident in the physical condition of the cottage. I bear the marks of our marriage, too.

"Why do you want to know if I'm going out on the water?" he demands.

"I—I was worried. If the weather is bad, it'll be dangerous."

He tightens his grip, his fingernails digging into my skin. "You think I don't know my way around the sea? I've been fishing these waters since I was a boy."

My wrist throbs, my skin flashing hot as the pain crashes over me, my knees buckling beneath the weight of my belly and the pressure of his fingers.

I grab the edge of the table with my free hand, struggling to steady myself.

"I know. It's the babe. This close, I'm just nervous. I'm sorry—"

Words fail me as the pain crests, and I babble nonsensical things, anything to get him to let me—us—go, to stop this escalating into something more, something far worse than bruises on my wrist.

Tom releases me with a muttered, "Women," under his breath.

My wrist throbs as he shifts his attention to the food I prepared for him.

He digs into the johnnycakes with vigor, his anger momentarily forgotten.

He eats quickly, and I go about my morning routine straightening the kitchen, sounds breaking into the daydream I slip into like a well-worn dress—his fork scrapping across the plate, the chair sliding across the floor, the heavy footfalls that follow him out the door, until I am alone once more in the cottage on stilts.

WALKING FROM OUR HOUSE TO THE RESTAURANT WHERE I WAIT-ress, my feet treading the familiar sandy ground, I pass lines of men trying to pick up extra work for the day. I'm lucky to have my job at Ruby's with the Depression going on, the opportunities few and far between, and even more so for women. But Ruby's nothing if not loyal, and she's kept me on in good times and bad.

As the "Southernmost City," Key West is the end of the road, the farthest you can venture in the United States before your feet meet water. Such a distinction brings all manner of people: wanderers, criminals, people wanting to get lost, people wanting to get found, as though anything is possible down here at the edge of the world—for most of us anyway. It used to be, you had to have a boat to get here, but now there's the railroad that runs over the ocean, connecting the little islands that make up the Keys to the mainland and Miami, the total journey spanning over one hundred and fifty miles and a few hours' time, an ambition Mr. Henry Flagler—one of the richest men in the country when he was alive—was ridiculed for when he announced the project decades ago. But Mr. Flagler pressed on, and the railroad was built, bringing jobs to people like my father—native Conchs—and men who came down to the Keys searching for work who laid the tracks for the Key West Extension with their bare hands.

The railroad's one of the greatest things man's ever built, Daddy would say. *Can you imagine? Flying over the ocean in one of those big machines?*

I couldn't.

What sort of men dreamed of building things like floating railroads? What sort of people rode in them?

Daddy told me there were two kinds of people in this world:

The people who built things with their own two hands, and the kind of people who enjoyed the things others built. But then the Depression came, proving to be the great equalizer.

A long time ago, before I was born, Key West was the largest and wealthiest city in Florida. But even before the rest of the country felt the effects of the crash in '29, Florida struggled. Money and credit ran out, and problems have plagued the citrus crop. Now, people are out of work, hungry, and desperate, the city bankrupt, our fortunes anything but certain, thousands moving north with the hope of a better life.

There's some help from the government, which I suppose is better than no help, but it's never quite enough. They're trying to fix up the city, shipping veterans from the Great War down to the Keys to work on a new piece of highway linking Grassy Key and Lower Matecumbe.

At the corner of Trumbo Road and Caroline Street, I pass the railroad station as I have nearly every day for the past nine years. Beyond it lie the new docks. The Florida East Coast Car Ferry Company offers daily service to and from Havana, Cuba. They load dozens of freight cars onto the boats, taking them, cars, and passengers across the sea. Flagler's vision of connecting New York City to Havana is made possible by a few days of travel on his railroad plus several hours' ferry journey from Key West.

The familiar worn sign comes into view when I arrive in the parking lot of Ruby's.

Our proximity to the railroad station and the ferry terminal inspires visitors, the locals attracted by the possibility to gawk at the newcomers and take advantage of Ruby's low prices. Ruby doesn't hold much with pretensions, and it shows, the decor simple, the food hearty. It's the sort of place whose measure you take as soon as you walk through the doors, a restaurant that relies more on the food to recommend itself than the atmosphere.

We keep a steady pace of customers from the moment I arrive to midday, and I move from table to table, an ache settling in my back, the baby pressing down low. In the free moments when I'm able to sneak a break, I stand in the rear of the restaurant, leaning against the wall to relieve some of the pressure. The smells coming from the kitchen are nearly too much for my stomach, but at this point in the pregnancy, I'm so eager to take some weight off my feet it hardly matters.

The front door opens with a loud clang of the overhead bell, an awkward crash, the flimsy wooden structure no match for the large man whose hand rests on the handle. Heads turn, the noise rising above the sounds of the kitchen, the diners' conversations. The newcomer's cheeks redden slightly as he ambles through the door and gently guides it closed behind him.

I don't have to look to know which table he's taken. For the past several months, he's become a regular fixture in the restaurant even as he keeps to himself and his corner. The only thing I know about him is his first name—John—and even that was offered reluctantly months ago.

"Your favorite customer is back," Ruby says with a wink from her perch in the kitchen as she wipes her hands on the apron tied around her waist. As far as bosses go, Ruby and her husband are about as good as you can get. They pay a fair wage considering the times, and they have a tendency to keep an eye out for the staff from the kitchen they run. If a customer gets too friendly or too rowdy, Ruby and Max are always ready to swoop in. Ruby's not exactly what you'd call sociable, and she's content to keep to the cooking and leave the greeting and serving to me and the other waitress, Sandy, but over the years she's become more than just my employer—a friend of sorts, I suppose.

"Must be payday judging by how many of them have trickled down here this weekend. He seems hungry today," she adds.

"He always looks hungry," I retort, ignoring the amusement in Ruby's voice and the gleam in her eye.

"It's funny how he always eats here, isn't it?" Ruby drawls. "Real curious."

"It must be for the key lime pie," I reply, keeping my tone bland. "Everyone knows you make some of the best key lime pie in Key West."

The key lime pie isn't just a popular choice because Ruby's is the best in town. People still have to eat as well as they can, and pie's one of the cheapest things on the menu.

Ruby smiles. "I'm sure that's what brings him here—the key lime pie."

John is always polite, definitely quiet, but no one who gets within a few feet of him can miss the fact that he's clearly seen some ugly things in his time and carries them in a manner that suggests for him the war is far from over. He shouldn't make me nervous—he always tips better than most, and he's never given me any trouble—but there's something about him that reminds me so much of Tom that it nearly steals my breath when I'm around him.

When I set his food on the table before him, it's as though another man sits in his stead, with the same immense size, the power to use that physical advantage to inflict harm, and I instinctively wait for his meaty hand to seize my wrist, for him to overturn the plate of food because it wasn't hot enough when I brought it to him, to throw his meal at me because he's tired of eating the same thing every day and don't I know how hard he works, what it's like out there on the water, don't I appreciate all the food he puts on my plate when so many have so little, when people are hungry, how can I be so ungrateful, so—

And suddenly, I'm not back in the little cottage where all manner of sins are hidden by man and mangroves, but at Ruby's, my breaths coming quickly now.

"You all right?" Ruby asks.

I shudder. "I am."

"If waiting tables is getting to be too much this close to the baby coming, we understand. I could come out from the kitchen to help more. Or maybe Max could try his hand at it."

I'm lucky they didn't fire me when I began showing; I can hardly afford to lose this job considering no one else would hire a woman in my condition.

"I'm fine, but thank you. Besides, we need the money."

It's difficult enough to feed two mouths right now; I haven't quite figured out how we're going to manage three. Then again, it hardly seems worth fretting over. Life happens whether you're worrying about it or not, and it seems presumptuous to think we have much of a say in how things play out.

I trudge toward the new arrival, refilling a coffee cup or two along the way, prolonging the encounter as much as I can.

A wave of nausea hits me again, and I sway.

"Do you need to sit down?"

Surprise fills me.

The only things I've ever heard John say in addition to his name pertain to his order, as though God only gave him a certain number of words to use each day, and he'd already expended his quota before he sat in my section.

He's a big man with a thick neck, broad of shoulder, and tall, so very tall. His body strains against the fit of his threadbare white shirt and his ragged overalls, his large hands clutching the silverware, making it seem dainty in comparison, his table manners at odds with his rough appearance.

His voice is surprisingly gentle for such a big man, the words coming out cool, crisp, and not from around here.

"I'm fine," I reply, letting go of the table instantly. "Thank you, though."

His cheeks flush again as he angles his body away from mine. On his weekend trips into Ruby's, I haven't seen him in the company of the other veterans working on the highway. They never fail to acknowledge him with a nod of their heads or a tip of their hats, but they move past him as though he has erected a barrier around himself. He is one of them, and yet, he is not.

Much of the town has given the veterans a wide berth, complaining of general drunkenness and disorderly conduct when they come down to Key West for the weekends. In the tight-knit communities up on Matecumbe and Windley Keys where the population is smaller and the days—and nights—quieter, they're probably even less welcome. These are difficult times, and when you're at your lowest, fear and uncertainty have a nasty habit of making you close ranks and view outsiders with suspicion, even if you're cutting off your nose to spite your face. For all we need the railroad and highway to bring the tourists in, you'd think the locals would be a little nicer to the people working on them, but then again I've given up on trying to understand why people do the things they do.

People are a mystery, and the second you think you have them figured out, they surprise you.

"How much longer?" John asks, straightening in his seat, his gaze on my swollen belly beneath the worn apron. His eyes are a rich brown, a shade darker than his hair, framed by long lashes most women would envy.

I flush at the matter-of-fact manner in which he asks the question.

Pregnancy has a way of exposing your most private intimacies to the world whether you'd like them to be exposed or not.

"A few weeks," I reply.

The baby kicks again.

John's eyes narrow slightly as though he is attempting to work something out in his mind. "You shouldn't be on your feet so much."

I don't spend much time worrying about "should." As much as Ruby has some affection for me, she's running a business here, and there've been times when this job has meant the difference between us having food and going hungry when Tom's hit the bottle too hard to go out to sea or drunk his pay away.

"Can I take your order?" I ask, ignoring the intimacy.

"I'll have eggs and bacon," he answers after a beat. "Black coffee, too, please."

He orders the same thing every time he comes in here.

"It'll be a few minutes," I reply.

I lean forward and brush a speck of food from the table left from one of my earlier customers, and my sleeve rides up on my forearm, exposing the dark purple bruises that decorate my skin.

Five fingerprint-sized bruises, to be exact.

I tug the sleeve back in place, my cheeks heating.

"What happened?" he asks, his voice low.

"Nothing," I lie.

You can tell he's not a local, because I doubt there's anyone left in Key West who doesn't know that Tom Berner gets a little rough with his wife when he drinks—and when he's stone-cold sober.

"Can I get you anything else?" I struggle to keep my voice steady, to plaster a polite smile on my face.

I don't want his judgment or sympathy; have no use for well-meaning words that would do more harm than good. What's between a man and his wife is a man's business, or so they tell me. I am Tom's wife, Tom's possession, to do with as he wishes.

The baby will be his whether I wish it to be or not.

John shakes his head in response to my question, letting me know he doesn't need anything else, and he is once again the taciturn stranger to whom I have grown accustomed.

The bell above the front door rings, and the room quiets considerably more than usual as new arrivals stroll in.

The woman is far more elegant than our typical fare, in a dress that looks like it came from Paris or some fancy city like that. She's beautiful in an almost untouchable way, as though she sauntered off the pages of *Photoplay* or one of those other Hollywood magazines, her hair an inky black, a slash of red across her lips, her skin flawless. The dark-haired man beside her strides in like he owns the place, while she appears as though she's skimming through the water, gliding through life.

Railroad folk for sure. I've never seen a dress like hers in all my life.

They sit at one of the empty tables in my section, and I head over to my next customers, but not before the daydream sneaks up on me again, and I envision Tom out there in his boat on the sea, the wind whipping around him, the waves growing stronger, a storm brewing in the distance, lightning cracking through the sky, thunder booming, the heavens unleashing their righteous fury.

I close my eyes for an instant and offer the prayer that has run through my head for much of my nine years of marriage.

I pray the sea will keep my husband and he will not return to me.

Two

※

Mirta

"Milk?"

I glance up at the blond waitress, struggling to form a response to her question.

What kind of wife doesn't know how her husband takes his coffee?

From the moment Anthony led me into Ruby's Café, all eyes have been on us. My dress is too formal for such a simple place, my jewelry ostentatious, my features darker than those of the other customers.

I have never felt more out of place in my life.

"I'm not sure," I reply, stumbling over the unfamiliar English, my stomach churning, the breakfast I ate hours earlier on the ferry from Havana to Key West leaving a metallic taste in my mouth. The entire journey, I feared I would lose my battle with the nausea and upend my eggs and fruit on Anthony's flashy black leather shoes. I hardly slept during the ferry ride, the question of whether my husband would choose that moment to consummate our marriage weighing heavily upon me. In the end, though, my worries were for naught. However Anthony chose to spend the journey, it wasn't in my bed.

The waitress's brow rises at my response, the milk jug hovering in midair. Her eyes widen as her gaze sets on my ring finger, her reaction to the diamond not far off my own when Anthony presented it to me weeks ago.

"Milk, please," I decide, taking a wild guess while Anthony is outside making a phone call.

The waitress leans forward to pour the milk in Anthony's waiting coffee cup, a wisp of her nearly white blond hair escaping the bun atop her head. She's pregnant, her stomach jutting out of her petite body with an aggressive force that suggests the baby could be due at any moment, the coffeepot seemingly too heavy for her slender wrists and hands to bear. Her skin is chapped and red, nearly raw in places.

She appears to be about my age—in her early twenties, perhaps, or a few years older. Far too young for the tired set of her eyes, the hunch of her shoulders.

And still—she's quite lovely.

She reminds me of one of the watercolors that used to hang on a wall in my parents' house in Havana—muted, faded colors giving the distinct impression of loveliness, an ephemeral quality to her beauty. There's a nervousness to her movements, though, a jittery frenzy of limbs at odds with her serene countenance.

Belatedly, I flip the diamond on my ring finger around so it's no longer visible, a hint of shame pricking me at the ostentatiousness of the stone, the clothes *he* paid for. If fate had turned out differently, would I have ended up like this woman: my clothes worn and threadbare at the seams, eyes tired and filled with desperation?

"We're newlyweds," I offer as an explanation for my milk faux pas, even though it explains so little. Even newlyweds have some prior relationship history, a shared affection and understanding.

The waitress's mouth opens as though she has something to say, but she closes it almost immediately, her attention no longer on me, but on Anthony, striding through the door, all long-limbed confidence and brawn.

He is a handsome man, my new husband, as glitzy as the diamond on my finger, the sort women can't help but admire, the type men gravitate toward in smoke-filled clubs where less reputable dealings and questionable stock tips—the little to be had these days—are passed between glasses of rum. His reappearance in the restaurant earns him a fair number of stares, his natty suit as out of place as my dress.

He is a handsome man, and—*most importantly*, to my parents, at least—he is a wealthy and well-connected man, though rumors of the sources of his amassed fortune run the gamut from the decadent to the truly criminal. These days, it hardly matters. Money bought him a wife whose family had run on desperate times. I never learned what he and my father settled on—whether it was gold, or property, or some other manner of valuing his only daughter—but my thoughts on the situation hardly mattered.

"Did you order lunch?" Anthony asks me, our language another barrier between us.

I am most comfortable in Spanish, he prefers Italian, and so we must do with English, the only language we have in common.

How are we to build a life with so many differences between us?

"No, I didn't order yet. I wasn't sure what you'd like. Your coffee is here." I gesture toward the cup, waiting to see how he reacts to the drink. I know so little about him: his likes, his personality, his temper.

The waitress walks away during this exchange, hips swaying as she manages the tray in her hands.

"I talked to my friend on the phone," Anthony says. "We'll drive up on the highway and catch a ferry that will take us the rest of the way to Islamorada. The staff has readied everything for us."

I twist the ring around my finger once more, unused to the weight of it, the sharp prongs holding the diamond in place that occasionally dig into my skin. What sort of man buys his wife a ring like this in times like these?

Anthony's dark brows knit together, his gaze on my hands. "Is it too large?"

"Pardon me?"

"The ring."

I stop fidgeting.

"Is it too large on your finger?" he clarifies. "We can take it to my jeweler when we get to New York if you'd like to have it resized."

New York is to be our final destination, by way of the Florida East Coast Railway in a week or so after we've honeymooned at Anthony's friend's house in Islamorada. I've never been to New York, know not a soul, yet somehow it is to be my home, where I am to bear his children, live out the remainder of my days. No matter how many times I tell myself this is to be my future, I can't quite reconcile how my life has changed so suddenly and with such finality. I can't picture what our days will entail or how I will learn to be this man's wife.

Will my family visit? My parents? My brother? Will my new husband ever take me back to Cuba? His business interests brought him there initially after the revolution in 1933, but he's said nothing of his long-term plans, whether he intends to return.

Will I ever go home again?

"The ring is fine. Beautiful. I don't think I thanked you properly," I add, remembering my mother's earlier advice that marriage would be easier if we were able to find common ground between us, if he found me agreeable.

Powerful men are busy men, Mirta. They do not wish to be bothered with problems in the home or the trivialities of your day, the vagaries of your moods. Your aim should be to make your new husband happy, to alleviate the pressures of his life, to make him proud.

Her words came to me as she buttoned me into a white lace gown, the pins holding the dress in place pricking my skin. She shoved a bouquet of ivory flowers in my hands, last-minute instructions for a whirlwind wedding. Of the wedding night, I received no advice.

"When I saw it, I knew it was perfect for you," Anthony says, and I stifle the urge to grimace.

It's hardly the sort of jewelry I would have chosen for myself. It's too big, too gaudy, too much. In these times, with the political fortunes such as they are in Cuba, we've all learned to survive by not calling attention to ourselves. I can hardly fault him for the mistake, but still, I add it to the pile of small indignations I am accumulating surrounding this marriage.

"I like the restaurant," I say suddenly, eager to do anything but talk about the ring.

"Really?" He glances around the crowded seating area. "I worried it might be too plain for you. I'm sure you were used to finer establishments in Havana. But I thought it would be easy since it's so close to the ferry. You hardly ate on the trip."

"No, it isn't the sort of place I normally frequented," I admit, even though the novelty is precisely what makes the restaurant so intriguing.

When my father supported President Machado, our position was secure, and we lived within the insular world of Havana society.

Two years ago, everything changed.

Cubans grew tired of Machado's dictatorship, and economic

worries fueled by the crisis in the United States and a political movement led by many of the university students spurred tensions and violence within the country. The troubles building, the Americans intervened diplomatically, and eventually, Machado was ousted and forced into exile by a group led by some of his army sergeants. His followers—the Machadistas—have been hunted since the military coup, their bodies scattered throughout Cuba, hanging from lampposts, dumped along roadsides, burned to death in town squares.

By the grace of God or some other unseen hand of fortune, my father survived, but he made the mistake of backing the wrong candidate for power, and now Fulgencio Batista—elevated to colonel—pulls the strings in Cuba and is the one to whom we must ingratiate ourselves.

My older brother Emilio has been tasked with overseeing our sugar business, with forging a better relationship with the new regime, cozying up to Batista. Our father's close relationship with Machado has left him in disfavor, though more fortunate than many of his friends who lost their lives, so now Emilio must set the course for the family.

"Once we might have spent our days out in society," I reply, choosing my words carefully. "More recently, we spent a fair amount of time at home. There was a circle of families who, like my father, lost their position after the revolution in '33 that brought Batista to power."

Anthony and I have spent the last couple of years living on the same island, but we weren't really living in the same country. The casino and hotel business might have brought him to Cuba thanks to Batista's new ties with the Americans, but he was little more than a visitor, shielded from the horrors the rest of us feared.

"I wondered how you spent your days and nights," he says. "I would see you out in Havana, but you were always coming or going. I never saw where you ended up."

I flush. "No doubt my final destinations were far less interesting than yours."

"Perhaps." He smiles. "I didn't think ladies wished to frequent nightclubs and casinos."

"It's hard to know what you'd like when so many doors are closed to you."

Something that might be understanding flickers in his gaze.

While it is far easier to be a man than a woman, in this we likely share a common albeit tenuous bond—there is a difference between earning money and being born with it, and no doubt my husband with his likely ill-gotten gains knows a thing or two about having doors closed to him.

And still—somehow his path crossed with my father's enough for them to play cards, for Anthony to suggest a marriage between us. There are so many questions burning inside me, but my mother's voice is in my ear once more, so instead of demanding the answers I crave, I settle for making polite small talk.

"Do you do much business in the Keys?" I ask him.

"Some, although not as much as I once did. The ferry and railroad have certainly been useful additions to the region. We'll soon see Key West as a major trade route—after all, with its close proximity to the rest of the United States, Latin America, and Cuba, there are untold opportunities for success."

Given the rumors about my husband's business interests, it seems he has a knack for finding chances to make money. They whisper that Anthony was a bootlegger before the United States government ended Prohibition two years ago, smuggling alcohol and contraband between Cuba and the United States.

My new husband is said to be a friend of Batista, as are so many of these Americans now planting their flag in Havana, a fact that must have greatly influenced my father's decision to marry us off. In these times, having a man in the family who has the ear of the most powerful man in Cuba is a great incentive indeed.

"Do you travel much in your line of work?" I ask in yet another attempt to piece together our future. In my experience, most men are more than eager to talk about themselves as much as possible, but my husband is remarkably close-lipped about his life.

This might be the most we have spoken together in succession.

"Sometimes."

I wait.

Once it becomes clear he isn't going to elaborate, I try again.

"Do you enjoy traveling?"

For a moment, he almost looks confused by the question. "My interests have become more spread out as the years have gone by, and it's important I keep an eye on them. You can hire good people to work for you, but it's helpful to maintain a personal interest, to remind them what's at stake."

"And your interests in Cuba? Do you intend to go back?"

"I have business there, of course—the hotel and casino. You would like to visit your family. You will miss them."

There's no need to pose it as a question; he has a very good sense of how much my family means to me and how far I am willing to go to protect them. My father wanted me to marry Anthony, and so I did, because following my family's wishes without protest is what I have been raised to do.

I envy men the freedom to choose their own spouses. They snap us up as though they are purchasing a piece of fruit at the market, and we are expected to have no say in the matter.

Anthony's speaking of the house where we are to spend our honeymoon, and while I sit there, watching his full lips move, I cannot really hear anything, am able to do little more than nod as though I understand, as though I am here with him, when really I am out to sea, drowning, lifting my arms in the air, asking someone to save me while people pass me by.

"Does that suit?" Anthony asks, and I jerk my head like a marionette.

How will I survive this strange marriage?

Three

Elizabeth

"Call me Eliza," I purr. "All my close friends do."

This is not strictly true—I am Elizabeth in all circles, most frequently *Elizabeth Anne Preston* when my mother is vexed, which she often is. It hardly matters, though; on this train, I can be Eliza if I like. Besides, the line does the trick as I'd hoped. The college boy sitting across from me on the Florida East Coast Railway train flushes as I lean back in my seat, the pale curve of my leg flashing his way before I cross my ankles again, his attention momentarily drawn away from my face.

Who said the trip to Key West had to be boring?

For much of the over-fifteen-hundred-mile journey since I boarded the train in Penn Station, it was one small, depressing, no-name town after another, the view offering little to recommend it. Finally, the scenery changed. Brown and gray became aquamarine and sapphire, Mr. Flagler's railroad eventually living up to its vaunted reputation. Flagler and my grandfather were friends of a sort in their lifetimes—well, acquaintances, if I'm being truthful.

No matter how much my mother wishes it were otherwise, even in our heyday we didn't have Standard Oil money. The last name Preston might mean something in this country, but the value is diminished considerably when you're a mere cousin to greatness, your family status relegated to invitations to the odd wedding and funeral, a reunion every few years.

College Boy and I have been doing this dance for five states, at least. He's traveling home, on break from some fancy university in Connecticut, and I'm, well, more than a little antsy for the journey to be over.

We started our flirtation when the train left Penn Station in New York City, my unease over the length of the trip mollified by the sight of his broad shoulders and elegant suit. We exchanged pleasantries, engaging in the familiar game of which families we had in common, boys in his fraternity whom I've known throughout the years. The car is busier than anticipated, likely due to the Labor Day holiday weekend and the sale the railroad is advertising to entice business, but we've sought out each other like two magnets drawn together, sharing cigarettes and a flask of whiskey as the train rolled down the tracks.

At Key Largo, I allow him a peek at the barest hint of cleavage, my dress several seasons past fashionable, hardly the only castoff in my closet.

There are those who would say I should endeavor to not draw attention to myself, but I've never been much for what other people say, which I suppose is part of the problem. So a red dress it is to match my hair and lips, the color attracting the regard of every man in the carriage save one.

The man in the gray suit.

I noticed him when he boarded the train in Miami and slid into the seat across from mine with little fanfare. I noticed him even more when he proceeded to *not* notice me back for the next several hours while I conjured up in my mind all the possibilities of who he could be.

Unlike the other passengers, who began looking out the window as soon as we neared Key West, their attention diverted by the view, the majestic Atlantic Ocean on one side, the equally stunning Gulf of Mexico on the other, he's engrossed in whatever he's reading as though he has no interest in the scenery.

"Did you see that?" College Boy asks, his expression filled with excitement. "Look at the fish below."

The corner of the man in the gray suit's mouth quirks. Almost a smile.

"Neat," I drawl, my gaze not on the school of fish swimming in the water a couple dozen feet below but on the man sitting across from me. That half smile is the closest thing I've seen to a human emotion since he boarded the train. And still—

He doesn't bother glancing up from his papers.

What can possibly be so interesting about some dusty old pages anyway?

"I'm going to see if I can get a better view in the observation car," College Boy announces.

I dismiss him with a wave of my hand, his affections easily won, my attention firmly on the man in the gray suit now, the challenge too delicious to ignore. The journey's almost over. Surely, he'll look up.

I lean forward in my seat, giving my book a little shove off my lap, making absolutely no effort to conceal my intent.

The book hits the train floor with a thud.

Something that sounds a lot like a sigh escapes from the man in the gray suit.

I wait.

He moves, his big body uncoiling as he leans forward to pick up the book I've dropped. I shift in my seat, advancing at the exact moment he does, perfectly aware that the movement puts him in direct line of sight with the impressive décolletage of my strained dress.

He emits a noise—somewhere between a sharp inhale of breath and a sputter—and my lips curve.

Gray Suit hands my Patricia Wentworth novel back to me wordlessly.

His eyes are a lovely, solemn shade of brown; his hair is a neat close-cropped blond intermixed with strands of brown, and perhaps, a touch of steel. He must be thirty, at least.

He's not handsome, not in an obvious way, but he has the look of a soldier about him, all square-jawed goodness.

"I've been waiting for you to notice me," I say in a breathless voice, fluttering my lashes, trying to summon a suitable blush, my skills rusty. My social life has become one of the casualties of this Depression, my technique not what it once was when men flocked around my skirts and danced attendance upon me.

Gray Suit doesn't respond, but he straightens in his seat slightly, his gaze pinning me.

"Did you notice me?" I ask.

His lips twitch. "Sure did."

Another bat of my eyelashes. "And what exactly did you notice?"

He snorts. "That you're trouble."

I wait for the rest of it. Despite their protestations, I've learned most men like a bit of trouble. You could say I've cultivated a study of it, if you'd like.

When he doesn't reply, I lean in closer, allowing him to get a whiff of my French perfume—the last of it, anyway, which I assiduously diluted with water to eke out the remaining scent.

"And what's your opinion on trouble?"

"I don't have time for trouble." He smirks. "And certainly not the barely legal kind."

"I'm twenty-three."

"Like I said."

"How old are you?" I retort.

"A lot older than twenty-three. I don't have time for spoiled girls with more time on their hands than sense." He gestures toward his paper. "There's enough trouble in this world. No point in searching for more."

If I was easily deterred, I wouldn't be here on this train, and I've yet to meet the man who could resist a pair of fine legs and a hint of cleavage. Everyone knows these are desperate times, and in desperate times, everyone plays it a little fast and loose—among my set, at least. When you've lost it all, it's hard not to feel as though there's little to be gained by following the rules, by playing it safe.

My heartbeat picks up as I lean forward again, on the precipice of tipping out of my chair entirely, my lips inches from his ear. Goose bumps rise over my body at the scent of masculine soap and skin.

"You might like it," I tease.

Gray Suit doesn't flinch at my words or pull back in alarm. Instead he holds steady, the only discernible motion in his body a tic in his jaw.

In the beginning, this was merely a game, one I've been playing since God gave me breasts and hips, and Gray Suit wasn't wrong: at the moment, I have more time on my hands than anything else. But in the space between my approaching him and now, my lips inches away from his warm, tanned skin, the game has changed.

I want to kiss him.

I pull back with a jerk.

He doesn't look at me, as much as look through me.

"I don't believe I would like it," he replies in that accent that could be from anywhere, really.

I open my mouth to offer up some retort, but the words fail me, the bravado I've clung to for so long eluding me.

Emotion clogs my throat, embarrassment hot on my cheeks, and I rise from my seat on unsteady legs, choosing a different seat from the one I previously occupied, away from College Boy, away from everyone, my gaze trained on the water rushing below the tracks.

My father owned shares in this railroad once upon a time when I was still a girl living in a gilded world. Before the crash. Before we lost everything. Before he killed himself.

I pull the letter from my pocketbook, the envelope worn, the paper creased, reading over the words there, clinging to the faint thread of hope that brought me to Key West.

The rocking motion of the train lulls me to sleep.

FOUR HOURS LATER, WE ARRIVE AT THE MAIN TERMINAL IN KEY West, and I wake to the sounds of passengers moving around me. At some point, someone draped a blanket over my shoulders.

Gray Suit is nowhere to be seen. Now that the journey is over and I'm *here*, I can't quite muster the energy for flirtations.

I step off the train, bag in hand, the humidity in the air a shock to a girl's system. The water is within walking distance, palm trees peppering the landscape, so different from what I'm used to back in New York.

There's comfort to be found in the hustle and bustle of the city, in the anonymity of bodies brushing against you on the street, the buildings around you forming a phalanx of sorts. There are boundaries in the city, streets forming a map for you to follow, putting one foot in front of another and carrying on.

I always avoid the section of streets down near Wall Street, the ones I used to walk with my mother on our way to visit my father in his office. Another life.

I take the letter out of my pocketbook once more, rubbing my fingers over the Key West postmark.

My stomach rumbles, eliciting a sound that would make Mother cringe. There's a diner off in the distance, a weathered white sign with faded lettering proclaiming it to be:

Ruby's Café.

And in smaller letters below, the auspicious moniker:

Best key lime pie in town.

I slip the letter back into my pocketbook, opening my change purse and quickly counting my money. My heart sinks.

As I stuff the meager supply back in the purse, my fingers brush against something metallic, the platinum prongs of my engagement ring digging into my skin, sharp enough to draw a drop of blood.

I take a deep breath and set off in the direction of Ruby's Café.

Four

Helen

Labor Day weekend keeps us busier than normal, a steady stream of locals, tourists, and veterans enjoying their time off, distracting me from the discomfort brought on by the baby.

In that strange in-between transition from lunch to dinner, the restaurant crowd thins, and I duck outside and sit on one of the wooden benches in front of Ruby's.

A gleaming black car is parked near the restaurant, the young woman I served earlier standing beside it, her husband nowhere to be seen.

"Is everything all right?" I ask.

"Flat tire," she replies, her words tinged in an accent I recognize from the Cubans who frequent Key West, enjoying the close proximity and the ferry service between the two places. "My husband went to find someone to fix it."

I've never been to Cuba myself; Tom always said we would go when we were newly married. After all, his fishing often took him to the island, and he would disappear for weeks at a time, returning to me smelling like rum, cigar smoke, and the hint of a woman's perfume. Eventually, though, the promises became less and less frequent until I gave up on the idea entirely when I realized I was likely better off not knowing what he did down there.

The elegant car's front right tire is indeed flat, a jagged gash the obvious source of the problem.

"Did y'all get in an accident? That's a nasty cut."

"No."

"Did this happen while you were eating in the diner?"

"It might have. We aren't certain, but we didn't notice anything wrong with the car until we came to leave. It certainly wasn't like that when they unloaded the car from the ferry."

"Sorry for the rough welcome. It's not the greatest neighborhood, to be honest. We get our share of rowdies pouring out of the bars on Duval Street. A car like that draws some notice." I gesture toward Ruby's behind me. "You can wait inside if you'd like. Get a break from the mosquitoes."

"I'm fine out here, but thank you. I need the fresh air. It's been a long day with the ferry crossing."

"Is Key West your final destination?"

We get our fair share of people passing on to other places. One of my favorite things to do when tourists come through the doors is hear where they're headed. Sometimes I'll look up the places on the map in the public library, imagining what it would be like to go there myself. I've had hundreds of adventures that have taken me all over the world. If a place strikes my fancy on the map, I'll ask one of the librarians for a book about it. When Tom's away, those hours spent reading in the cottage are some of the happiest I've ever experienced. When he's home, the books go back in their hiding spot. Tom says too much reading in a woman—which is any reading at all, really—is a dangerous thing.

"We're headed up to Islamorada," she answers. "For our honeymoon. Then to New York later on."

Islamorada's not the sort of destination I envisioned for someone so glamorous, but I suppose if they're searching for privacy on their honeymoon, they'll certainly find it.

Her gaze drifts to my stomach. "How much longer?"

"A couple weeks. It's my first," I add, fielding the question about other children before she can ask it. It's such a seemingly innocent discussion that can bring so much pain.

Her gaze lingers on the simple tin band on my ring finger. "You and your husband must be very happy."

I lay my palm over my stomach. "I have always wanted to be a mother," I say simply.

As scary as this change in my life is, as uncertain as the future that lies before us, my love for this child is the only thing I don't doubt. I don't tell her about the losses preceding this one, the times I couldn't be sure if it was Tom's fists or my own body failing me, how desperately I prayed for this babe, even as it felt like a wholly selfish wish considering the life I had to offer my child.

Her brow furrows at my response, and there's something in her expression—

"Are you all right?" I ask again.

Her eyes well with tears. "It's nerves, right? Every new bride experiences this."

"I don't know," I answer truthfully, surprised by her candor, her manner at odds with her flawless appearance.

When I married Tom at sixteen, I practically ran down the aisle with excitement, and look where that got me.

"Do you think he's a good man—your husband?" I ask. "A kind man?" He seemed polite enough at the restaurant—people tend to show the truest parts of themselves when they're dealing with those who serve them, and I've certainly waited on a ruder person—but

I've given up thinking of people in absolute terms. People are what circumstances make them.

"We married quickly. There wasn't much of a chance to get to know each other."

I can't help it—my gaze drops down to *her* waistline.

Her cheeks flush. "My family wanted us to marry."

"I wish you the best, then." I pause. I don't normally share so much with strangers—or anyone, really—but despite the obvious differences between us, there's something about her that is so familiar. I know what it's like to feel alone. "Marriage is complicated. It's no easy thing to bind yourself to another, for their moods to dictate yours, for your needs to come second to theirs, to bend yourself to the will of another. It's exhausting," I confess.

"I'm sure. My name is Mirta," she offers after a beat.

"I'm Helen." I try to smile. "I hope your experience is different."

"I'm sorry yours isn't." She swallows. "Was it always like this?"

I think back to the beginning, nine years of marriage eclipsing my memories of when we were young and Tom used to visit me at Ruby's, when he returned from the sea smelling like salt, and fish, and sun, and freedom, and I loved nothing more than to bury my face in the curve of his neck, wrap my arms tightly around his body, his strength a sturdy barrier that I thought would keep the world's problems at bay.

There were happy times, weren't there? There had to have been. They're muted and faded now, as though they belong to another person, as though *I* am another person, but they existed once. Somehow, though, those moments drifted away before I realized it, and the other parts of our marriage that used to be sources of shock and fear became ordinary events.

"No, it wasn't," I reply. "It was a different time when we married. We were poor, of course, but it was a different kind of poor. We had a good run before things started to go bad. We had a little house and maybe one day we'd have a baby, and there were plans to be made."

We had hope back then. Even after things got bad, Tom had his boat. He used to say a man who was willing to work with his own two hands could do anything. But it turned out the boat wasn't enough. He had the ability to catch food, but fish weren't useful for much when people didn't have money to buy them.

"He changed," I answer finally, decisively now. "Or life changed us."

And at the same time, there are plenty of good men in this world who lost everything like the rest of us and didn't start beating their wives or drinking away the remainder of their paychecks. Maybe those qualities were always inside Tom, and I never saw them.

"How do you know?" Mirta asks, her face pale, her eyes wide.

So young.

"How do you know if you've married the sort of man who would change?" I finish for her.

She nods.

"I'm not sure you can know. Did you want to marry him?"

Was she like me—swayed by a pair of broad shoulders? Did she have fanciful thoughts of ocean air, the breeze blowing in her hair? Did she seek adventure? Was she so recklessly in love that she knew her own heart but not his?

"I don't know. I wanted to be a wife. To have a family. I thought I'd have more say in the matter."

I want to do more, say more. Despite the differences in our circumstances, I remember what it felt like to be a new wife, trying to build a family and a home with little to guide me. At least I had the benefit of moving down the road from my parents when I married Tom. I can't fathom what it must be like to move to a new country with a spouse who is little more than a stranger.

There's a commotion behind me, Ruby calling for me.

"My break's over. I should get back to work."

"Thank you for talking to me." Mirta leans forward and wraps her arms around me in a quick hug, and when she pulls back, I check to make sure none of the grime and grease from my day got on her stylish dress. "Thank you," she whispers again. "And good luck. I hope everything works out for you and your child."

"Same to you."

I linger for a moment, struggling for the right words to give her, but none come.

The helplessness is the hardest part, that sensation of being trapped by life, by circumstance and all the things out of your control wearing you down day after day, month after month, year after year. It's enough to make you want to run away and never look back. It's enough to make you rail against the world.

I see it in her eyes, a spark, a flash of anger, hot and sharp, transforming her into someone else entirely. Someone I recognize.

I smile back at her.

"YOU HAVE ANOTHER ONE," RUBY TELLS ME WHEN I WALK BACK into the restaurant.

The new customer is young and pretty. At first glance her clothes are fine, but there's something slightly off about the way they fit, as though they were made for a younger girl, a body still on the cusp of womanhood.

The hemline is shorter than what's fashionable, the belted waist tight despite her slender frame. Her necklace is lovely, though, adding a dash of style to the whole ensemble you typically don't see in these parts.

Definitely not from around here.

A traveling case rests on the ground next to her, appearing as though it was fine once but has seen its share of better days.

"Runner," Ruby predicts.

"Clothes are too nice for a runaway."

Ruby snorts. "Rich kids got problems, too."

They probably do, but when so many of your struggles revolve around money, it's hard to envision any other sort.

"She looks like she's in trouble," I murmur.

"Or like she came down here for a getaway like the rest of them." Ruby's gaze sweeps over the restaurant. "It'd be a shame if a storm comes and all their vacation plans are ruined."

She doesn't say the rest, but I hear the unspoken worry in her voice—if a storm does hit us, the restaurant will lose out on the business we all desperately need, too.

I walk over to the newcomer's table. "Good afternoon. Welcome to Ruby's Café. What can I get you?"

"Coffee, please. Black."

"Anything else?"

The girl hesitates, her teeth sinking down on her lower lip. "No, thank you."

I revise my earlier assessment. Maybe she was rich once—her clothes and natty little suitcase certainly have that appearance about them—but now she looks hungry and scared.

"I'll be right back with the coffee."

I pour her a coffee in the back and add a slice of key lime pie from the kitchen.

Ruby shakes her head as I walk by with the plate in hand. "You're a soft touch, Helen."

"She's a kid."

"And you have one on the way. Sooner than later, judging by how that baby's dropped in the last week or so."

"And I hope if my child is ever hungry, alone, or scared, someone will do right by them."

She sighs. "I'll add it to your tab."

Tom will wonder why I bring him less this week, but I suppose I'll deal with that later.

I walk over to the table, stopping to take another order on the way, and set the key lime pie and coffee in front of the girl.

Her eyes widen. "There's been a mistake. I didn't order any pie. The coffee is fine."

"It's on the house," I reply, and because I recognize the determined glint in her eyes, the pride there, I lie and say, "No one's ordering it, and we'll have to throw it out at the end of the day. You're saving me the trouble, honestly. The scent makes me sick. I haven't been able to go near the stuff."

I can't tell if she believes me or if she's too hungry to care, but she picks up the fork, scooping up a bite of the pie, her eyes closing for a moment as she swallows it.

There's an art to the girl's movements, a daintiness that reaffirms my impression that someone once taught her to dine as though she is at a formal dinner, her posture erect and graceful. You can tell a lot about a person by watching them eat.

"Good, right?"

She flashes me a bright smile. "Yes. Thank you."

"Is there anything else I can get you?"

"Actually, I'm looking for someone."

"Most everyone in Key West comes through Ruby's at some point."

"Best key lime pie in town," she mutters under her breath.

I grin. "Can't argue with that. Who are you searching for?"

"He came down here for work, I think. That's the problem. I don't know exactly."

She pulls a letter out of her purse, the envelope crinkled and worn. Masculine handwriting slants across the page.

Boyfriend, most likely.

It takes everything in me to resist telling her that I've yet to meet the man who's worth chasing all the way down here, but for her sake, I hope she's found the exception.

She hands the envelope to me, and I study the writing. The postmark is from Key West, the letter addressed to a Miss Elizabeth Preston, no return address.

"What line of work is he in?" I ask.

"I don't know what he's doing. He fought in the war. Last I heard, he came down here to work with some other veterans."

I give the letter back to her, doing a quick sweep of the restaurant to see if any of the veterans are dining here.

"The veterans work in camps to the north. They like to come down to Key West on their days off, let off some steam, and your sweetheart might have sent that letter when he was here, but they live up on Lower Matecumbe and Windley Keys."

A line forms on her brow. "Matecumbe. I think I saw that stop on the railroad."

"There are two ways to get there—the railroad or the ferry. For the ferry, you have to take the highway to No Name Key. The ferry leaves from there, and it takes you up to Lower Matecumbe Key in a few hours. It's unpredictable—sometimes it doesn't run, other times it's late—but God willing, it'll get you there."

An unladylike curse slips out of her mouth. "That far?"

Tourists don't quite comprehend what it's like down here until they're faced with it, the islands connected tenuously like a string of pearls, the complication of getting from one place to the next impeded by water, poor stretches of road, and undeveloped areas. The railroad has made it easier, of course, and when the highway's fully up and running, it'll be better, but you're still subjected to Mother Nature's whims and man's limitations.

"Unfortunately, it is that far. I used to visit my aunt there in the summers when I was a little girl. There are a couple camps on Lower

Matecumbe Key, I think. They built them last year. One up on Windley. The ones who come in here aren't what you'd call friendly with the locals. They mainly keep to themselves."

She tucks the letter back into her purse, the pages well-worn and creased as though they've been read over and over again. That kind of devotion is pretty hard to discourage.

"Thank you," she replies. "You've been very helpful."

I know when I've been dismissed, but I waver, the faint quiver of her lower lip and the hunch of her shoulders doing the deciding for me. "Word of warning? The camps can be pretty rough. They're no place for a girl like you. The journey north isn't an easy one, either."

"I can take care of myself."

"I'm sure you can, but no man's worth chasing if he doesn't want to be caught. If he came down here to get lost, he doesn't want to be found."

She doesn't respond, but then again, she doesn't need to. The stubborn glint in her eyes says it all.

I sigh. "If you need a place to stay, you'll want to do so up on Upper Matecumbe or Windley Key. Lower Matecumbe Key is pretty sparse from what I remember. My aunt has an inn on Upper Matecumbe. Islamorada. Right before you get to the train station. It's nothing fancy, but it's clean and cheap. I can give you the name of the place if you'd like."

A flash of relief fills her green eyes.

The girl hands me a pen and the envelope of her crumpled old letter. I scribble down the address on the back of the envelope alongside the name.

Sunrise Inn.

"Thank you. I'm Elizabeth," she adds with a belated smile.

"Helen. Where are you from, Elizabeth?"

"New York City."

The location doesn't surprise me as much as the distance.

"You're a long way from home. You come down here by yourself?"

"Yes."

"You be careful down here. I don't know what the city's like, but don't be fooled by the pretty beaches and blue sky. You can get into a lot of trouble if you don't know where you're going, if you trust the wrong person. People are as desperate here as they are all over the country. Desperate people do dangerous things."

Despite my reservations, I can't help but admire her courage and tenacity. How many times have I considered leaving, only to be stopped by all the reasons I shouldn't, all the obstacles in front of me?

Out of the corner of my eye, I spy one of my other tables signaling for me.

"I'll be back to check on you in a few minutes," I say, loath to leave her.

When I return ten minutes later, she's gone, change on the table for her meal—including the pie—and a little extra for a tip I doubt she could spare.

Five

Elizabeth

I shade my eyes from the sun, tears threatening. The clouds come and go, providing some respite, but it's not nearly enough. It was hot inside the restaurant, the fans doing little to cool the place, but now that I'm outside again, the sticky air is nearly unbearable, the breeze not providing much comfort.

How am I going to get to Matecumbe Key?

It's ridiculous, of course, to be so discouraged by the waitress's words. I made it all the way from New York City on my own. These last few hours shouldn't seem insurmountable, but they do.

I was so sure he would be in Key West.

I set down my suitcase on the dusty ground, the weight of it suddenly too much to bear.

A mouse scurries past me, its little tail wiggling in the dirt.

I shriek.

When my parents presented me with the elegant set of luggage on my sixteenth birthday, my initials affixed on the exterior, I envisioned taking the suitcases with me on stately ships, using them on my travels to Europe, Newport, Palm Beach, and the like. I certainly didn't predict such an ignominious end.

I pull out my change purse, counting the money there again, the mouse long gone. There's barely enough for food and lodging; adding train fare will likely erase my remaining budget for this trip. Then what? Only one person I know has funds to spare, and I doubt he'll help me once he learns I've run off.

I rummage through my bag, my fingers grazing the diamond ring, searching for my handkerchief—

"Can I help you?" someone asks.

"I'm fine, I—" I glance up, and the man in the gray suit from the train is standing in front of me, peering down at me from an unfairly high perch.

Bother.

My fingers curl around my old handkerchief, and I rub the fabric beneath my eyes, praying my makeup isn't smearing, my cheeks burning from the indignity of it all.

Of all the people to see me so low, why did it have to be him?

"I'm fine," I repeat more forcefully this time. "Thank you," I add, because Mother always taught me that good girls are polite girls, even if my interest in being "polite" is only marginally more than my interest in being "good."

At best, hopefully, it will see him on his way.

"You don't look fine," he points out rather inelegantly.

"Thank you for that observation. But I am."

I wait for him to excuse himself.

He doesn't.

"You can leave," I say, "polite" and "good" firmly abandoned.

"You weren't so eager to be rid of me earlier."

Is that a smirk on his face?

"I was bored," I reply. "A long train ride will do that to you. Everyone goes a little crazy when they're cooped up for so long."

"Bored? Hardly. You had your fair share of admirers."

"You can hardly call them a fitting conquest."

"So you had to collect more?"

"Why is it that when men approach women as conquests to be won they are lauded, but when women decide to go on a hunt of their own, they're branded as too aggressive, too eager, too greedy? Your sex didn't corner the market on ambition. Or a love of the chase."

He laughs, surprising us both, I think.

"You have a point there. Speaking of conquests, where's your friend from the train? Still mesmerized by the fish in the ocean?"

So he *was* paying attention earlier.

"He's elsewhere. Now please go. We've made the requisite small talk; we've danced around insulting each other. I don't have time for this, and as much as it pains me to disabuse you of any illusions you had, I really wasn't interested in you for anything other than an opportunity to pass the time."

But he doesn't go. Instead he leans against the porch railing next to me, crossing his arms in front of his chest.

"Well, then, now that we've established you aren't hopelessly in love with me, you can satisfy my curiosity as to why you're standing out here at one of the hottest times of day, wearing the same dress you had on earlier on the train, your bags beside you, looking utterly lost. Are you waiting for someone?"

"No, I'm not waiting on anyone. I came here alone."

Why won't he go away?

"You're joking. I assumed you were visiting family . . . friends . . ."

"I came down here to find someone," I answer after a beat. "I thought he'd be here, and he isn't. So now I'm leaving. You should do the same."

"So if he isn't here, where is he?" he asks.

I consider lying or refusing to answer altogether, but I'm too tired to be bothered, so the truth comes out instead.

"Lower Matecumbe Key, I think. Or Windley Key. I—I don't know, exactly. We lost touch. But I've come to understand that's where the veterans' camps are."

"He fought in the war?"

"Yes."

"Those camps—that's no place for someone like you."

"I can take care of myself," I repeat for the second time today.

If they only knew what my life was like back home; Key West is no match for New York City. A girl doesn't survive these days without learning to keep her wits about her.

"I'm sure you can take care of yourself, but Matecumbe is hours away. You have a journey ahead of you."

"I am aware of that. I've made it this far from New York. What's a few more hours?"

"A great deal down here. How do you propose to get there? The train won't run anymore tonight."

A sharp stab of disappointment fills me. "Are you sure?"

"Last train left the station an hour ago."

"There's always tomorrow, then," I say with false cheer. Surely, there's a local shelter where I could stay. Not ideal, but I can think of worse possibilities, and it would hardly be the first time I've considered such an option.

As his gaze sweeps over me, his eyes narrowed slightly as though he can see the wear in my clothes as plain as day, he is likely realizing the tightness of my bodice has little to do with an attempt to play the coquette and far more to do with the fact that the gown was made for me years ago.

"Do you have a place to stay tonight?" he asks bluntly.

"I'm fine."

He shifts back and forth, his brow furrowed—

"I have a car." He gestures toward a Studebaker parked up the road. "I'll take you to Matecumbe Key."

"You're joking."

"I'm not. We don't have much time if we're going to catch the ferry, though. Are you interested?"

"You were unforgivably rude to me on the train earlier and now you want to help me?"

"I don't like being toyed with. Haven't the patience for it. On the train, you wanted a mouse to play with. Now we've established we have absolutely no romantic interest in each other, I think I can manage a good deed or two, and you definitely could use the help."

He reaches into his breast pocket and shows me a badge.

Agent Sam Watson. Federal Bureau of Investigation.

"You work for the government?"

"I do."

I'm not sure if that's a point in his favor or not, though likely not. I assess the risk of getting into a car with a strange man, the waitress's earlier admonition to be careful down here ringing in my ears. Despite what others may say, I'm not entirely reckless. But, still, there's the inescapable fact that I have next to no money and I need to head north as quickly as possible.

Besides, considering who is coming after me, I could do worse than the company of a federal agent. Hopefully, even Frank would pause before going after a government man.

"I'm Elizabeth," I say, the decision made. There's a risk to leaving with him, but a greater one to getting stuck here.

His lips curve.

"No Eliza?"

"Eliza to my friends only," I lie. "The waitress at the diner recommended an inn near Islamorada. She said it was a good place to stay."

"What's the name of the place?"

"Sunrise Inn."

"I usually stay at the Matecumbe Hotel, but I know it. You'll be in between the camps there. I'll see you safely to Matecumbe. You have my word."

"Your word as a government man?"

"My word as a gentleman."

"Why are you helping me?"

He shrugs. "I'm going that way anyway. Besides, I bet you'll get into trouble if left to your own devices, and maybe I don't want that guilt on my conscience."

"I am perfectly capable—"

He makes an impatient noise. "I'm sure you are, but a girl by yourself at night in a place like this with nowhere to go isn't exactly prudent. Especially if you have as little money as I bet you do. I'm happy to do what I can to help. Are you planning on staying at this inn?"

"Yes."

He glances up at the sky, the clouds threatening once more. "If we're going to leave, we should do so soon. I have business up in Upper Matecumbe Key, and I've already spent too much time lingering here. Besides, they're predicting rain this evening, and I'd rather not get caught in a storm."

"What business?"

"I'll tell you about it on the drive. Are you coming?"

Suspicion fills me.

"If you were headed to Matecumbe Key anyway, why didn't you get off at the station in Islamorada? Why come all the way down to Key West to turn back around and go north?"

"For one, because my car was down here. Secondly, I was told a man I needed to see would be down here. I missed him. He's headed up to Matecumbe Key. I don't want to miss him again, so I can't exactly sit around and wait. Leave or stay, it's no matter to me, but if you're coming with me, you better tell me now."

"Fine. Thank you."

He smiles. "Smart choice."

Infuriating man.

Sam takes my bag without a word, carrying it toward the Studebaker. He opens the door for me with one hand, and once I'm settled in the creamy leather seat, he lifts my suitcase into the car's trunk before coming around back and climbing into the driver's seat.

He starts the car, and we head on our way.

Does Frank realize I've left New York? Has he sent his men after me? He probably doesn't lose much, and I shudder to think of his reaction when he realizes he's lost a fiancée.

If Frank's people do figure out that I bought a train ticket to come down here, at least their search will be contained to Key West and not where I'm truly headed. Unless, of course, he realizes who I'm looking for. Hopefully, by then, though, we'll be long gone.

It's good to put some distance between Key West and me, to fall off the map.

"Where are you from?" I ask when Sam maneuvers the car onto the road.

"Are we to make small talk now? I thought we were fellow passengers by necessity—yours—rather than choice."

"True, but you already know I bore easily. Besides, I figure I should know a thing or two about the man with whom I am to share a car—and ferry—for several hours."

He sighs. "I'm from Jacksonville, Florida. Born and bred."

I wrinkle my nose as I remember the tiny town Mr. Flagler's railroad passed through, the scenery offering little to recommend it.

I lean closer. "And what does a man like you do in Jacksonville?"

"You can stop the femme fatale act, you know. You aren't very good at it, and now hardly seems the time."

"Not very good at it—" My cheeks heat.

"Relax, gorgeous. I'm not saying you're not a stunner; but I'm not a boy, and I haven't fallen at a woman's feet in a very long time. I have no intention of doing so anytime soon. You don't even realize you're doing it, do you? Or is it your way of getting the upper hand when you're nervous?"

That wretched man.

"Fine. What do you do for the FBI?" I ask, my tone flat, the purr removed, my body language infinitely less inviting.

A smile tugs at his mouth. "I investigate things."

"What sorts of things?"

A pause. "Criminal things."

"Bank robbers, and the like?"

"No, not bank robbers."

"Gangsters, then," I guess.

He doesn't confirm or deny it, which I take as confirmation enough.

"Are there many gangsters in Key West?"

We certainly have them in New York, but I confess, I'd always envisioned the Keys as a sleepy little place, hardly a hotbed of criminal activity.

"There are several worrying smuggling routes."

"So you're here on business, then? Not pleasure."

"Yes."

"That sounds dangerous—chasing gangsters."

"Sometimes. Most of the time, it's fairly tame—a lot of desk work."

"Do you like it?"

The men of my acquaintance devote their lives to business, to making money, and I can't imagine one of them choosing such a path. They're more inclined to skirt the law than defend it.

"It's a job." He pauses. "Yes, I like it."

"There must be a measure of certainty in it. People will always commit crimes."

"Yes, they will."

It might not be the most glamorous job, but in this climate even I can appreciate the benefits of such security.

"And you like catching them?"

"I like bringing them to justice. Enjoy knowing there is one less danger on the streets. There's a sense of relief that they will answer for their crimes."

He has that look about him, the straitlaced do-gooder. There's a slight edge, though, and I suppose you cannot spend your days pursuing criminals without getting down in the muck and mire, too.

"And what do you do with your time?" he asks me, turning the tables quite neatly.

I shrug. "The same as anyone else, I suppose."

"And what's life like in New York City?"

Which answer should I give? The "before" answer—when life was parties, and laughter, and fun—or the "after" answer—when we were as desperate as everyone else?

"These days, likely very similar to what the rest of the country experiences. Not enough jobs to go around; not enough money, either."

"What sort of work do you do?"

Had the question been posed to me a few years ago, I would have laughed. Now, it brings a tinge of embarrassment.

"I marched myself down to the employment bureau a couple times. Tried to get a job."

"And what did you find there?"

"Far too many women in the same desperate straits. Women with experience, women with children to feed." I shrug. "They offered me a position working the counter of one of the department stores because I was pretty."

Even in a depression, it seems there's some sort of work for beautiful women.

"I tried my hand at it, but to tell you the truth, I was terrible."

"You don't say."

"I didn't have the patience for it. All that standing around and waiting for someone to approach you. And the money wasn't nearly enough to improve our situation. There are always other things a pretty girl can do."

"I can imagine," he replies, not a drop of humor in his voice.

"Somehow, I don't think you can. It's easier for men, isn't it? Thank heavens I wasn't born a homely girl in addition to being a single one, hungry and desperate, consigned to doing extra washing and dreaming of a future that will never come."

This depression is hard on all of us, but it's hardest on the women still. So many women dreamed of marriage and having families, but these days fewer and fewer people are getting married. Others dreamed of careers, only to be scolded for taking jobs away from men.

"They say that the worst is over," Sam replies.

I'm hardly surprised one of the government's employees buys the lies they're selling.

"They would say that, wouldn't they?" I retort. "It can't get any worse when you've already lost everything." I stare out the window, watching the scenery pass us by. It is beautiful here—untamed and wild. For all that Manhattan is heavily populated, New York society is actually quite small, and when we lost everything, there was no privacy to be had, our failures laid out for all to see. I can understand the appeal of coming down here to disappear, the respite from the whispers and gossips. With the ocean at your back, the sun on your face, the sand beneath your toes, there are worse places you could end up.

Surely, I'll find him this weekend.

I have to.

Six

※

Mirta

After lunch, once someone helps Anthony patch the tire, we are back on the road, continuing our journey north as we pass most of the drive in silence until we arrive at No Name Key. There we board a ferry to Lower Matecumbe Key, the sun nearing its descent. Anthony is quiet, a grim expression on his face for much of the journey. He's obviously displeased by the delay brought on by the flat tire, and I struggle to lighten his mood, until I simply give up entirely and doze the remainder of the trip. When I wake, it is to the sight of my husband's brown eyes staring down at me, watching me. We disembark the ferry and are back in the car again for another short drive before we arrive at the place where we are to spend our honeymoon.

The residence is a surprise: a large, white beach house with a wraparound porch and dark shutters. Towering palm trees frame the entryway, adding to the secluded setting.

Romantic.

"The old money is at Flagler's fishing camp on Long Key," Anthony comments. "Vanderbilts and the like."

He needn't say more. There are some things no amount of money can buy, and it's apparent that respectability is as impregnable in the United States as it is in Cuba.

He parks our car, and we are greeted by a skeleton staff that will see to our needs while we are here. We make our way through the house, and one of the caretakers—he introduces himself as Gus—leads us up to the master bedroom and sets down my suitcases near the wooden armoire opposite the bed. I am greeted by pale green walls, large windows offering a view of the ocean and sandy beach.

"There's no electricity in these parts, but you can use the kerosene lamps at night. You're lucky—the house has plumbing, which is rare around here," Gus says.

My gaze darts to my husband.

Anthony leans against the doorframe, his arms crossed in front of his chest. He removed his jacket when we left Key West, the top down on the car, the air heavy with an impending storm, the palm trees swaying in the breeze. His white shirtsleeves are rolled up to expose his tanned forearms, a sprinkling of dark hair there. His gaze is on me.

The caretaker leaves the room as quietly as he entered, and we are alone, the great big bed between us.

Surely, he can't mean for us . . . Heat rises along the back of my neck.

"Would you like to go for a swim?" Anthony asks, a smile playing on his lips as though he can read my mind and my desire to do anything to prolong the time before my wedding night. We didn't spend the night together in Havana after our businesslike marriage. Anthony said a casino hotel was no place for his wife, and I don't think either one of us was comfortable with taking a room under my parents' roof. Awkward enough to share such intimacies with a stranger, even more so in the house where I grew up.

Tonight it is, then.

"It's nearly dark," I say.

"Not quite, though. There's probably an hour of daylight left. We have the beach to ourselves, or so I'm told," Anthony adds, excitement in his gaze that could almost be described as boyish.

I suppose when you live in New York City, the beach is still a novelty, and on the bright side, it buys me a reprieve from marital relations.

He leaves me alone, and I change quickly into one of the bathing suits I purchased for my trousseau.

Anthony waits for me at the bottom of the stairs, clad in his swim trunks, a towel wrapped around his neck.

Did they stow his luggage in a separate bedroom? Will we share a room while we're here or maintain separate bedrooms like my parents have throughout my life? Is this the sort of thing one discusses with a spouse, or does it happen organically, through some mutual, unspoken agreement?

"Ready?" he asks.

Hardly.

I follow him to the water.

WE WALK ALONG THE BEACH, THE WAVES BREAKING BESIDE US. A breeze comes off the water, alleviating the heat slightly, but the air is stickier than I'm used to, pregnant with humidity. Anthony moves to the spot closest to the water, and something about the movement is reassuring—that act of kindness, that chivalry, the fact that he cares enough to spare me this small indignity.

He is rougher around the edges than the men—boys, really— I'm used to. While there's nothing outwardly objectionable to his manners, the way he carries himself, it is impossible to miss the fact that he comes from a different world than the one I inhabited in Cuba.

What sort of man have I married?

"It's beautiful here," he murmurs, his gaze sweeping over the water.

It *is* beautiful in a wild, rugged sort of way, although in truth, I'm not sure anything holds a candle to Cuba.

Our pale pink home in the Miramar neighborhood in Havana occupies nearly the entire block, trees surrounding the landscape. The house has been in our family for generations, and one day it will be my brother Emilio's, the place where he raises his children. I used to spend hours swimming in the pool in the backyard, my skin growing wrinkled from the water. Whenever I think of home, I see those sturdy walls, the bright Cuban sky.

"You've probably seen your share of beautiful beaches," Anthony adds.

"I have."

Cuba, for all of her faults and foibles, is unquestionably stunning. Maybe that's the problem; there's a double-edged sword to beauty and all the interest—good and bad—it attracts.

"Will you miss it?"

"I'm sure I will. There aren't many beaches in New York, are there?" I ask, changing the subject.

"Not in the city, no. But there are other parts of the state that can be nice."

"Where did you grow up?" I'm eager to learn more about his background.

"Brooklyn."

"Was it nice?"

"Growing up? No, I'm not sure I would call it 'nice.' But it made me who I am today."

"And now? What's your life like? Things must be different."

"Money doesn't buy everything."

Spoken like someone who has an ample supply of it.

"Doesn't it, though?" I ask.

"It doesn't buy you a good name."

"It bought you a society wife."

The gleam in his eye is more affection than avarice. "It did."

"Albeit a tarnished one," I joke.

"You're not tarnished to me."

The intensity in his voice surprises me.

"It's a tradition of sorts in my family, you know," I say, attempting to lighten his mood.

"Is it?"

"The first known Perez ancestor won himself a title and a wife in his bid for respectability."

"Was he a disreputable sort?"

"Allegedly."

"What manner of sins was he guilty of?"

"Women. Piracy."

Anthony smiles. "I would have liked him, then."

I laugh. Very few people are so accepting of their flaws, but then again, a great deal of power affords you such privileges.

"And his bride?" Anthony asks.

"A lady whose family had fallen on desperate times. She boarded a ship and sailed halfway across the world to do her duty."

"So it was duty between them?"

"Legend has it they loved each other, but who can be certain? Who really knows what goes on in a marriage besides the people inside it?"

"She must have been scared," he muses, and I have an inkling that we aren't merely talking about the corsair and his wife.

"She likely was, but she did her duty anyway. We women are made of stern stuff."

I gesture to the necklace around my neck, the family heirloom my father gifted to me on my wedding day.

"The corsair gave her this."

For luck, my father said.

"May I?" Anthony asks.

I nod.

He lifts the necklace, rubbing his fingers against the gold heart, the red stone. He releases it without comment, grazing my skin.

He doesn't back away.

I'm so nervous I can scarcely remember to breathe.

Our first kiss was at our wedding—simple and chaste, given the audience—and we're about to experience our second.

Anthony leans down, erasing the distance between us, his lips brushing against mine, softly, a featherlight caress.

A tremor fills me.

I suck in a deep breath, my heart thundering in my chest, and he deepens the kiss.

The ocean swells around us, the wind whipping my hair around my face. His kiss is brash, confident, seductive.

Exactly like him.

I know enough from talking to my cousins and friends to recognize that he wants me, can feel the desire in the tension in his body, the way his hands move over my clothes, gripping the fabric of my bathing suit, clutching me toward him as though he's desperate for me.

No one has ever kissed me like this.

Anthony releases me with a gleam in his eyes.

I raise my fingers to my mouth, my lips swollen to the touch.

He smiles. "We'll do just fine."

I wish I were so sure.

DINNER IS A FEAST OF LOCALLY CAUGHT SEAFOOD, THE CONCH AND snapper the best I've ever tasted. I'm too nervous and tired to eat much, but Anthony had a crate of champagne sent down from New

York, and he toasts our marriage in an extravagant fashion. After dinner, we separate, and Anthony decamps to the library with a cigar while I go upstairs to prepare for bed.

I dab perfume at my wrists and neck after I bathe in the house's round tub and choose the most elegant nightgown from my trousseau.

The bedroom was transformed by an unseen member of the staff while I bathed, candles lit around the room, white petals scattered about the bed and the floor, matching the snowy bedspread.

I walk over to the bed and grip the post, nerves dancing in my stomach.

A novel sits on the nightstand Anthony seems to have claimed for his own—Steinbeck's *Tortilla Flat*.

So much for separate rooms.

I flip through the pages, a bookmark indicating his progress halfway through the book.

I can't resist the urge to snoop. A pocket case of the cigars Anthony smokes sits inside a drawer in the nightstand, the tobacco a familiar odor—clearly, in this, too, he prefers Cubans. Beside the cigars are stacks of cash, the amount of it staggering. Back in Cuba, my father kept money in a safe for emergencies. The fact that Anthony sees no need to secure it speaks to both his arrogance and his wealth, and perhaps the security of his position. If he's as connected to the mob as he appeared to be in Cuba, many must fear him too much to steal from him.

There's a handkerchief; I lift it to my nostrils, the scent of Anthony's cologne hitting me instantly. I glance down. In the back of the drawer—

Cold black metal stares back at me.

I slam the drawer shut.

I shouldn't be surprised a man like Anthony has a gun, but there's a difference between all the things that keep you up with worry at night and seeing the reality with your own two eyes.

The bedroom door opens.

Anthony has removed his vest in addition to his jacket, unbuttoned the first two buttons of his white shirt.

I swallow.

He's no longer the man I kissed on the beach hours earlier; the sight of the gun, of that part of his life, has brought the old fears crashing through me.

Can he be a good man, a kind man, and live with violence as such a part of his daily life?

"You're beautiful." Anthony's voice is a low whisper. "Hell, 'beautiful' doesn't do you justice."

My nightgown is sheer white lace, leaving entirely too little to the imagination. And still, modesty aside, my mother counseled me that pleasing my husband would make my marriage more bearable—the gleam in his eyes, the manner in which his gaze rakes me over, assures me I have succeeded.

"Come here," Anthony commands.

I walk toward him on shaky legs, heat spreading throughout my body. Between the gown's immodest slashes and dips of fabric, the hazy, filmy gauze covering my skin, I'm practically bare before him.

I stop out of reach. I can't make myself take that final step.

"You're scared."

"I've never done this before."

"I'm not going to hurt you." He sighs. "I know what they say about me."

"It's not only that."

"But it doesn't help, does it?"

"No. It doesn't."

"Where I'm from, there's an advantage to people fearing you, to thinking you capable of about anything," Anthony replies. "With fear comes respect; otherwise, the world tears you apart. When I was a kid, I watched my father get shot on the street because he owed the wrong people some money. It wasn't even a lot of money, but it was enough for them to make an example of him."

"I'm so sorry—"

"It taught me that in order to be safe, to keep the people I loved safe, to hold on to the things I built, I had to be strong, too. Strong enough that no one could take anything from me again."

The world he describes isn't so different from the one I grew up in; politics in Cuba is a particularly bloodthirsty sport. And still, I very much doubt my father is capable of the things this man has done.

I open my mouth, then close it again, not sure I'm ready for the answers to the questions running through my mind.

"You can ask me anything. You're my wife."

The sincerity in his voice surprises me. As does the reverence he injects in the word "wife."

"My parents loved each other before my father was killed. Very much. I'm not interested in a bloodless society marriage."

"How is this supposed to be a real marriage?" I sputter. "We know nothing of each other."

Anthony closes the distance between us and reaches out, trailing his fingers down my arm as though he is attempting to soothe a skittish colt.

Goose bumps rise over my skin.

"I want more from you," he says. "I want everything."

"You didn't—" I suck in a deep breath, gathering my courage. "We haven't—"

"Why haven't I bedded you yet?" he finishes for me.

My cheeks burn.

"Not for lack of desire, I assure you," he replies, his tone wry.

"Then why?"

"Because our marriage got off to a shaky start, and I don't want to risk our future by rushing you into something you're not ready for. When you end up in my bed, I want it to be because you want to be there. Because you want me." Anthony leans forward, pressing a kiss to my forehead. "Good night."

My body is a riot of emotions and unfamiliar sensations, the desire his casual caresses have ignited sending off sparks inside me.

"That's it?"

He grins. "I think it's best if it is for now. I want to make you happy in this marriage, Mirta. Just give me a chance."

He walks away, and I am left staring at his retreating back, torn between relief and disappointment.

I spend the night reading Anthony's copy of *Tortilla Flat*, wondering if he will return to the bedroom, worrying over where he has gone and what he's doing.

At some point, I fall asleep, and when I wake, the book is back on the nightstand, the bookmark moved from the spot where Anthony had marked it to where I left off, his side of the bed empty.

Where is my husband?

Seven

⁘

Elizabeth

It's dark when we arrive at Upper Matecumbe Key, our surroundings considerably less welcome than the ones we encountered in Key West. Here the area is relatively barren, the landscape populated by an odd rickety cottage on stilts. So far I've counted more wild animals than people, the heavy brush home to all manner of creatures.

After our initial attempts at conversation, Sam and I descended into silence for the rest of the journey, but despite my best efforts to ignore him, the closer we get to our final destination, the more I struggle to stay quiet, the starkness of our surroundings setting off a whole host of questions inside me.

Perhaps it looks better in the light of day with the glittering sun to recommend it, but at the moment, I can't see it. What would possess someone to come down here?

"Did you fight in the Great War?" I ask Sam.

"I did."

"You must have been little more than a boy at the time."

"I was eighteen. Marched myself down to the nearest recruiting station."

"When you came back—were you—"

"Affected by what I'd seen?"

"Yes."

"How could I not be?"

"How did you move on?"

"I don't know. I don't think of it much, I suppose. I just did."

Sam navigates a turn down an even rougher road than the one we were on.

The farther we drive, the more I begin to doubt the wisdom of coming here without a better plan.

"Are you going to tell me more about what brought you down here from New York City?" Sam asks.

"That's personal."

He gives a sharp laugh. "As though you haven't been trying to excavate my past for the last few hours?"

"It's not as though you gave me much to work with," I retort.

"You got more than most." He grins, the gesture softening the harsh planes of his face, making him appear years younger. "Has anyone told you you're pretty observant?"

"Hardly."

"Well, you are. It's a good quality; it'll serve you well in life."

"Unfortunately, it's yet to be of much use."

"Why did you come down here by yourself?" Sam asks. "There wasn't a family member who could travel with you?"

"There isn't anyone else."

"If you'd like me to accompany you to the camps, I'd be happy to. There are hundreds of men working and living there. Some of them can be a little rough around the edges. It's not the sort of place you want to be alone."

"I've spent some time in the company of men. I'm not afraid of a little rough language and crass behavior."

"If 'rough language' is the worst you're expecting, then you haven't spent very much time in the company of these sorts of men."

I frown. "'These sorts of men'?"

"You should be prepared. The stories coming out of those camps aren't good. Do you even have a plan to find this man you're looking for?"

"I haven't exactly come up with one. Yet."

"Then let me propose that we start out tomorrow morning."

I arch my brow. "'We'?"

"Yes, 'we.' I told you I'd help, and I meant it. You're going to need someone who knows the area and has a vehicle. From what I understand, there are two main camps where the veterans live on Lower Matecumbe Key and another up on Windley Key. We can start with the one on Windley and work our way down. While most of the veterans live at the camps on Lower Matecumbe, the one up on Windley is where the hospital is. If the conditions are as grim as people say, the odds that he's received medical attention at some point are high."

To his credit, as far as plans go, it's certainly more than I've come up with.

"How do you know so much about the veterans' camps?" I ask.

"I spend quite a bit of time down here. You pick up things."

"In your search for bootleggers, gangsters, and smugglers?"

"You'd be surprised by how often those things overlap. But yes."

"Prohibition's over."

"It is, but that doesn't mean the criminal element has disappeared. It hasn't even been two years since the law changed. A lot of people aren't prepared to alter their ways. Just because they aren't smuggling rum from Cuba doesn't mean they aren't still involved in criminal operations. Look at what the mob's trying to do down there, the influence they hope to build. Do you think they aren't doing the same in the Keys? There's still money to be had, and many of them are too greedy or desperate to give up their less savory activities."

"How did you get involved in this kind of work?"

"You could say it's in my blood, I suppose. My father was a detective."

"It must be fascinating."

I think of the novels I like to read, the mysteries solved by intrepid investigators.

"It has its moments," he replies.

"And the case you're on now—how did that come about?"

"We were part of an agency task force with other groups like the Coast Guard and the Bureau of Prohibition to crack down on the rumrunners. When Prohibition ended in '33, we still had a list of people we knew were involved in criminal elements and part of larger organizations. We've been monitoring them, and given the different trade routes that intersect down here, particularly between the United States and Cuba, there are many opportunities for smuggling."

"It's a whole other world," I muse.

"It's not the Manhattan society set, no."

Surprise fills me that he so aptly identified my background. I hardly seem like a debutante at the moment. "Is it that obvious?"

"It is if you're paying attention."

"So you did notice me on the train."

"Of course I noticed you. I wouldn't be very good at my job if I hadn't. A pretty girl certainly isn't a hardship to look at."

"You didn't seem that interested."

"I don't mix pleasure with business."

A knot tightens in my stomach at the word "pleasure."

"Never?"

"Never."

"How boring," I tease.

He laughs. "Whatever you want to say about my job, I'm not sure 'boring' is the word I'd use."

His hand is devoid of a ring on that all-important finger, but that means little. Still, I can't quite envision him with a wife and family at home. There's little softness to be found in his demeanor or his countenance.

"Is there a woman waiting for you at home?" I ask, my curiosity getting the best of me.

"No."

"It must get lonely, then, traveling the country by yourself, chasing criminals."

"Sometimes."

"This man you're hunting down here. Is he dangerous?"

"Undoubtedly."

"Are you ever afraid?"

"It's hard to do this job if you're scared all the time. There's danger, sure, but most of these men are bullies at heart. They want you to fear them, because fear gives them power. The trick is to treat them as though they are only men, to diminish them until their threats and boasts mean little at all."

"You like it—the chase."

"I do."

"Men."

"Like you don't feel exactly the same way."

"Me? I'm hardly chasing criminals across the country."

Although, I can't deny it sounds exciting.

"I saw the way you played with that poor boy on the train, batting him around like a cat with a toy on a string."

I sniff. "A cat?"

"You liked it. Liked the thrill of the hunt. It's the same urge even if it's conducted with a peek of your—"

"You really have no idea how to talk to ladies, do you?"

"I didn't realize I was talking to a lady."

First I was a cat, and now I'm—

"I figured you fancied yourself an adventuress of sorts," he adds. "Much more interesting than a lady."

"How many ladies have you known?"

"If you mean society matrons and the like, none."

"I've little use for society matrons these days," I admit. "I've sort of been cast out of that world anyway."

"Did you shake things up too much?"

"Something like that. Apparently, there are some rules that aren't meant to be bent or broken."

"It's their loss, then. I bet you make a very dull society that much more fun."

He turns down another road, glancing out the window, the roar of the ocean growing louder.

"How much longer until we're there?" I ask. It's so dark out here; many of the ramshackle houses don't appear to have electricity.

"I'm not sure," Sam replies. "The man at the gas station said it should be up ahead."

If my reputation hadn't already been ruined, this—being alone with a strange man at this late evening hour—would likely do the trick.

And at the same time, I don't care. There are no judging stares out here, no whispers to fill my ears with how far my family has fallen, about the honor that has been squandered away. There is only freedom.

If Frank has come after me, it'll be that much harder for him to find me.

I take a deep breath of the ocean air.

"THIS IS IT," SAM SAYS AS WE PULL INTO THE PARKING LOT.

It's too dark to judge whether the Sunrise Inn lives up to its name and offers a scenic view, but the exterior appears clean enough, and at the same time, not too expensive for my dwindling finances. The money I saved by driving up with Sam rather than taking the train will help a great deal indeed.

I've been poor for so long, six years since the Great Crash that set everything in motion, that I've forgotten what it's like to not worry about such things, to stay in some of the finest hotels money can buy without blinking an eye. It's strange how quickly everything can change. How your life can be on one path, and suddenly, you're on a completely different one with little to no warning at all, ill-prepared for the challenges ahead.

I follow Sam into the inn after he parks the car, dragging my elegant case behind me.

"Let me get that for you," he offers.

"I have it." The least I can do is carry my own suitcase.

Sam's lips quirk at my reply, but he doesn't argue the point any further.

We're greeted by a man who introduces himself as Matthew and secures us two rooms next to each other, offering to send up a light snack from the kitchen.

The pie and coffee from Ruby's were hardly filling, but I plead exhaustion over hunger, needing to conserve my funds—I've certainly grown used to the nagging emptiness in my belly.

My body is stiff as I climb the stairs to my room, the hours on the train, on the ferry, and in the car taking their toll. We part ways at the entrances of our respective rooms, and I walk into the bedroom and shut the door. The room is small and sparsely decorated, but clean enough, the walls paper-thin by the sounds coming from Sam's room, as I envision him going about the same routine I am: opening his suitcase, removing his nightclothes, stripping the travel-mussed clothes from his body.

Once I have finished, I sink into the cool, crisp sheets, the sound of the ceiling fan whirring overhead mixing with the waves outside the inn.

We agreed to meet tomorrow morning to head over to the veterans' camps together. No matter how many times I said I was fine to go on my own, Sam insisted he was happy to accompany me.

It's enough to make a girl think a guy's sweet on her, although in his case, it's likely more a matter of duty than anything else, and while I enjoy preserving my independence in theory, I haven't the luxury for my principles at the moment.

There's a rustle on the other side of the wall, a creak of wood, a soft thud.

I fall asleep.

Eight

***

Helen

It's late in the evening by the time my shift ends, the people on the streets changing from locals going about their daily lives to tourists and troublemakers searching for a good time.

My entire body aches as I walk out the side door of Ruby's, my feet already protesting the trek home. My apron pocket is filled with a good amount in tips; we kept busy most of the day, the holiday weekend drawing a larger crowd than normal.

The sky is a cloudy one, the moon nowhere to be found, the prospect of rain in the air.

A forgotten copy of the *Key West Citizen* litters the ground, a storm warning on the front page. It was a popular topic of conversation in the diner this evening; hurricane predicting—guessing, more like—is its own sport around these parts. It's the fishermen who usually know best. When you live and die by the water, you learn to read her tells. If Tom thinks the storm is going to miss us, I'm inclined to agree.

A rustle sounds in one of the bushes, and I steel myself for whatever manner of wildlife is about to greet me. We share this island with all forms of animals—alligators, deer, snakes, and rats—and while I've never begrudged them the space, the dark night is hardly the time I wish to cross paths with them.

But it isn't an animal that greets me.

It's a man.

Another rustle.

Two men.

I recognize them from earlier today; they lingered over their coffee and pie for longer than most, leaving behind an ashtray of stubbed-out cigarettes.

"Evening," the one closest to me calls out, his hat pulled low over his face, moving with the languid ease of a man with booze in his belly loosening his limbs.

"Good evening," I reply automatically, my gaze drifting from the first man to the second and back again.

"There's no need for any trouble," the first man says. "We want the money in your pocket, and we'll be on our way." His gaze drifts down to my stomach and back to my face. "No need for any harm to come to you or your baby. No need for any fuss."

I open my mouth to scream for help, but there's no sound, panic and fear closing up my throat, my feet rooted to the ground, my body tense.

The smell of gin coming off him makes my stomach turn. It fairly oozes from his pores, as though he bathed in it, that sticky, sweet, sweaty scent that reminds me of Tom when he's gone off on another bender.

As hard as I try to make myself move, run, scream, it's as though I'm frozen in place.

"Did you hear me? Give us the money. Now."

There's an edge to his voice, a warning in that word "now" that I recognize intimately, the threat there altogether familiar.

We need the money, and I don't want to think about how angry Tom will be if I come home empty-handed, but—

What choice do I have?

I reach into my pocket, fisting my fingers around the coins, my hand trembling as I hold the money out to the man.

With a quick step, he's in front of me, his skin on mine as he wrenches the change from my hand.

I flinch at the contact. My chest tightens.

"Is that all?" he asks.

There's little else to be had. My wedding ring isn't worth anything, but I begin tugging at it, trying to force it off my swollen knuckle.

The man in front of me takes a step back.

A man's voice fills the night. "Leave."

I turn, and my customer from earlier—my regular, John—strides forward.

"Come on," the attacker wheedles in response, his accomplice hanging behind him. "We're not going to hurt her. Don't want no trouble here."

"Then leave," John says. "Give her back the money. Get out of here."

The attacker shifts back and forth on his feet, fiddling with the pocket of his worn pants.

"This is your last chance," John threatens.

"Let's go, Henry," the accomplice calls, taking another step back. "Not worth it."

"Shut up," Henry growls, slipping his hand into his pocket.

John takes another step forward.

Henry pulls his hand out of his pocket.

Oh God, he has a knife.

John jerks his head my way, and I realize I've said the words out loud.

"Please," I whisper, moving toward John, grabbing his forearm, trying to tug him back toward me, my body shaking.

Even though the two men are no match for John in size alone, with their number advantage and the size of the knife, the odds have become considerably tighter.

"It's only money," I plead. "It's not worth—"

John moves before I can finish my sentence, advancing on the closer of the two men—Henry—with quick, assured strides, likely aided by those long limbs.

Henry slashes forward, knife in hand, aiming for John's belly.

Henry's arm moves higher, jerking up, and John groans, his fist connecting with Henry's jaw with a loud crack.

Henry's head snaps back, but instead of falling over, he lunges forward, the knife once again connecting with skin.

Another groan fills the night.

Blood drips from a slash in John's clothing, running down his chest.

The sight of all that red breaks me out of my stupor, and I shout at the top of my lungs—

"Help! Help! Please!"

For a moment, Henry's accomplice seems frozen by indecision, weighing the odds of jumping in and joining the fray, but then he runs toward the wooded area, away from the fight.

There must be someone still lingering around the front of the restaurant. If I go and get help—

The men circle each other once more, and then I see it in the corner, a stray piece of wood Ruby never got around to cleaning up.

I move quickly, grabbing the wood, swinging, swinging, until it connects with Henry's head.

THE WOOD FALLS FROM MY HANDS, AND I STARE DOWN AT THE man slumped on the grass in front of me.

I sag to the ground.

"Are you all right?" John asks.

"I—I think so."

"Is there any pain in your abdomen? Any pressure?"

"No."

"Any bleeding?"

"I don't think so." I rise slowly, accepting the hand John holds out to steady me. He releases me once I'm on my feet again. "Is he—" I take a deep breath, my heart racing. The money Henry tried to steal is spread all around his body. Blood trickles from his hairline, running down his face. "Is he—? Did I kill him?"

John leans over the body for a moment, checking his pulse. "No. Just knocked him out."

He bends down, scooping up the money strewn about the ground, and gives it to me.

I stare at it for a moment, a spot of red on the corner of one of the coins. My fingers tremble as I take the change from his outstretched hand and shove it into the pocket of my apron.

"You shouldn't have grabbed that post. You shouldn't be lifting anything that heavy this late in your pregnancy," John says.

I gape at him. "He was stabbing you." I take a deep breath, steadying myself. "Besides, I carry trays of food all day. I was hardly going to be brought down by a piece of wood."

"You shouldn't be carrying heavy trays, either," he retorts.

"And you shouldn't have fought him. You heard them—they only wanted the money."

"You don't know what they wanted," he counters. "It could have been a lot worse. Let me walk you home, at least. Do you live nearby?"

"It's only two miles away."

He shoots me an incredulous look. "You walk two miles by yourself every night after work?"

He doesn't tack on "in your condition," but he might as well have.

"Are you well enough to walk?" he asks.

"Of course. Are *you* well enough to walk? You're bleeding."

"I'll be fine. Ready?"

As much as John unsettled me before when he'd come into Ruby's, after the attack, the company is welcome even as I put a little more distance between us than is necessary.

"Yes. I didn't thank you earlier for coming to my aid. Thank you."

My legs quiver as I walk, my steps slower than normal. I place a hand protectively over my stomach, saying a silent prayer for the baby to move.

John matches his pace to mine, and I notice for the first time that he has a slight hitch in his stride.

His jaw is clenched as though he's in pain, his gaze trained to some point off in the horizon.

I stop, and he does the same.

There's a flutter in my stomach, followed by a kick, strong and steady.

I settle my hand on my belly, at the spot where the baby kicks again, relief flooding me.

"The babe?" John asks.

I nod, tears welling in my eyes.

The baby shifts in my stomach, a jab here, another kick there. Never before has such motion brought such relief.

I begin walking again, and John trails behind me. He doesn't offer anything else to the conversation, and we drift into silence, our journey punctuated by the sounds of the night.

The weather is pleasant enough, but there's an undercurrent contained in the air, a taste on my tongue, a scent that suggests a storm is brewing despite Tom's insistence it would miss us.

"You're not from around here, are you?" I ask John. Most of the highway workers are transplants from other areas.

"No, I'm not."

"Do you like the Keys?"

"I've been worse places," he replies. "It's warm, at least. Pretty enough scenery if you don't mind things a little wild. It's about as good as any a place to recover."

"Were you injured in the war?"

He gestures to the leg he's been favoring. "Shot. Healed fine, but it stiffens up on me in the cold or at the end of a long day. Don't find much cold down here, so it suits me."

"I'm sorry."

He makes a noncommittal sound beside me.

"Really, thank you for helping me tonight. You're right, it could have been much worse."

"I didn't do anything special. Just what anyone would have done."

"I don't know about that. It wasn't your fight."

"The day we stop fighting for others is the day we might as well pack it all up and go home."

"I'm not sure many people see it the way you do," I reply.

"You must see all sorts of people coming through Ruby's. Did you recognize the men who tried to rob you tonight?"

"They were in there earlier this evening, but I don't think I've ever seen them before. We get a lot of men like that coming through our doors—hungry, a little mean."

"Did you grow up in Key West?" he asks.

"Lived here my whole life. My daddy used to work on the railroad."

"It's a hard way to make a living," he comments.

"Daddy was a hard man. A good one, but a hard one just the same."

"If it was anything like working on the highway, then there

wasn't a lot of room for softness. It's dangerous work. It can make you hard."

"Is that why you come to Key West so often? To escape?"

"Perhaps."

"Why'd they send you all down to the Keys?" I ask. "Surely, there are plenty of projects around the country for you all to work on. The weather might be good, but the elements aren't exactly welcoming."

"They didn't want us in Washington, causing trouble, reminding the American public—the voting public—that we weren't taken care of, that the government hasn't exactly lived up to its promises. They probably thought the Keys were far enough away to send us so everyone would forget about us."

A few years ago, many of the men who fought in the Great War went to Washington D.C. alongside their families to demand that the government pay the bonuses they were owed for their wartime service in an early lump-sum payout rather than making them wait years for the full payment in such desperate economic times. The papers referred to them as the "Bonus Army."

"Were you involved with the Bonus Army?" I ask. "The protests in Washington D.C.?"

"I was. I marched with them. A lot of veterans are out of work. Hungry. Losing hope. The government made a promise to them, had the means to help them, to give them the money they were owed by law. Instead, they shoved them aside."

"The images in the papers—"

They showed chains on the gates at the White House, men living in tents, guards patrolling the street, tear gas bombs released on the remaining veterans, their tents burned.

"The movement changed, of course," he says. "People gave up hope. Went home. Others came in who had no real affiliation to the war. Near the end we had people join us who were there to cause trouble.

"It's a shame what's happening to this country, the mess that's consuming us. We fought the war to end all wars. Lived through hell. We won. Only to come home to a different sort of hell. And the people who are in a position to do something? You have congressmen making almost nine thousand dollars a year while the people they're supposed to be serving make a fraction of that."

Nine thousand dollars is an unimaginable sum of money compared to the few hundred I make at Ruby's each year.

"Why not home? Why didn't you go back?"

"I tried. After the war. I'm not—" He takes a deep breath as though bracing himself for something unpleasant. "I'm not the man I was when I left. Everyone was happy to see us home, but once we were there, they didn't know what to do with us. Wanted to pretend we were the same people who'd left, that we hadn't seen the things we'd seen."

"Will you stay down here permanently?"

"I don't know. There are rumors they're considering closing the camps. Not that anyone's told us. They sent us down here like that was going to fix what's broken in us, and now they want to get rid of us again."

"That's not right."

"No, it isn't, but not much is in this world."

I can't disagree with him there.

"What do you do down in Key West?" I ask.

As soon as the question leaves my mouth, I regret it. I'm a married woman—it's fairly easy to guess what he gets up to down here.

"During the week, we're working on a stretch of highway between Grassy Key and Lower Matecumbe. On the weekends? The other guys like to go out. Sloppy Joe's and the like," he answers evenly.

"And you don't like to go out?"

He shrugs. "I went out plenty before the war. Drank myself to sleep enough nights after. Trouble's the last thing I need."

"What did you come here looking for?"

"Peace," he answers, before turning my own question around on me. "And you? What are you searching for?"

"I've never been anywhere else."

"Where would you go?" John asks. "If you could go anywhere?"

Away. Far away.

"Is it like they say?" I ask, sidestepping his question. "In the camps?"

"What do they say?"

"They talk of fights. Disorderly conduct. Drunkenness."

"Are there some men who came down to cause trouble? Sure. But there are good men, men working hard to send money back to their families. Men who simply need a break. We've all been through something that changes you, and most of us are trying to get by."

"I've noticed you keep to yourself. It must get lonely. Your family must miss you."

"I don't know about that. I do just fine."

"Are you married?"

It's pretty much impossible to spend your day waiting on people and not form a curiosity about their lives. Sometimes I wonder about them to distract myself from the other things on my mind, and other times, I genuinely want to know.

He's silent for a moment that stretches on in the night. "No. I never married. How long have you been married?" he asks me.

"Nine years."

"Long time."

Sometimes it seems like an eternity, as though my entire life has been defined by my marriage to Tom, and I suppose in a way it has. The girl I was before him belongs to someone else's memories.

I take a deep, shaky breath, staring up at the inky night sky. "I wonder sometimes—"

How my life would have changed if I'd said "no" when Tom asked me to marry him . . . If things would be different if I'd never gone out to the docks that day his boat was coming in full of fish and smelling of the sea . . . if I'd gone north to my aunt Alice the first time he hit me rather than believing him when he said it would never happen again . . . if we hadn't lost all those babies . . . if the Depression never came . . . Would our marriage be something different now if fate hadn't crashed into us so decisively? Or were we always on this course and I couldn't see it?

"What do you wonder?" he asks, and I realize I've stopped speaking entirely.

It's not like me to share such intimacies with a stranger, much less a strange *man*, but there's something soothing in his manner. Perhaps by offering so little of himself, he naturally invites the other person to fill the spaces where polite conversation would normally lie.

And truthfully, my days are spent asking others what they'd like, what they need, and I can't resist the urge to speak.

"It seems wrong, I suppose, to bring a child into all of this."

"Is there no one else? Do you have family?" he asks me.

"My parents are dead."

"I'm sorry for your loss."

"Do you think there's something better out there?" I ask. "Something better than this?"

Another pause. "I hope so," he replies. "What does 'something better' look like for you?"

I can hardly tell him the truth, about the daydreams and the rest of it. Good women don't dream of their husband's death.

"Somewhere far away from here. Somewhere safe."

"You could leave," he says.

The familiar yearning fills me at those words, at the possibility of them. How many times have I considered it? Planned it?

"How? Where would I go? With what money? A woman's place is with her husband."

At least, that's the pretty excuse that's used to cover up all manner of sins.

"Maybe a man loses his right to be called a husband when he raises his fists to someone he should be protecting."

Bitterness threads through me. "That's a nice thought."

"I've angered you."

Perhaps he has a little, poking and prodding at things he has no understanding of. It's easy to judge when you're on the outside staring in.

"I shouldn't have spoken as I did earlier," I say instead. This strange night has loosened my tongue. "What's between a man and his wife is no one's business."

"Wouldn't your friends help you? I've seen how the other staff treat you, how the owner dotes on you."

"Ruby has enough to worry about trying to keep a business afloat. She has mouths to feed. Responsibilities. She doesn't need to be concerned over my troubles."

"Maybe she's already worried about you and she'd be happy to help."

"And you? You said you'd left your family. Who helps you? Every time you dine in the restaurant, you're alone. Where are the friends you lean on? Since you've been coming in the restaurant, you've never said anything to me, never bothered to make polite conversation."

I hardly recognize myself, the ability to speak my mind heady indeed.

He looks momentarily abashed, the effect unexpected, transforming his face to something younger, softer. "You're right. I'm not good at taking my own advice."

"No, I shouldn't have said anything. That was rude of me—I apologize."

"There's no need to apologize. You're right. I could do better. And I'm sorry if I came off as rude at the restaurant. It was never my intention to give offense."

"Not rude. Just not particularly talkative."

"I've found it difficult to be at ease with people since I came home."

I smile despite my earlier annoyance. "You're doing a pretty good job of it now."

"You're easy to talk to."

"I suppose that comes with the territory in my line of work."

"It's more than that. There's something calming about you."

"Calming?"

He nods, tilting his head away from me.

I think I've embarrassed him, even as I am left with the unmistakable sensation that I have made a friend.

WE SPEAK LESS AND LESS THE NEARER WE GET TO MY HOUSE, JOHN trailing a step behind me as he follows my path. When we reach the last turnoff, I slow my pace. We're closer to the water now, but it's too dark and we're too far away for me to tell if Tom's boat is moored, if he's back from his fishing trip. His schedule has always been unpredictable, and I've done the best I can to anticipate his needs, to never be home too late in case he is waiting for me; no doubt he knows exactly how long it should take me to walk home from Ruby's, even if most nights he steps off his boat and heads to the nearest bar rather than darkening our door with his presence.

"I'll go the rest of the way by myself," I say, stopping in my tracks and facing John.

"Are you sure?"

"I am. It's up ahead. No one's out here anyway. Thank you for coming to my aid earlier."

"Thanks for coming to mine," he replies. "I'll be in Key West through the weekend if you need anything."

"I'll be fine."

He gives me a sad look as though we both know that isn't strictly true.

"Are you sure you don't need patching up?" I gesture at the general vicinity of his torso.

"I'll be fine," John replies, echoing my earlier statement. He takes a cigarette and a lighter from his pocket. "I'll wait here a time, make sure everything is all right."

"Good evening."

"Good evening," John replies with a faint inclination of his head.

I walk the last few yards to the cottage alone. When I round the bend to the building I call home, I spy a soft glow in one of the windows.

I grip the doorknob, twisting the handle as a chill slides down my spine.

With drink, there's a line, a tipping point between being drunk and dangerous and being too drunk to be of much harm to anyone. I pray Tom is simply passed out, his limbs sprawled out on the cottage floor.

The main room is dark, save for the glow of a kerosene lamp in the corner.

The front door shuts behind me.

The scent of bourbon hits me first, turning my stomach, the air heavy with it as though if you lit a match everything would simply go up in flames.

I swallow, cursing the loudness of my heavy footsteps as I head toward the bedroom.

I stifle a scream.

Tom's positioned right in front of the doorway, his body half in the shadows, a bottle dangling from his fingertips, half empty.

"Who walked you home?" he demands.

I quake at the boom in his voice, the sound of it bouncing off the walls of the little cottage, seeping inside me as the tremor grows.

"Wh-What are you talking about?"

How could he know?

"I heard voices." He rises from the rickety chair, the bottle abandoned with a thunk on the floor, the amber-colored liquid spilling over the floorboards.

It'll be hell to clean later, but Tom doesn't like a mess.

He moves closer, crowding me, his frame blocking out the light thrown off by the kerosene lamp. "Don't you lie to me."

Between the late hour, the full day of work, and the babe, my response doesn't come as quickly as it should, my mind and body sluggish.

"There were men outside Ruby's when I left work. They were drunk. Hassling me." I take a deep breath. Tom, like the rest of the town, distrusts the veterans. "Men working on the highway. One of Ruby's regulars saw it happen and came to my aid. He offered to walk me home so they wouldn't follow me."

Tom takes a step toward me, and I move without realizing it, my hip colliding with the sharp corner of the table in the kitchen.

My heart pounds.

"What's his name?"

"I don't know," I lie.

"You said he was a local."

"He's a regular," I reply, dancing around the "local" term.

"Who are his people?" Tom challenges. "Perhaps I need to have a word with him."

"I don't know. He mostly keeps to himself."

"Now that's not exactly true, is it? Seems like he wanted something with my wife."

"I'm nine months pregnant," I whisper, the plea in my voice unmistakable.

When we first married, I thought it was sweet that he worried about me so much, that he cared where I was. But the more out of control the world around us became, the tighter Tom held on to things at home, until he became more jailer than husband and I realized it wasn't sweet at all.

"It was nothing," I babble. "He was doing me a kindness."

Tom raises his hand.

"Please."

I scan the room, searching for something to use to defend myself, something—

Tom drops his hand to his side.

"He take an interest in you?"

My head wobbles, my teeth chattering.

He moves so quickly, his reflexes so fast, that I wonder if he's been putting on this whole time, if he isn't nearly as drunk as he's pretending to be.

His big hand spans the width of my neck, lifting my chin up so our gazes meet.

"Don't you lie to me."

"I'm not. I'm not lying. I promise. Just let me go."

"Who do you belong to?"

Tears spring in my eyes, fear and shame surging inside me. "You."

"That's right. You better not forget it. I hear stories about you carrying on with men at Ruby's, and you'll never see that baby again. Do you understand me?"

The pressure of his hand against my face jerks my head up and down, until he releases me with an impatient noise.

I take a step back, the reprieve from his hands a welcome relief, and Tom grabs me, clamping down on my wrist, his fingers digging into the old bruises.

He likes to do this: let me go so that I have a taste of freedom, only to snap the leash again so I am back under his control.

"It was wrong," I whisper. "I shouldn't have let him walk me home. I'm sorry."

Tom's nails dig into my skin, the scent of him sending a wave of nausea through me, my stomach rebelling at the odor of fish, salt, sweat, and bourbon.

Please don't hurt the baby.

Tom's grip tightens, and my knees buckle, my vision narrowing, a tunnel of blackness greeting me as the pain becomes more than I can bear.

"You won't see him again. He tries to talk to you again, you tell me and I'll handle it."

I don't bother arguing with Tom about the difficulty of my keeping such a promise, the likelihood that John will come into the restaurant again; at this point, I would say or do anything to stop the pain shooting through me.

His grip on my wrist tightens.

I fall to the floor, cradling my stomach with my free hand, and Tom releases me.

The baby kicks.

A tear trickles down my cheek.

How did we go from a couple embracing on the docks, love beating in my breast, to this?

"I'm leaving tomorrow for a fishing trip. I'll be back in a few days."

His absence brings an immediate sense of relief, a gulp of air in my lungs, but still—

"The storm—"

I try to tread carefully, existing in half sentences and thoughts, whittling down my existence to the least likely to make him angry.

"Storm's nowhere near us," he retorts. "I heard the latest report. It'll be fine."

The sad thing is that as much as I want him gone, I'm also afraid. What if the baby comes early, what if—

He must have read the fear in my eyes, because his expression darkens. "Who puts food on this table?"

"You do," I whisper.

"Damn straight."

The floor is hard against my back, and I try to push myself up into a seated position, try to make my legs move, but the weight in my stomach upends my balance and pushes me back again.

Tom makes a sound of disgust and gives me his hand, and despite the desire to turn away, I take it, letting him pull me off the ground. When I'm standing on my own, I pull out the change, still stained with John's blood when those men stabbed him.

I place the coins in Tom's outstretched palm, fighting the wave of anger, the desire to take back the money and squirrel it away somewhere.

He does a quick scan and slips the change into his pocket.

"I'm going to bed," he announces, and after nine years of marriage, I know I am to follow him.

We fall into our evening routine in silence, our earlier fight fading into the background.

I wince as I remove my clothes, slipping the worn cotton nightgown over my head, my wrist throbbing with the effort.

There's a moment when my head hits the pillow that I fear Tom will roll over and face me, pressing himself on me, his body looming over mine. At this point in my pregnancy, our marital intimacy has lessened considerably, but there's still enough of a spark of fear inside me to have me lying as still as possible, regulating my breathing, hoping he believes I have fallen asleep.

My husband doesn't take "no" for an answer.

Minutes pass, a creak of the bed, a rustling of the sheets, and I hear it—a soft snore, and another, and another.

I stare up at the ceiling, the baby moving around in my belly, the pain in my wrist lessening not one bit. The night is quiet, the water a distant sound, the creatures that inhabit the mangroves surrounding our cottage scurrying around. I rise from the bed with a wince, padding to the front cottage window, my uninjured hand pressing against the small of my back to relieve some of the pressure from my midsection. I stare out at the sky, up at the moon, the stars, imagining a life as far away from here as I could get.

Paradise.

Through the trees, I see a spark of flame—like the end of a cigarette.

It's too dark to make out the man holding it, but I know it's him, and I wonder if John can see me in the moonlight, if he knows I'm standing here watching him.

I remain at the window far longer than I should, far longer than is wise, before returning to my place beside Tom in bed, before I close my eyes, and I remember the sensation of holding that post, of swinging with all my might, and the satisfying crack of hearing the wood strike Henry's skull as I watched him fall to the ground.

When I dream, I am back in the woods outside Ruby's Café, and this time Tom is on the ground, blood seeping from his skull, his eyes lifeless, as I stand over him, the post in my hand and vengeance coursing through my veins.

Nine

SUNDAY, SEPTEMBER 1, 1935

Mirta

When I come downstairs for breakfast the next morning, Anthony is seated at the spacious dining room table, a cup of coffee in front of him, a newspaper folded beside his plate. Someone has cut an arrangement of flowers and put them in a vase at the center of the table, the china and linens the same creamy color.

Anthony glances up from the paper with a smile.

"Good morning."

"Good morning," I reply.

Where did he sleep last night after he left me alone in the bedroom?

He rises as I walk toward the table, pulling out the chair across from his for me. Before I sit, Anthony leans forward, the scent of his aftershave filling my nostrils, and kisses my cheek.

"You look beautiful," he whispers, his lips grazing my ear.

My cheeks heat. "Thank you."

I sit down in the chair, waiting while he slides it forward, the domesticity of the moment rattling me once more. He must be a dozen or so years older than me, but we have, what—forty more years of this? One day, there will likely be children seated at the table with us. I am truly no longer Mirta Perez, but someone else entirely.

"How did you sleep?" Anthony asks as one of the staff emerges from the kitchen, setting our breakfasts of pancakes, eggs, and bacon in front of us.

"Well," I lie, not courageous enough to admit to the inordinate amount of time I spent thinking about our new relationship. "How about you?"

His lips curve. "As well as could be expected, I suppose. Would you like the paper?" Anthony gestures toward the folded sheet next to his plate.

In Cuba, my knowledge of current affairs and politics came from my father's table discussions, from the fear and uncertainty that surrounded our days. It seems wise to learn more about the country I am to inhabit.

I scan the headlines, my husband's gaze on me. The paper talks of violence and death. A man named Frank Morgan has apparently started a crime wave in New York, and I can't help but wonder how often my husband's name graces the pages of these papers with similar stories about his involvement in such matters.

I set down the paper.

"I could get used to this, you know," Anthony says. "Starting my day with you seated across from me at the table."

Gus, the caretaker, walks into the dining room, saving me from formulating a suitable response.

"I apologize for interrupting your morning," he says. "I thought you should know—the storm's getting worse."

"Are you worried about it?" Anthony asks him.

"Can't say for sure right now. People are boarding windows. 'Course, it could miss us entirely. Right now it seems like it'll hit closer to Cuba."

"We got out of Havana in time, then." Anthony turns to me. "Do you want to call your family?"

A lump fills my throat. "I'd like that."

Storms are hardly a novel occurrence in Cuba, and while my family will be prepared, I've lived through enough hurricanes to fear them.

"Are we safe here?" Anthony asks Gus. "The Key West newspaper said it's a few hundred miles away."

"We might see some winds, rain. Water will be choppy. You won't want to take the boat out. Hopefully, the worst we'll get is a day or so of bad weather. I'll watch the barometer to see if the pressure falls and keep an ear out on the radio. Talk to some people. The fishermen spend their lives on the water. I'd trust their word over that of the Weather Bureau any day. Worst case if it does get bad, we can board up the windows."

In Cuba, the staff handled our storm preparations, but I remember my father's worry over the damage the storm could do to the sugar crop, his livelihood frequently threatened by weather and politics.

Gus excuses himself, and we are alone once more.

"What are your plans for the rest of the day?" Anthony asks me.

"I haven't any."

"You could walk on the beach again. Better to get in as much good weather as we can."

He frames the idea as though we are to spend the day apart, and while his suggestion isn't uncommon—my father certainly spent his days away from my mother, content to occupy his time with work or his social circle—the notion of being married to a stranger, of welcoming a stranger into my bed, is hardly appealing.

"Perhaps we could spend some time together today," I suggest. "Get to know each other better."

"I didn't realize you wanted to know me better—yet."

"We're married. We're to spend our lives together. It seems only natural."

Even if everything about this situation is entirely unnatural.

"Then what do you want to know?" Anthony asks.

"How do you picture our lives together? How will we spend our days once we are in New York?"

"I hadn't really thought about it, to be honest. This concerns you?"

"No, I suppose I have a hard time imagining what my days will be like. I always saw myself as a wife, but that was in Cuba. With my family and friends around me. I thought I'd marry one of the boys I grew up with, and we'd move into a house down the street from my parents."

"You didn't want to leave."

"I agreed to marry you," I say evenly, reluctant to untangle the giant gnarl of emotions inside me. It's not as simple as whether or not I wanted to leave home. The future afforded to me given my family's fall from grace was a narrow one, and I took the best opportunity I could, even if it's hardly the future I envisioned for myself.

"While I enjoyed the time I spent in Havana," Anthony replies, "my business is in New York, and if I am absent for too long, my enemies tend to get restless, try to move in on what's mine. I've already lingered longer than I should have."

A shiver slides down my spine at the word "enemies."

"Have you many?"

"Enemies?"

"Yes."

"I suppose. You don't get rich without leaving some bodies along the way."

I realize I must have gone pale by the chuckle that escapes his lips.

"I've unsettled you, my little proper society wife." His gaze narrows speculatively. "I take it you did read some of the articles in the paper. The world I live in really isn't all that different from politics. People want power because they think it makes them untouchable. They'll do anything they can to make sure that power is never taken away from them."

"Does your power make you untouchable?"

"No one is untouchable. It would be foolish to believe otherwise. That's the thing about power—you never have enough. It always keeps you wanting more."

"I suppose if you put it like that, it's not all that different from the social whirl," I muse, trying to lighten the mood, remembering the unspoken hierarchy in Havana, the power we wielded with a flutter of our skirts and a snap of our fans. Better that than the memories of bodies on the roadside, insects buzzing around them, the scent of death and decay that comes from power.

"No, I suppose it isn't," Anthony replies. "I watched you out and about in Havana. I saw how heads turned when you walked by. Even after your family's scandal, you were still a force to be reckoned with in the city. You'll do fine in New York."

"I'm not sure about that."

"You will. And at the end of the day, if they don't like you, it won't matter. They will respect you."

"Because I'm your wife?"

"Yes."

"It must be nice to be so confident," I remark, my tone dry.

"It was a hard-fought skill, I assure you." He leans in as though he's telling me a secret. "I was rather scrawny when I was younger. I know a thing or two about being powerless, poor, remember it well enough to never want to be in that position again."

"And now they all fear you."

"Not all of them."

"But enough of them."

He doesn't bother contradicting me.

"Still," I reply. "It sounds exhausting."

"What do you mean?"

"All those enemies must come at a cost. Do you ever get tired of paying it? Don't you worry one of your enemies will strike at you?"

My father believed he was untouchable once, thought Machado's friendship would keep his fortunes secure. He never saw the coming wave of power that ushered in Batista, never envisioned our futures would end as they have. If the last two years have taught me anything, it's that your life can change in a moment even if you never saw it coming.

"This is hardly a conversation for one's honeymoon. Would you like to go for a short walk?" Anthony says, changing the subject. "I have some business to conduct, but I have a few minutes beforehand."

"I didn't realize your business interests were significant here."

"It's a useful shipping route."

What is he shipping?

"Are we to have the sort of marriage where we confide in each other? Tell each other our secrets?" I ask.

"Have you secrets I should know about?"

I shrug, registering how his gaze drifts to my shoulder with the motion.

Are husbands and wives meant to flirt?

He smiles. "I'd worried I lost her, you know. When I saw you walking down the aisle toward me on our wedding day, you looked utterly terrified, like you were walking to your death."

"Worried you lost who?"

"The girl I saw in Havana."

"This isn't Havana."

"No, but you dazzle just the same."

Now it's my turn to laugh. "That is a terrible line."

He rises from the table and holds his hand out to me. "Maybe it isn't a line at all."

I place my hand in his, wishing I could silence the doubts in my mind, the questions.

Why did he have to go all the way to Cuba to gain a wife? Surely, there were American girls who needed husbands and were willing to ignore a sullied background and whispers of ill-gotten gains?

So why me? Why marry a girl he barely knew? Was it his powerful connections in Cuba, his friendship with Batista, that enticed my family? Or did he offer my father money to marry me?

We walk through the open doors overlooking the patio, our hands linked, heading to the beach a hundred feet away, within sight of the house.

"My meetings shouldn't take too long," Anthony says. "We could take the boat out afterward if you'd like."

"That sounds lovely. I wouldn't have pegged you for a sailor, though."

"I'm not," Anthony replies ruefully. "But surely one of the staff can show us the ropes."

"My brother Emilio used to take me on his boat. I loved it."

He grins. "Then perhaps you could show me the ropes. Are you close? You and your brother? I didn't get the opportunity to spend much time with him when I was in Havana."

"When we were younger, we were. We played together constantly. Sometimes our cousin Magdalena would join us. We'd spend all day in the backyard, pretending we were pirates, having adventures. They were some of my happiest memories. But Magdalena grew up and moved to Spain. And Emilio—he works too much now, is too serious to spend time with his little sister. As our father has gotten older, he's given much of the responsibility of the business to Emilio.

"Emilio wanted to be a doctor. Before this mess with Machado. Our father was convinced he would outgrow the desire, but he never did. Then the choice was taken away from him."

"He did his duty, and you did yours."

There's a question in his tone, one I have no desire to answer. How do you answer a question like that without an insult?

"I asked about you before I approached your father," Anthony continues. "No one said your affections were tied, but . . . did you leave a lover back in Cuba?"

In this moment, I wish there had been a sweet boy who pressed gentle kisses to my lips and read me poetry on lazy Havana afternoons. I wish there had been something to acclimate me to this man who sees too much and pushes too hard.

"No, no one special."

"And if there had been?" he asks.

"Would I have chosen duty or love?"

Anthony nods.

"I don't know."

"I suppose I should count myself lucky then that I didn't have a rival for your affections."

"'Rival' implies more effort on your part. You swooped in and snapped me up before we'd even been properly introduced."

He laughs. "And I prefer this plainspoken version of you to the blushing, simpering debutante that greeted me after the wedding."

"I didn't blush a lot in Cuba," I admit. "And certainly no simpering."

"Then please don't do so with me. I want the real version of you. Not who you think I want you to be."

When he leans toward me this time, I'm ready for him, meeting him halfway as his arm hooks around my waist, pulling me against his body as his lips meet mine.

His grip tightens on my waist, his mouth slanting over mine, deepening the kiss, leaving me breathless and dizzy.

"You're good at that," I say when he releases me, my heart pounding insistently, my lips sensitive and swollen.

Satisfaction gleams in his eyes.

"You've likely had a great deal of practice," I add, shamelessly fishing for the truth.

He doesn't bother refuting my claim, and I can't fault his honesty.

"You don't lie, do you?" I ask. "Not out of politeness or consideration. Not to spare someone's feelings."

"No."

"So if you aren't a liar, then what is your biggest flaw?"

His lips curve. "Some would say greed."

He's right in front of me again, his fingers skimming my jawline, and this time, I'm the one who leans into the kiss, whose lips brush against his first. A soft gasp escapes his mouth, and a thrill fills me at the realization that I have caught him unaware.

There's power in that; my life as a wife will likely be far easier if I can turn his head, if I can keep his attention.

Not to mention, I like it.

This time when we finish kissing, he doesn't release me, but instead intertwines his fingers with mine.

"I have to go to my meeting." The regret in his voice winds its way through my heart. "Will you be fine on your own?"

"Of course," I reply. "Will you be meeting your associates here?"

"No. There's a house up the road that we're using for the meeting. I'll be back soon."

With a quick kiss to my cheek, he's gone, walking back toward the house, his hands shoved deep in his pockets, his collared shirt stretching across his frame.

It takes me far longer than it should after he's left to collect myself, to turn my attention back to the water steps away from me.

It's strange how different beaches can be, how their individual characters can make them so distinct.

Cuba is beautiful.

Islamorada is something else entirely.

The landscape is peppered with heavy brush, rendering my dainty sandals practically useless as the ground scrapes at my feet. Branches snag at the skirt of my dress. There's an almost sinister quality to the scenery, as though the flora and fauna aren't afraid to snap back at us interlopers and swallow us whole.

A swishing sound in the mangroves makes me jump. A dark snake slithers past me, inches away from my exposed feet, its body undulating in the dirt.

I scream—

A man emerges from the mangroves at the edge of the property, wearing a pair of ratty overalls with a dirty shirt beneath them. His hair is matted with sweat and sea, a cigarette dangling from his mouth.

One of the gardeners, I imagine, his tanned skin roughened from days spent working under the sun.

I give an embarrassed laugh. "I'm sorry I screamed. I must have startled you. There was a snake, and, well . . ." I gesture ruefully toward my ridiculous footwear. "I didn't exactly pack for these conditions."

He doesn't speak, merely stares back at me.

I hurry past the spot where the snake crossed in front of me.

The weight of his gaze follows me as I walk toward the mangroves, heading for the opening to the stretch of beach. In Cuba, I was friendly with the staff—most of them had been with the family since I was a little girl. Our gardener, Carlos, taught me all about flowers, and I helped him plant at the start of each season. If I were back home, I would walk up to the man and introduce myself. But here, the rules are different. I am an outsider, noticeably so. The staff keeps their distance, and not just because I don't quite fit in, but more likely because I am Anthony Cordero's wife.

People are deferential, and it isn't only because of his wealth. They fear my husband.

When I look back, the man is gone.

Ten

Elizabeth

I wake early and dress quickly, eager to start the day.

I walk to Sam's room next door and knock. From my place in the hallway, I can hear the sound of furniture creaking, the rustling of linens, heavy footfalls padding across the floor. The door opens with a creak, and Sam peers through the crevice, his hair mussed, dressed only in his undershirt and a pair of slacks.

"What time is it?" he asks, his voice husky with sleep.

"Just after eight."

A wince.

"I've always been an early riser," I chirp, letting my eyes wander as I look my fill. There's something utterly delicious about a rumpled man, and in his sleepy surliness, Sam doesn't disappoint.

"I'd have guessed you debutantes lounge around in bed for hours."

"Ex-debutante, remember? Besides, I could never sit still long enough to lounge." I grin. "Wouldn't have taken you for a late riser, though."

Sam rakes a hand through his hair. "I've been on a job for a few weeks now. Sleep's been hard to come by."

"Sin never sleeps?"

"Something like that."

"This man you've been hunting has to be pretty dangerous to keep you up at night."

"He is."

"Well, if he's as bad as you say, are you sure it's a good idea to take the morning off? Are you still interested in going with me to the camps today?"

"I am. I can spare a few hours. Just give me time to get dressed."

"I'm going to walk down by the water. I'll meet you in front of the inn in"—I take in his appearance, the cross expression on his face, and factor the late hour at which we arrived last night—"thirty minutes?"

"Fine." Sam closes the door without another word.

I descend the steps quickly, flashing the man behind the desk who checked us in last night a smile.

"Storm's coming," he calls out as I walk by.

Sam mentioned something about a storm yesterday. Hopefully, it won't rain too much before we make it to the camps.

As soon as I step out of the inn, the sound of the ocean hits me, the unfamiliar landscape lending itself to the sensation that I have traveled to a distant land. I couldn't be anywhere more distinct from Manhattan if I tried. The beach is narrow, the skinny strip of sand bordered by mangroves and swamp. Debris litters the sand—pieces of wood, an empty glass bottle, parts of crates broken up and adrift on the shore—remnants of civilization in a notably uncivilized place.

And still, despite the slender island, the strange little beach, it's not an entirely unpleasant place. The sun is bright, the air still, the sky clear. It's beautiful in a wild, wanton sort of way that calls to something inside me yearning to be free.

A girl walks down the sandy path toward the beach. She stops a few feet away from me.

"I was beginning to think I was the only one out here at the end of the world," I say in greeting.

"Not quite the end of the world," she calls back, walking closer toward me. "Though, perhaps, one of the less-inhabited corners of it."

She speaks with an accent that in addition to her glamorous attire furthers the notion that she's not a local.

I appraise the girl quickly, taking in the trim dress better suited for a stroll on Fifth Avenue, the ostentatious diamond on her ring finger, the sublime rose-colored shoes. She looks and smells like money, and for a moment, I let the scent waft over me, remembering how good it tasted on my tongue—oysters, and exotic fruits, their flavor sweet and tangy running down my throat, champagne, the odor of perfume from Paris. I almost want to stroke the fabric of her dress, if only to feel something other than this cheap, worn material against my skin.

"You're not from around here, are you?" I ask.

"No, I'm here on my honeymoon."

"Congratulations."

She doesn't respond with the lovesick smile of a newlywed or the smug expression of a woman who's snared a prime marital catch. In fact, she doesn't say anything at all, so I fill the silence myself.

"I'm Elizabeth."

After my family's disgrace, my old friends proverbially flew south for the winter rather than have their good reputation tarnished. Not that I can entirely blame them—a girl's good name is everything, or so they tell me.

She smiles, and I detect a hint of loneliness there, too.

"Mirta. It's lovely to meet you."

"Interesting spot for a honeymoon, Mirta."

"We married in Havana. We're on our way to New York City. We're here for a few days, but my husband thought it was a convenient stopping point."

"What a small world. I came from New York. What's your husband's name?"

If there was a single man with a respectable fortune—or a single man with an obscene fortune and a less than respectable reputation—my mother kept tabs on him up until recently.

"Anthony Cordero," she answers.

Shock fills me.

The name couldn't be more out of place, the images it conjures up made for the grit and muck of the city, the parts girls like me are only supposed to read about in the newspaper. While a man of Anthony Cordero's ilk hardly runs in the same tony circles my mother once inhabited, his name is instantly recognizable to most New Yorkers. It also hits uncomfortably close to home.

"You're joking."

Her chin lifts, and there's a spark of defiance in those brown eyes. "I'm not. I know what people say. We have gossip in Cuba as well."

"That doesn't bother you?"

"I haven't decided."

Well, well, well, not merely a proper, boring debutante.

"What's he like?" I ask, curiosity getting the best of me.

A flush settles over her cheeks.

Not boring at all.

"That good?" I tease.

The blush deepens.

I grin. "I'll take that as a 'yes.' I've seen his picture in the paper. He seems handsome enough if you like that sort."

"And how did you end up down here? Islamorada is a long way

from New York," she says with the practiced subject change of someone who has spent a fair amount of time in society.

I smile at her attempt to sidestep my admittedly rude remarks. I like her.

"Did you come down here with your family?" Her gaze searches my bare ring finger. "A husband?"

"No, just me."

Her jaw drops. "You came down here by yourself?"

"Why not? I wasn't going to ask for permission."

There's no mistaking the envy that sweeps across her features.

I smile. I know this girl. I used to be this girl: pampered, sheltered, hemmed in by society's rules and expectations. I rebelled, of course, but the tension within her is unmistakably familiar.

"That kind of freedom must be nice," she replies.

"It is."

"A little scary, too."

"It is," I admit, unsure why I'm sharing this with her. "I'm engaged to be married."

"Congratulations."

"That might be precipitous. It's not exactly what you would call a love match."

"Is that why you're down here by yourself?" she asks. "To run away?"

"Maybe."

"Then I wish you luck." She glances back over her shoulder before turning around to face me. "I should return to the house. We're staying up the road. The big white house with the black shutters. If you're bored, you should come by and visit."

"I don't want to impose on your honeymoon. No one likes a third wheel."

Not to mention, I very much doubt Anthony Cordero would welcome me into his home.

"My husband has some business to conduct while we're here," Mirta replies. "I don't think he'll be around very much, and I'd like the company. Besides, you might get lonely after a while by yourself."

Despite the risk, the desire for a real friend gets the best of me. "I'd like that, then."

Mirta walks away, her dark hair blowing in the breeze, the skirt of her dress kicked up by the wind.

Once she's gone, I am alone once more.

I gaze away, out to the sea, a storm somewhere off on the horizon. I wade into the water, lifting my skirt higher than I'd normally dare, exposing my calves, my knees. A wave tumbles right in front of me, the salt water spraying my face.

Despite the early hour, the sun beats down, warming my skin, but with the water pooling around my legs, the breeze whipping my hair around me, it isn't stifling at all; instead, I want to shed my clothes and go farther out to sea.

I glance around me.

Now that Mirta has departed, there's not a soul in sight, and thanks to the earliness of the morning and the remoteness of this stretch of beach, it's unlikely anyone else will see me. Given his disheveled appearance, Sam probably won't be ready to make our way to the camps yet.

The decision is made with speed, the ocean too tempting, my lack of care already a foregone conclusion.

I spent far too much of my life playing by the rules my parents set for me, expecting to make a good marriage, certain my life would be like my mother's used to be—filled with parties and laughter and ease. I didn't strictly follow the path they established, of course, because I'm me, and it seems somewhere along the way I inherited the Preston stubborn streak, but I mostly kept it within the acceptable margins, earning myself a few punishments, count-less exasperated sighs, and much hand-wringing.

But then the crash came.

And everything changed.

And I stopped caring, because none of it mattered anymore. I was ruined by the actions of others, so why not do it properly? Why not live on my terms rather than someone else's if it's all out of my control anyway?

I walk toward the shore, lift the cotton dress over my head, and lay it gently on the sandy beach, out of the water's reach. The frock was pretty enough long ago, when my curves were less extravagant, the floral pattern not as faded. Now it's several seasons out of what-ever passes for fashion these days. Still, it's one of my best dresses.

I wade back into the water, letting out a little whoop as it covers my legs.

"Elizabeth."

I move slowly, turning, the moment drawing out on an exhale, until I'm staring at Sam dressed in another neat suit, his jaw dropped.

The chemise really isn't all that scandalous—it's tattered white cotton, hardly tantalizing silk and lace—but the tic in Sam's jaw suggests otherwise.

"What—What are you doing?" he sputters.

"Swimming," I reply, the words coming out on the tail end of a laugh. "Having fun. You should try it sometime. It might change your life."

My smile deepens at the heat that flickers in his gaze.

Not so disinterested now, is he?

Sam shoves his hands in his pockets, stalking toward the water's edge, his gaze surveying the landscape as though he's searching for any and all possible threats.

He stops several feet away from me, the breaking waves licking at the toes of his sensible—boring—black leather shoes.

"I thought we were supposed to be visiting the camps, not playing around," he grumbles.

"I was more than ready earlier. You were the one who was still sleeping. Are you going to join me?" I tease, splashing the water around me.

He shifts, fixing me with an expression I suppose is meant to be stern. "I thought we'd formed a truce of sorts last night. No flirting."

"Oh, honey, flirting is like breathing. You shouldn't take it personally."

A speculative gleam enters his gaze. "You're not what I expected."

"What were you expecting?"

"Hell if I know. I thought you society girls were demure."

"They threw me out, remember?"

"I can't hazard a guess why."

I sigh. "Fine, let me put you out of your misery. I can practically feel your embarrassment from here." I walk toward the shore, waiting for him to do the gentlemanly thing and turn around.

He doesn't.

Instead, his gaze rakes me over from head to toe, the damp fabric of the chemise clinging to my legs, a few wet spots where the sea splashed against my torso. Now that I'm no longer in the ocean, my decision to go swimming seems foolish, a hint of salt sticking to my clothes.

I stop, and Sam bends down, picking up my dress and handing it to me wordlessly.

There's a moment when our skin brushes as he gives me the dress, his hand twitching, and I regain control of the situation, but it's swept away by the curve of his lips, the sardonic smile affixed on his face.

"You're going to be wet and miserable all day."

"In this heat? I'll be dry in ten minutes."

I slip the dress over my head, the rough cotton dragging over my skin causing goose bumps to rise. When my dress is righted, the buttons down the front redone, I meet his gaze once more.

"Are you ready?"

Sam leans forward. His lips graze my ear. "You missed a button."

I glance down, and sure enough, midway down my cleavage a button hole gapes open. I refasten it, and by the time I've finished and glance up, Sam's back is already to me as he moves away, leaving me little choice but to follow him.

We walk up to the inn's parking lot, to his car, and Sam opens the door for me as I slide into the passenger seat.

Once he's seated beside me, the key poised in the ignition, I can't help myself—

"I'm to be married," I blurt out.

I've no idea why I say it, only that it seems like it needs to be said.

Sam doesn't respond.

"Let me guess, you pity the man who would be saddled with me?"

He turns the key in the ignition, the engine humming to life. "I didn't say that. And I don't think it."

"Then what do you think?"

"That he's lucky bastard," he says, shocking me. His lips quirk. "And I hope he's ready for a bit of trouble. More than a bit," he amends.

"You think I'm trouble?"

"You know it. And unless I miss my guess, you like it."

Maybe I do.

"You must love him a great deal to agree to be tied down," Sam muses. "I wouldn't have thought you wanted that. You seem like you're searching for freedom more than anything."

Now it's my turn to be silent, his words hitting uncomfortably close to the truth. And at the same time, there is a loneliness to being wholly on your own that I didn't anticipate. Perhaps I wish to find the person with whom I can be free.

Eleven

TAT

Helen

I wake the next morning before the sun is up, fixing Tom his breakfast before he goes out fishing. It hardly seems like a day to be on the water, a storm threatening, but after last night's argument, I know better than to further provoke him—the bruises on my wrist are reminders enough of the consequence of his temper.

After Tom is gone, I set the cottage to rights, scrubbing the spilled bourbon from the floor with salt water, straightening pieces of furniture knocked askew. I'm more tired than usual by the time I walk the two miles to Ruby's Café, a persistent drizzle and a gray sky my companions along the way.

Despite the weather and the early hour, business is steady throughout the morning. Every so often, the door opens and a man lumbers in, and I tense.

Did Tom decide to check on me after all?

"Thought the weather might put them off," Ruby comments as I set down my tray with a wince. "They keep coming, though. It's shaping out to be a busy weekend. Must be that special Labor Day fare the railroad's running."

"Must be," I murmur, barely resisting the urge to lift my hair off my nape and fan myself. Between the pressure from the baby and the heat, the dizziness worsens with each passing hour. I wore a long-sleeved blouse and skirt today in an effort to hide the bruises, but at the moment, I'd almost rather face the prying stares than suffer another minute.

"You look terrible," Ruby comments.

"I didn't sleep well last night." There's no point in hiding it. My skin is even paler than normal, dark circles under my eyes.

Sympathy threads through her voice. "It's hard toward the end. I remember those days and don't envy you them."

The front door to the café opens, and I jerk—

A couple walks in, smiles on their faces, their cheeks pink from too much sun, eyes bleary from lack of sleep.

Tourists.

"You seem jumpy today. You expecting somebody?" Ruby asks.

"I—"

The door opens again, and this time I don't have to turn to the entrance to know who it is. Ruby's appraising smile and the slight curve of her lips settles the matter for me.

"Busy day for key lime pie," she says, a twinkle in her eyes.

My mouth is suddenly dry, words stuck in my throat. I take a deep breath and head over to John's table.

I'M WAYLAID TWICE BEFORE I GET THERE—ONCE WITH A REQUEST for more coffee and the second time because one of my tables' food orders is ready. By the time I make my way to John, my wrist is smarting again from carrying the heavy tray laden with food, a faint trail of sweat on my brow.

John is dressed in a clean white shirt and a pair of dark pants, his appearance a marked change from what I'm used to. This morning he looks like he could be sitting in a church pew listening to a Sunday sermon.

It must be lonely living alone in the camps. He appears older than me, but he's still young enough that he might want to have a family someday. Does he have a woman down here? Did he leave a sweetheart back home?

John glances up from the table when I am at his side, his gaze running over me, starting at my face, traversing the length of me, and back to the heavy tray in my hand.

"Are you well?" he asks, his voice low.

"I am," I lie.

There are more tourists than locals at the diner at the moment, but I can't take the chance that someone will mention to Tom that I was speaking to a strange man. Not after last night.

"And you?" I ask.

"I patched myself up."

"Good. I'm glad. Is there anything else I can get you?" I offer a half-hearted attempt at a smile. "Key lime pie?"

"Didn't come here for the pie. I wanted to see you. Make sure you were doing well after everything. I was worried about you."

"I'm fine."

"Was he there when you got home last night?"

I glance around the restaurant. Bobby from the bait stand is seated in one of the corner tables. He and Tom occasionally share a beer together after work. Two tables over, one of Tom's fishing customers is enjoying a meal with his wife. Near the entrance, Tom's brother's best friend dines with a friend.

"I can't talk." I lean forward, trying to keep my expression neutral as though I am merely taking a customer's order. "Tom will be upset."

"Then meet me out back."

"I'm working," I hiss.

"Don't you have a break coming up?"

"I—"

"You convinced me. I'll have a piece of key lime pie. Thank you," John says in a voice loud enough to carry to the next few tables. He lowers his tone. "Ten minutes."

I don't respond, heading to the back and giving the cook the order for a slice of pie.

"He seems chattier than usual," Ruby says, coming to stand next to me.

"Mm-hmm."

"Are you going to take your break soon? You seem like you could use it."

My gaze flickers to John sitting alone at his table, his back to me. I would be a fool to meet him. I'm grateful for his help last night, but I don't need someone swooping in to rescue me from my life.

"Helen. You really don't appear well."

"I'm tired, the baby—"

"I heard Tom was out drinking last night. Max saw him leave Duval Street looking worse for the wear. Did he cause problems when he came home?"

"There was some trouble outside the restaurant last night. Two men tried to rob me." I jerk my head toward the table where John sits. "*He* helped me. Walked me home to make sure I got there safe. Tom didn't like it."

"What kind of trouble?"

I tell her about the men, about what happened.

"From now on, you're not closing by yourself. And if you see them around here again, you tell me." Her expression darkens. "Tom hurt you, didn't he?"

"He—It's nothing that hasn't happened before. Nothing I can't handle."

"He's no good."

"Sometimes he is," I say, driven by an irrational need to defend my husband. After all, I made vows, didn't I?

For better or worse, in sickness and in health. What's your word worth if you take back the promises you make? But there were promises Tom made, too, ones that were broken.

What is this if not "worse"? The man I married isn't the man I'm married to now. It's like there's a sickness inside him, eating away at those good parts I fell in love with so long ago until there's nothing of the emotions I once felt for him, only fear and regret.

"He hasn't been good since he was a boy, and even then he had a wicked streak in him," Ruby retorts. "You couldn't see it. Young love, and all that nonsense. He was always a wild one. Thought he could do whatever he wanted and the hell with everyone else."

"Things have been difficult lately. Fishing isn't what it used to be. He's under a lot of pressure."

"Lots of people are under a lot of pressure. And lots of men don't beat their wives."

"I know. When the baby comes—"

Things will change. They have to. We'll be a family. Tom will drink less. Things will get better. I'll stop fantasizing about my husband's death.

"When the baby comes, nothing will change," Ruby replies, gentleness in her voice. "Do you want your child to grow up seeing its mother hurting? Do you want to spend your days worrying that one day he'll use his fists on them, too?"

"I would never let someone hurt my child."

"Helen. No matter how hard you try, as long as you're with him, you'll be in danger. It's getting worse, isn't it?"

"It is. But is leaving supposed to be easy? He'll kill me if I try to leave and he catches me. He told me last night that he'd take the baby away from me."

"Oh, honey. You could go to the police."

"What will they do? How is Tom different from other men? Do you know how many nights Tom has spent in the jail sleeping one off only to be released in the morning with a smile and a wave? Sometimes he takes the sheriff out fishing, shows him the best spots to catch marlin."

"Is there somewhere you could go?"

"Tom would find me."

After all, there aren't many places I could hide. Nearly all of my childhood friends moved north when things got bad, when tourism dried up and the fishing industry changed and the only money to be had was smuggling booze or running guns.

"No one can tell you what to do, Helen; you have to decide for yourself. But he's got you thinking you're backed into a corner, that you have nowhere to go, no options but him, and that's not true. You have friends, people who would help you, and most importantly, you're smart and you're stronger than you give yourself credit for. No one could live the life you've been living and not be brave.

"Before I met Max there were men. Some good, others not so much. The bad ones will make you believe you're nothing. They'll make you small because that's the only way they'll ever see themselves as amounting to anything. It's a lie. The second you stop believing the lie is the second you take their power away from them."

"I'm having a baby. Tom's baby. If I leave, he'll come after us. I've seen what he's capable of when he's angry—I don't want to consider what he'll do. Even if I could leave, if I could escape somewhere, how would I support us?"

"You're doing a pretty good job of it now. How much of the money you make here does Tom drink away in a bottle? I didn't say it was easy, but, honey, nothing about life is easy or ever has been. You got steel in you, and it's time you believed it."

This baby inside me is a ticking clock, and where I'd almost convinced myself this marriage was something I deserved, the vows a promise that shouldn't be broken, it's not only me anymore. I want better for my child. I want better for myself.

"You and the baby can always stay with me and Max."

It's kind of her to offer, but I can't bring that kind of trouble to their doorstep, and in many ways, Key West is really a small town in its own right.

"What about your aunt?" she asks. "Your momma's sister?"

"We write to each other, but I haven't seen her since I was a little girl. I can't bring these problems to her—"

"Sure you can. You worry about getting safe. The rest will fall into place."

My mother passed away seven years ago, and I never miss her more than in moments like these, when I'm in need of advice, comfort. Maybe she would have told me my place was with Tom, that every man gets a little free with his fists when he's had too much to drink, but whatever words she would have given me, the absence of her is the hardest part. She wasn't a soft woman, my momma, couldn't be married to a man like my father if she was, but she loved me, and I wish more than anything that she was still here, to help guide me through this new phase in life.

But she's not here.

There's just me, and this baby.

What if there could be something else? Somewhere for the two of us? What if I could be free? I'm scared, but more than anything, I'm tired. So tired.

"I'll take my break now, Ruby."

Our gazes lock, and she leans forward, wrapping her arms around me, giving me a swift hug—the first I've experienced in all the time I've known her.

"You do right by that baby. You do right for yourself."

THE FRESH AIR HITS ME WHEN I OPEN THE BACK DOOR OF RUBY'S, the freedom from the various odors escaping from the kitchen much needed, and I sag against the building's exterior.

The sound of footsteps coming around the corner startles me. In the daylight, the back of the restaurant doesn't seem as ominous as it did last night, but I've learned my lesson not to be too lax.

My heartbeat slows as John comes into view.

He stops a few feet away from me. His limp is less pronounced in the morning; in all the times he's come into Ruby's, I never really noticed it until last night.

"You're in pain," he says, his gaze searching.

"It's the baby. It's uncomfortable."

"I worried about you last night. I shouldn't have let you go into that house alone. I should have gone in with you to make sure it was safe."

"That's the last thing you should have done. Trust me. It only would have made things worse."

"It's not only the baby bothering you. Did he hurt you?" He says the words with a mixture of fury and disbelief, as though he cannot understand how such a thing is possible even though the evidence to the contrary is right in front of him.

My mind reels from my conversation with Ruby. It's the leaving that scares me most. I can't stay in Key West. But leaving is a difficult proposition when you don't have a car and you don't have much money. Leaving seems impossible when you're walking away from all you've known, when the stakes are life and death.

I was a girl when we married, barely more than a child myself. Tom has been my whole world; he has made himself my whole world in all sorts of little ways I never even realized, like telling me what to wear, or what to eat, or who I should be friends with. But as hard as it is to envision my life without him, I can't see staying with him, either.

In the distance, the sound of a hammer hitting a nail over and over again echoes like gunfire.

I jerk.

They're boarding up houses and businesses in preparation for the storm. If she comes, they'll applaud their foresight; if she misses us entirely, they'll grumble as they pull down the boards.

It's funny how one man's paradise can be another's prison.

I can't stay another day in mine.

"I'm leaving him."

The words escape my lips before my mind catches up with the reality of them, but as soon as I say them, I am filled with a sense of rightness even as fear seeps through.

"Where will you go?" John asks.

"My aunt lives up north—Islamorada. I haven't seen her in years, but we write letters." Letters I've always hidden from Tom, since he didn't approve of Aunt Alice and her independence. "She might know of a place I could stay."

Getting to Islamorada is the difficult part; it's about an hour drive to the ferry landing, and then there's the ferry—

"A guy I grew up with lives down here part of the year," John says. "He lets me borrow his car when he's not around, when he doesn't need it. I'm planning on leaving this morning—driving up to No Name Key and taking the ferry back to camp. It would be no trouble for me to take you to your aunt's." He glances down at a surprisingly elegant timepiece. "Ferry leaves around eight. If we hurry, we might be able to make it."

And like that, I leave my husband.

WE BARREL DOWN THE HIGHWAY LIKE THE DEVIL IS ON OUR HEELS. For all I know, perhaps he is. I left with nothing other than the clothes on my back, a fistful of tips and my unpaid wages—with a little extra from Ruby—shoved into the pocket of my dress. I briefly considered returning to the cottage to pack a bag, but there wasn't enough time and it wasn't worth the risk of encountering Tom. The ferry is unpredictable enough as it is; better to leave now when there's help to be found and a chance of escape than miss this opportunity.

I glance at John behind the wheel of the Plymouth, wondering if he's regretting his decision to help me out, if he's afraid Tom will come after us. How would the law view a man interfering in the business of a man and his wife—helping to take his child away from him? In these parts, people take care of their own, and for an outsider like John, the price to pay is steep indeed.

"I'm sorry," I say.

"Why?"

"I keep laying troubles at your feet."

"It's no trouble. You saved me last night. Everybody needs help at one point or another. There's no shame in that."

He says it so matter-of-factly, but it's not that simple, is it? The world has expectations of you, of how you are to shoulder your burdens with grace, of the role you play, and as soon as you don't live up to those expectations, it's easier for others to cast you aside rather than change how they view the world.

We are defined by what we do for others, by our relationships, by what we have to offer. A married woman has a measure of security a single one does not; a pretty girl a better chance than a plain one. A soldier who comes back from war triumphant is a hero, whereas one who is broken by the effort is forgotten.

The road is rougher the farther we head away from Key West,

the landscape changing and becoming more desolate as we continue on. I haven't been this far north in years, and it's a whole other world. Despite the small space, it appears you could go days without another soul in sight.

"Thank you for helping me regardless," I reply. "You know it's strange that we've ended up together like this. Of all my customers, you were the one who was always a mystery. Most of the time people sit down at your table and offer more details about their lives than you want to know. But with you, it was the opposite."

"I didn't used to be quiet. But it's hard talking to people when you lose the art of talking about nothing. People ask how you're doing, but they don't really want to know if you're struggling or not; they want the answer that enables them to go about their day without feeling guilty."

I never thought about it that way, but he's right. There are greetings, and casual questions I ask throughout my day, but they're done out of habit more than anything else. They're expected. A routine that makes everyone more comfortable, the answers as rote as the questions themselves. A script we've all memorized.

"It seemed easier than pretending I was someone I wasn't, than unburdening myself on others," John adds.

"Everyone needs help at one point or another," I say, repeating his earlier words. "There's no shame in that."

"And no one ever helped you get away?"

"It's not that simple." I twist the little tin wedding band around my finger, not quite ready to remove it. Despite the physical act of leaving, it seems as though I'll always be tethered to Tom.

"Did you ever consider living elsewhere?" John asks me.

"When I was younger, all the time. That was one of the things that first drew me to Tom. We used to go out on his boat, and we'd talk about sailing away, moving down to the Bahamas, or going to Cuba, seeing the world."

"What happened?"

"Life, I suppose. Do you like the work you do on the highway?" I ask, changing the subject away from my lost dreams.

"I do. It's hard work, but at the end of the day when your head hits the pillow there's not a lot of room for much else in your mind."

"It must be difficult going to war."

"Going to war was the easy part—people prepare you for that. Coming home was the hard part. There's this buildup before you leave. Your head is filled with ideas of what it will be like, of what you can accomplish, a desire to sacrifice yourself for something bigger than yourself. And whatever you expect, war is something else entirely. But at least there's a mission, a focus, and you're surrounded by people who come from different walks of life, but who you're connected to by this bond no one else will ever understand. And then it's all over."

I take his hand. He jerks beneath my touch, and I can't tell who is more startled by my action—me or him—and then he exhales, his whole body shuddering with the effort, and for a beat he is still.

I can't remember the last time I touched a man who wasn't Tom, but the hurt in John is unmistakably familiar, and the desire to offer comfort is instinctive.

After all, what more do we want than for someone to see us as we are, to acknowledge our pain, and to offer a moment of relief?

I give him a quick, reassuring squeeze before I snatch my hand back.

How long has it been since I made a friend?

"Is your wrist bothering you?" he asks.

"How did you—"

"You were favoring it earlier when you were carrying the tray in the restaurant. And the older bruises made it clear he was rough with you."

"He wasn't always."

"He shouldn't ever be."

For a moment, I seize that thought; I imagine living in a world of such comforting absolutes. But the moment flits away from me, carried off by the wind blowing through the open car window.

WE ARRIVE AT THE FERRY JUST IN TIME. JOHN PARKS THE CAR, coming around behind the back of the vehicle to open the passenger door for me. I wince as I try to get up, the sheer size of my stomach sending me toppling back.

"Are you all right?" John asks.

"Give me a moment."

I take a deep breath, pushing off from the car seat. John takes my elbow, holding me steady as I rise to my feet, his fingers blessedly avoiding the bruises Tom left on my arm.

"You folks waiting on the ferry?" a voice calls out.

"We are," John answers.

"Good timing. Storm's coming. This is the last trip. Y'all better hurry."

I move as quickly as the babe will allow; John rests his hand on the small of my back, guiding me, supporting me.

When we get on the ferry, the car loaded as well, my stomach lurches, the water surprisingly choppy.

We wait while the rest of the passengers board quickly, the ferry filling with men who work on the highway. A few acknowledge John with a tilt of their head, but whether they recognize him as a friend or acquaintance, or simply the fact that he is one of them, is difficult to tell.

John stands stiffly beside me, his gaze scanning each new arrival, and it isn't until the fourth or fifth passenger that I realize I'm doing the same thing—searching for Tom in the faces of all these men. Not that a ferry ride will stop my husband. If he figures out where I've gone, it'll be easy enough for him to take his boat to Matecumbe in search of me.

A few feet away from where I stand, a big man lumbers on board, his head bent, the span of his shoulders broad, his body as recognizable as my own. Panic fills me, and I move behind John, pressing my body against the railing, praying he doesn't see me.

How could Tom have found me so quickly?

He raises his head, and my heart stops for a moment, the breath knocked out of me.

"Helen?" John says, his brow furrowed.

I grip the railing, glancing out over the water. For one utterly terrifying moment, I consider what it would be like to jump overboard and take my chances with the sea.

But the man turns before I truly consider it, and there's a flash of something on his features—an expression I'm intimately familiar with—and then it's gone, and I realize it isn't Tom at all.

Only a stranger with a similar manner of carrying himself.

The surge of relief hits me so quickly I could almost cry.

Man after man hops on the ferry, some big, some slight, but none of them are Tom.

We cast off, pulling away from the dock, the water slapping the side of the boat.

Suddenly, it's all too much, and I lean over the railing, sickness overtaking me.

When I'm finished, a square piece of fabric enters my line of sight, and I take it wordlessly, surprised by the fine cloth, the initials painstakingly embroidered in the corner. Did a girlfriend make this for him? A fiancée?

I clean myself up discreetly before facing John.

"Thank you." I hope my cheeks aren't too red, my embarrassment great indeed.

"Of course. Have you been sick throughout the pregnancy?"

"In the beginning, but then it went away. Lately, it's come back with a vengeance. The sea isn't making it easier." I grip the railing as the boat rocks once more.

"They say it helps if you focus on a steady point," John suggests.

"Helps with what?"

"The seasickness."

"And if there is no steady point?"

The weather has kicked up considerably in the last few hours, the wind wailing, waves battering the ferry, the crest rising higher and higher.

"Then you plant your feet and hope for the best."

The water tosses the boat to and fro.

"Hold on to the railing. I've got you," John shouts.

The boat jolts, and I lurch forward, John lunging to catch me.

Suddenly, we slow until we're at a near crawl.

I grip the railing more tightly, dread settling in my stomach like a ball of lead.

"Why are we slowing down?" I ask John.

What if Tom has come after us?

"Let me see if I can find out what's going on. Will you be fine if I leave you here by yourself?"

I nod.

Around me, people have taken notice of our decreased speed as well, murmurs and shouts rising from the crowd.

There's open water all around us, and I scan for the *Helen*, to see if Tom has flagged down the ship, but all I can see are the riotous waves that look like they could consume us.

What have I done?

Footsteps echo behind me, and John's voice—

"One of the propellers broke. That's what slowed us down. With only one left, the trip will take hours longer than we thought."

I lean over the side of the ferry and lose the rest of my breakfast.

Twelve

Elizabeth

It's late in the morning by the time we're on the road. Silence fills the car as we drive to the first of the veterans' camps, and suddenly, I can't take it anymore, the need to fill my head with something other than my worry overwhelming.

I stare out the window. "What a strange little place. You could almost stand in the middle of the road and put both of your arms out and touch the water."

Sam chuckles. "Somehow I can see you doing just that. You'd probably cause an accident."

"You know, I'm not only a troublemaker. I have other qualities. Besides, it's hardly my fault if men can't keep their wits about them in front of a pretty girl."

"I thought we already settled the matter of you being more than 'pretty.' And you're right. Men do utterly absurd things when women are involved."

"Perhaps men do utterly absurd things on their own and merely like to use women as a convenient excuse for their foolishness. Are you speaking from experience, pray tell?"

He grins. "I might be."

"I can't fathom the woman who'd get under your skin."

He shoots me a curious look. "What's that supposed to mean?"

"I didn't take you for the romantic sort."

"Whereas, let me guess, you fall in love weekly."

"Only on Tuesdays. Mondays I'm far too busy, and falling in love on a weekend is too prosaic."

"And Wednesdays?"

"Oh, I'm usually bored with them by Wednesday, and on to the next one. It's a very delicate balance."

"I see that. And who was the last man you fell in love with? The fiancé?"

His tone is mild, but I detect a note of interest there buried beneath the layers of insouciance.

I pause, as though I'm conjuring a man up from legions, when really the answer is so simple it twists my heart.

I shake my head. "No, not him. Billy."

There's only the slightest pang when I say his name now, as time affords.

"Billy?"

"William Randolph Worthington III."

He snorts. "Billy."

"Yes, Samuel. Billy to his friends."

"And naturally, you were very good friends."

"As a matter of fact, we were. After a fashion."

"And you loved him?"

"Everybody loved Billy."

"But he, what, bored you a day later?"

I give him a tight smile. "Something like that."

"What really happened?"

"Why do you care?"

"Maybe I want to pass the time."

"What time? This place is so small, we'll be there in a minute."

"So entertain me for that minute."

"Have I ever told you how much I hate being ordered about?" I retort.

"You didn't need to. Your manner fairly screams it."

"And still, you try."

"Because you like a challenge. I bet Billy didn't challenge you."

He didn't, not really, but that's beside the point.

"Billy was lovely. Billy's mother less so."

"She didn't approve."

"Hardly."

"Why?"

"Do you really have to ask?"

"You're likable enough."

"Such effusive praise," I snort.

"So why didn't Mrs. Worthington II like you?"

"She probably thought I'd thoroughly corrupt her son. Scandal can be contagious."

"I thought scandals were regular occurrences around your set."

"Not my sort of scandal. People want to gossip about you when you're high enough for them to envy you, but when you fall, they want nothing more than to forget you."

"They were afraid," Sam says. "Afraid your family's misfortunes would be contagious."

"Perhaps. When all else fails, be a cautionary tale." I shrug. "It's ridiculous, really. The Depression has largely avoided families like the Worthingtons and their ilk. Fate is a capricious thing; there's no accounting for whom it affects. One family is spared, while the next is utterly decimated."

"If he'd loved you, Billy would have stood by you."

I laugh. "Does knowing that make it any easier?"

"If you'd loved Billy, you would have never let him give you up."

"And how would I have achieved that? If a man's made his mind up to go, I very much doubt there's anything a woman can do to stop him."

"Then you underestimate yourself. I don't believe any man can walk away from you without regretting it."

I open my mouth to speak—

Confounding man.

"Besides, look at you now. You've come all the way down here searching for a man. That's not someone who's easily deterred. So if Billy was the great love and you've given him up, what's brought you down here? The fiancé? Did he run off before you could walk down the aisle?"

"I'm trying to find my brother. Half brother, actually. His mother was my father's first wife."

She died of cancer; my father married my mother a scandalous eight months later.

"We lost touch with him a few years ago," I add. "The war—he wasn't the same when he came back from the war. He sent letters occasionally, but he disappeared from our lives."

"You couldn't have been more than a little girl when he left."

"I was. I remember what he was like before, though. Flashes of memories, at least. He was my hero. He had the best laugh. He was always bringing me treats, sneaking me sweets my mother didn't want me to have."

"What did he do over there?" Sam asks.

"He was a doctor when he volunteered. He went into medical service."

"He must have seen a great deal of death."

Almost forty million people died during the course of the Great War, and I've often wondered how many saw my brother in their final hours.

"He must have. He never spoke of it to anyone, though. When the war was over, we waited and waited for him to come home, and he never did. We received a letter postmarked from London that arrived much later saying he was alive. A few years passed and he showed up on our doorstep. I barely recognized him. He stayed for a night or two and he was gone again. Over the years, he would show up unexpectedly and disappear again. Finally, he stopped coming around."

"Do you know where he was living during that time?"

"No."

"And then you got a letter from him with a Key West postmark."

"Yes."

"And you thought the prudent thing was to board a train and drag him home yourself?"

"There were exigent circumstances."

"Such as?"

"That's enough of my secrets," I answer instead.

"Why is it so important you find your brother?"

"He's all I have left."

"You have no one else?"

"My mother isn't well," I say in a tone that makes it clear I'm done sharing.

"When did you last hear from your brother?" Sam asks.

"A month ago."

I don't add how the letter appeared on the same afternoon Frank proposed, or tell him how I felt when I opened it and saw my brother's familiar handwriting, how it seemed like the answer to all of my prayers, as though my big brother could sense my distress and was rescuing me like he did all those times when we were younger.

I don't tell him my brother is the only thing standing between me and a marriage I'm desperately trying to escape.

"There's the camp up ahead," Sam says.

AT FIRST GLANCE, THE CAMP ON WINDLEY KEY—CAMP ONE—IS A soulless place devoid of color, everything arranged in cold, austere angles with military precision. Upon deeper examination, it's a soulless place devoid of color that stinks to high heaven.

"I heard the conditions were rough," Sam admits. "But I wasn't expecting this."

I don't speak as he parks the car, my gaze on the camp, my heart sinking at the sight before me. A few tents dot the landscape in rows, meager-looking shacks with canvas-covered roofs beside them doing little to improve the conditions.

Men walk around, their shirts grimy and soaked with sweat, the cheap fabric sticking to their bodies. A faint buzzing fills the air, and a man slaps at his skin, killing a mosquito with the flat of his hand.

What kind of disease breeds in a place like this with all manner of vermin crawling about, men crammed in such tight and unsanitary quarters?

There's a uniformity to the men—they all appear tired and worn down, as though they are one tragedy away from losing everything.

I wait while Sam turns off the car, comes around the side, and opens the door for me. The heel of my sandal sinks into the ground as I get out of the car, and Sam supports me, his palm warm against my skin.

I lean into him, taking a deep breath, the air in the camp heavy and cloying.

Curious glances are cast our way, and Sam steps closer to me, settling his hand at the small of my back, hovering there reassuringly.

I search for my brother's face among these men, for a glimmer of recognition on their faces, but none stares back at me.

"How many men are down here working?" I murmur to Sam.

"Several hundred."

It's a small enough island that it seems like everyone knows everyone around here, even if there's a tension between the veterans and locals. And still—it's been years since my brother and I last saw each other, the picture I carry with me hopelessly outdated, the face of a boy before he went to war.

"Stay close," Sam urges. "I'm going to see if I can find someone who's in charge."

I wrap my arm around his, bringing my body against his side. Sam stiffens against me in surprise, and for an awkward moment, I think he's going to pull away, but he doesn't.

The camp is far rougher than I ever imagined; men loll about intoxicated, their sly glances and nudges making it clear that they are unused to many women in their presence. The stench in the air I can't quite place—and surely, don't wish to: fish, sea, sweat, and rot, and the sweet sickness that so frequently accompanies any number of maladies. I surreptitiously press my nose to my fist. I search for my brother, try to envision how his features might have changed, how the passage of time would have altered him.

Sam tenses beside me. "This was a bad idea."

We walk around the camp for a couple of minutes before Sam locates a man who appears to be in charge. Along the way I show the old photo to a few people, but no one recognizes him, or is even sober enough to notice.

"We're trying to find this man," Sam says, showing the photo to the man in charge.

He barely glances at the picture. "There's a storm coming. This isn't a real good time for a social visit. I gotta get these men taken care of."

"I'm searching for my brother," I interject.

"You see him here? There are other camps, though. Maybe he's on one of them. A lot of guys are gone for the holiday weekend. Down in Key West getting drunk or up in Miami doing the same. Besides, plenty of people come down here and then they stop showing up."

"My brother's not like that."

The look the man gives me is almost pitying. "They're all like that, darling."

"They were heroes once," I retort. "It seems like the least you could do is show them some respect."

"Sure. They'll tell you the same if you get enough drink in them. That was a long time ago. Those men who went to war—you wouldn't recognize them in the men who work here."

"How could I?" I snap as I gesture around the camp, my arm arcing out farther than I intended and nearly hitting Sam in the process. "Who would thrive in an environment like this?"

"Now, you listen here. We run a fine camp up here."

"A clean, orderly one," I say sarcastically.

"You want clean? Orderly? We do the best we can with what we've got here. We've got storms and mosquitoes, men getting up to all sorts of trouble, and right now, my hands are full. I shouldn't be a glorified governess to grown men, but I might as well be. Your brother isn't here, and unless I miss my guess, the fact that you're searching for him means he doesn't want to be found."

He leaves me and Sam standing in the middle of the camp without so much as a good-bye.

"Should we talk to more workers?" I ask Sam.

"It's a small enough camp that if someone had seen him, we would have heard about it."

"It's an outdated photo. Maybe his appearance has changed."

"Still. No one here recognized him."

"That man said a lot of people are out of town for the weekend." Should I have stayed in Key West? It seemed more likely for me to find him here, but at the moment, he's so far away.

He could be dead.

I try to dismiss the thought, but now that I've seen the conditions down here, I can't ignore that it's a distinct possibility. The living is hard, and I'm not sure he would have been equipped for something like this.

"We can come back another day," Sam says, the sympathy in his voice unmistakable.

"You think this is a fool's errand, don't you?"

"It could be, yes. I didn't like that man more than you did, but he wasn't lying to you. Some people come down here and disappear. Either by choice or not. I'm not saying your brother is one of those people, but you have to be prepared for that possibility."

"How do you know so much about life down here, anyway?"

"Work, mostly."

"What about your work? The man you're chasing?"

"I've put some feelers out at the inn. He'll turn up. They always do. Right now, let's focus on your brother."

We drive down to Camp Five on Matecumbe Key. It's smaller than Camp One, but still filthy, the same mosquitoes swarming around, the same indistinguishable stench in the air.

Bile rises in my throat. "How can they treat people like this? We wouldn't even treat our animals like this."

"This is what happens when you have a problem you don't want to deal with. You put it out of people's sight, out of their minds, get them out of Washington with the hope that they won't cause trouble anymore."

I was too young to care when the Bonus Army marched on Washington D.C., too full of my own drama and life to consider people so far removed from my own reality. It wasn't my problem, and even though my brother fought in the war, it was easy to view him as separate from all of this. Seeing what has become of so many of the soldiers now, I cannot help but wonder how many people made the same mistake I did, how many turned their backs on the veterans once the war drifted from their minds and they had their own problems to worry about.

We walk through the camp silently, eyes on us once more—mostly me, rather. Not that Sam doesn't attract his share of gazes, though, too. I get the impression that many of the men view anyone connected with the government with mistrust—not that I can blame them considering their experiences—and Sam in his somber suit and hat looks like the quintessential government man.

We meet another man similar to the official we spoke to at Camp One—impatient and brusque, his mind on the coming storm. He doesn't recognize my brother's photograph; nor do the dozen or so other men we ask. With each person we approach, I sink lower and lower, tears threatening, my voice wavering until Sam wraps an arm around my waist and takes over, directing his questions toward the men in a manner that makes me think he must be quite a good investigator indeed. I wouldn't say he has a way of putting people at ease, but he naturally commands respect seemingly without making an effort to do so. The men I'm used to throw their wealth around as though by virtue of it they are entitled to having the world spread before them. Sam is simply direct, lacking in pretense or artifice, and I watch, fascinated by the skill.

I admire the power in his job, the ability to command respect, to ask questions people answer. It gives him a quiet confidence I can't help but envy.

It's late in the afternoon when we finish up at Camp Five, and suddenly, the storm everyone has spoken of seems to make an appearance, the sky darkening, a raindrop falling on my dress. Then another. And another.

"Come on." Sam tugs on my hand, pulling me away from the camp and the men with ruined dreams in their eyes.

Water falls from the sky in heavy waves, and we run toward Sam's car parked in the distance.

Thirteen

It doesn't rain for long, but it seems like an eternity. I desperately need to stretch my legs, to get fresh air in my lungs after the misery of the camps we visited today. Beside me in the car, Sam seems restless, too, tapping a silent melody on his thigh with his fingers, a cigarette in his free hand. I shake my head when he offers me a smoke, my gaze trained out the window.

We wait outside the Sunrise Inn, and when the rain finally breaks, we walk to the little beach I explored earlier. I edge toward the shore, away from Sam, the water covering my feet as I struggle to steady my breathing, to replace the stagnant, sticky heat that has taken residence there since we visited the camps.

Even if I do find him, the truth is inescapable now—the brother I once knew and loved is lost to me forever.

No one is coming to save me from this mess.

Sam hangs back, but his gaze weighs on me between drags of his cigarette, his attention unraveling me more and more. What does he see when he stares at me? What did all of those men see?

A spoiled girl with no sense of the real world?

I have never felt less sure of myself than I do at this moment. All of the things that made me *me*—my family, my friendships, our wealth, my plans for the future—have been taken away.

I was so eager to leave New York, to escape the prying eyes and whispers, that it never occurred to me I'd miss it. At least you can get lost in the commotion of the city. I've never felt more invisible than in a crowd of people, but out here surrounded by this stark beauty, just me and Sam, I am stripped bare.

Now that the rain has ended, the weather has changed, and it's practically peaceful. The clouds appear as though they're tinged in a coppery glow. For all they worried about an impending storm at the camp, now that the rain has passed, the weather couldn't be calmer or more beautiful.

"Have you ever seen clouds that color?" I ask. "It's almost pretty here."

Sam shrugs. "You see beaches, I see smugglers in the mangroves."

"I doubt I've ever met anyone less whimsical than you in my life."

"I could say the opposite of you, I suppose," he counters.

"Life's hard enough as it is," I reply. "It's easier to go through it with a smile."

"It's not just the smiles, though, is it?" he asks. "You live on the edge and you like it."

I laugh because when he says it, it seems terribly glamorous, but the reality is that being a woman—even a reckless one—is fairly mundane. Something I've learned quickly since my family's fall from grace. The heroics are often saved for men who wager big and risk it all, rather than the women left to care for them and pick up the pieces when they've returned.

"And what do you call chasing criminals all day, if not taking risks? I'm not the only one who enjoys life on the edge."

He inclines his head as though subtly acknowledging the truth behind my statement. "No, I suppose not. Although, to put a finer point on it, you could say I'm more inclined to stop trouble than cause it."

"That sounds dreadfully boring."

"You'd be surprised." He steps closer, as though he's sharing a secret with me. "It starts with a target. Someone whose criminal behavior tests the bounds of lawful society. It can be wantonness, or recklessness, or general wickedness."

"General wickedness doesn't sound boring at all," I tease, batting my eyelashes at him, sinking into this moment, this delicious moment, when I can cast my troubles away for the space of a heartbeat.

He eyes me speculatively. "I can't tell if you flirt because you're too smart for the world you're stuck in and you're bored as hell, or if you have a mischievous streak you can't resist indulging."

"Maybe it's both those things. You'd be frustrated if your hands were tied. The running of this world is left to men, and quite frankly, I'm not impressed with what they've done with it."

He's silent for a beat, his tone gentler than any I'm used to hearing from him. "What happened to your father?"

I take a deep breath, releasing the words in a whoosh as though the effort could push them as far away from myself as possible. "He killed himself after the crash in '29. He had an investment firm on Wall Street. He didn't lose everything all at once, but it was a slow leak. A few weeks later, things were bad enough that he stuck a gun in his mouth and pulled the trigger in his office at home." The familiar tightness fills my chest. "I found him."

"I'm sorry."

"My brother George killed himself a few months later."

An oath falls from Sam's lips.

"There were debts, and after the crash, there were more," I add.

"None of us knew. My father maintained the facade that everything was fine, until there was no use pretending anymore." I can't quite keep the anger from my voice. Maybe some cleave to the Almighty in times like these, but I've found more fury beneath my smiles than anything else.

"Some people say the Depression is our punishment for our wickedness," I continue.

Sam's voice is almost unbearably gentle. "In my experience, lots of people say lots of stupid things. Fear and panic make them search for scapegoats."

"True."

"You must miss your family a great deal."

"I do miss them. It's strange—we weren't even that close, really. They were both so busy with work and I was so young. But still—it's not the same with them gone. My mother—she's not well. Her nerves, they say. She hasn't been well for a long time—since she lost my father and brother."

"You're responsible for her?"

"I am. I left her with our housekeeper while I came down here. She's been with the family forever, and stayed on when the money ran out. These days, there aren't a lot of options out there. For a while, we sold what we could to try to manage things. Cut back. We were shuttled from family member to family member like a set of poor relations. But not many people want to take on extra mouths to feed right now, and even less so when they come with such a stigma attached to them. We were running out of options, drowning under the weight of my father's debts. So I did what needed to be done."

"The fiancé?" Sam asks.

"Yes."

"And now you have regrets?"

"There has to be a better way. I'd leave New York if I could, but my mother doesn't want to go. Neither one of us is in a position to make enough to support us even if there was work to be had. Her treatments are very expensive."

"What sort of treatments?"

"Oh, all sorts. Baths and the like. Medicines they use that the doctors tell me will shock my mother out of her illness. They make her body quiver, which is terrifying to see, but they say they'll help. None of it seems to do much good, but it's better than the alternative, I suppose—putting her in an institution."

I went to one of the ones her doctor recommended, and the conditions were so horrific I vowed then and there that she'd never end up in such a place.

Sam doesn't respond but instead looks to the ocean. "How was the water earlier?"

I swallow past the tears threatening. "Surprisingly warm."

"Still interested in going swimming?" Sam asks.

"Right now? With you?"

He nods.

My heart pounds. "I didn't think men like you did things like that. You're always so serious."

"Go swimming with a pretty girl? 'Course we do."

I don't have time for such frivolous things—for emotion, for desire, for complications—but I also can't resist.

My hands tremble as I undo the buttons down the front of my dress, slipping it from my shoulders and letting it fall to the sand.

I don't wait for Sam to follow suit before pivoting and heading for the water. I wade deeper into the ocean, the water skimming my belly button, higher up, covering my breasts. The ocean floor dips and rises with each indent, and I wait for the moment when I'll put my foot down and meet nothing but water.

If Sam knew who I was engaged to, he would likely run in the opposite direction. Frank Morgan isn't the sort to turn the other cheek while his fiancée engages in an affair with another man. A little flirting kept carefully away from the circles he controls is one thing, but to actually kiss a man, for things to go further, is deadly serious.

I am bought and paid for, my body no longer my own, a bargain I've made to become Frank's wife in exchange for his financial support for me and my mother.

And suddenly, a sharp slice of anger cuts through me, filling my lungs, pouring out of me, until I want to throw my arms back and lift my head to the sky, and roar. I don't, of course—some things are simply inconceivable—but the urge is there, the anger at my father, my brothers, at my mother, Billy Worthington, who "loved" me enough to take me to bed and then cast me aside like garbage when my family lost their fortune, at all of the moves that led to my being in this position, the people who hemmed me into a space where I don't want to be.

I don't want to lie down in a marital bed of my making. I want to fight my way out. And in this moment, for the space of a breath or two, I want to wash the scent of desperation and loss from the camps off me, want to pour the defeat out of me, and do as I wish rather than as others wish me to.

When I glance over my shoulder, Sam is already in the water, his torso clad in his white undershirt, the waves covering the rest of his body from his hips down. He's more solidly built beneath those plain suits than I realized, his chest broad and muscular.

"This seemed a more pleasant idea before I got in the water," he grumbles, and I burst out laughing.

"You should see your face."

"It's colder than it appears."

"Pssh. It's like bathwater."

"And there are fish," he complains. "Skimming my calves."

I laugh again. "Need I remind you this was your idea?"

"Folly, more like."

I inch closer to him in the water.

"You needed this," I say, peering beneath the veneer of surliness he wears like a mask.

"I did," he admits. "Those camps—I wasn't prepared for that. I might have fought alongside some of those men. I know the things they saw and that they can change a man. How far am I from being right there with them, from sleeping in some godforsaken tent, drinking my problems away?"

"Your work sustains you. Gives you a purpose." I don't know how I know, just that I do.

"It does. Bad luck for them that the Depression came when it did. That men who were already struggling got hit with another tragedy. How many setbacks can a person take?"

"I don't know."

"I felt like I couldn't breathe back there," Sam confesses. "I want to help them, but where do you even start when things are that bad?"

"I know. The camps were the government's answer to helping, I suppose, even if they failed miserably."

"Were they helping? Or were they ridding themselves of a problem? Maybe they don't want the country to see how badly everyone is really struggling, how they treat the people who were once lauded as heroes. It seems like it would have been easier to pay them the damn bonus. I—"

The instinct to soothe is there, surprising me, and I close the distance between us, lifting my arms to his shoulders and resting there, not quite embracing him, but holding him steady.

"I'm sorry." I'm not sure why I'm apologizing or what I'm apologizing for, only that it's the sort of thing I've been taught to say when someone is hurt or upset, my words and my body the tools I have been given to ease another's sorrow.

Sam swallows, his Adam's apple bobbing with the motion. When he speaks, his voice comes out raspier than normal. "I shouldn't have brought it up. You must be worried about your brother."

A rush of shame fills me, because in this moment, my brother isn't the foremost thing on my mind.

I lean into the curve of Sam's body, the need to soothe transforming into a need to be soothed. I slide my hands lower, his heart beating beneath my palm.

Until this point, my relationship with Frank has been entirely platonic. Perhaps he believes I'm an innocent and doesn't want to push my boundaries. Much more likely, given his reputation, he has more experienced women for such matters and has no need of me for his urges. I am a doll to be displayed on a shelf, never played with, rarely touched, only to appear expensive and pretty, and more than anything, enviable.

But the second I touch Sam, the desire that has been coiled inside me rears its head, and I'm filled with so much want, it leaves me breathless.

Sam sucks in a deep, ragged breath, his expression hooded. He sweeps my hair over my shoulder, skimming the line of my chin, a tremor in his touch.

"Elizabeth."

My name sounds like the loveliest thing of all falling from his lips.

Triumph surges through me, and I tilt my head into his embrace, relishing the gentleness of the caress of his fingertips against my cheek.

I've been carrying other people for so long. Since when has

someone touched me like this? As though I was something break-able to be cherished or protected?

Billy certainly never did.

With him, I was expected to be the one to lead, as though I was Delilah to his Samson.

But here, Sam has taken over with the assurance of a man set about getting what he wants, and a thrill runs through me at the notion that I am the one being pursued rather than the one doing the pursuing.

Sam leans forward, closer, closer, his mouth inches from mine, his breath against my chin, pulling me toward him, my skin on fire, our lips about to meet—

A loud buzzing noise sounds overhead.

I jerk in his arms. "What's that?"

Sam moves quickly, stepping in front of me, our embrace broken, and I see a flash of the man who was once a soldier and is now a federal agent.

He tenses. "It's a plane."

A moment later, the little object comes into view, dancing between the clouds, something fluttering behind it.

We both glance up at the sky as the plane glides past us, the words printed on the banner trailing after it fully coming into view:

Hurricane Warning.

"It's probably one of the Coast Guard's planes," Sam says.

"Should we be worried?"

He's quiet for a beat too long, the silence dragging out between us, a damper on the moment between us earlier.

"I don't know."

I see what it costs him to be filled with indecision, to not have an answer.

It's the same expression he wore a few minutes earlier when he nearly kissed me.

Something that might be regret.

Coldness fills me, the water no longer welcoming, everything wrong suddenly.

And like that, with those two ominous words flitting in the sky above us, this little stretch of beach is no longer paradise.

Fourteen

Helen

It's nearly four in the afternoon when the ferry finally arrives on Matecumbe Key, the trip taking three hours longer than it should have due to the broken propeller. The seas were rough, the weather bad, an utterly interminable journey, my stomach unsettled.

Is Tom out fishing in this weather? Or is he in our cottage in Key West realizing I am not coming home? Or is he already on his way after me?

The ferry landing is connected to a small harbor where fishing boats are docked. A chill slides down my spine as my gaze runs over the dilapidated vessels, as I stand next to John, waiting to disembark, and scan the boats, searching for the *Helen*.

A line of cars is parked at the landing, passengers trying to board the ferry.

"Will they be able to get out?" I ask John.

"Between the propeller and the weather, not likely."

"Do you really think the storm will hit us?" I can't forget Tom's earlier conviction that we'd be fine. For all his flaws, he's always known the sea.

"I don't know. But for everyone's sake, I hope they're cautious about it. They've been pumping men into the camps these past few months, and many of them have no idea what it's like down here, have never been through a hurricane. Hell, even rainstorms flood the camps."

"What will they do with all of you if the storm hits?"

"There's supposed to be a train that will take us north."

His tone makes his thoughts on the matter clear.

"You don't think it will work?"

"It'll be a disaster. Any semblance of order in the camps is difficult on a good day. In a crisis, it will be impossible. Not to mention, if you can't get people out of the Keys entirely, where would they go? There's no high ground here. Just the water." He hesitates. "If it gets bad, promise me you'll head north. Go to Miami or farther up. In your condition, you don't want to take the risk of getting caught in one of these storms. At least you're closer to the mainland than you would have been in Key West."

"I will," I reply. "Hopefully, the storm will miss us entirely." I understand his concern, and the baby certainly changes things, but it's hard to explain to someone who isn't from here what it's like. You develop a healthy respect for Mother Nature—after all, you coexist mostly peacefully, and she directs your fortunes more often than you'd care to admit—but life goes on down here in fair weather or foul. When you're trying to survive, you don't have the luxury to leave when things are difficult. You dig in and make the best of it.

But I *have* left.

I'm still not sure of what to make of it. It's as though someone else got into the car, and onto the ferry, and sailed away from her husband, baby in tow.

What will I tell my child when it asks how I could have left? What would I have told my child if it asked how I could have stayed?

I give John directions to my aunt's inn, the wind from the open car window alleviating some of the nausea in my stomach as we drive down the highway. Motion never used to make me sick like this—another gift pregnancy has bestowed upon me.

The ferry landing is at the southwest end of the island next to the camp where John says he lives. We drive north, the highway and railroad covering the length of Lower and Upper Matecumbe Key. I haven't been up here since I was a little girl, but I have fond memories of playing in the water with my aunt, catching fish, chasing lizards, and building castles in the sand.

"It's not quite what I expected when they said there were jobs available down in the Florida Keys," John comments.

"What did you expect?" I ask.

"An island paradise, I suppose. A place to get lost, certainly. But nothing so desolate, so wild, so stark. There's no pretense to it, and while there are moments of beauty, there's also a deadly edge that sort of overshadows all else—the weather, the water. I can't decide if I like it or not."

"I can see what you mean. When I was a child, it felt like paradise because there was so much open space and it wasn't as busy as Key West. You could go a whole day without seeing another soul if you wanted."

"That does sound like paradise when you put it that way," he says.

"Don't you ever get lonely?"

"I do and I don't. I had friends, good friends, before I went off to war. And when I was there, there were men I considered to be brothers, men I would have sacrificed my life for. I miss that, I suppose. There are good men down here. But I told you, I'm not in a place to be much of a friend to anyone."

"What utter nonsense. What is this if not evidence of you being a good friend? You helped a complete stranger when many would have looked the other way—when many did look the other way."

"Not a complete stranger. I saw you at Ruby's for months."

"We never spoke about anything besides me taking your order."

"Maybe not, but you smiled at me. At others. It was nice. You always brightened my day even if you never realized it, and I'm sure I'm not the only one who felt that way."

Tom always said I talked too much to my customers, that I was too friendly with them, too familiar, but the truth is, I like talking to people, learning about their lives. You can live a fair share of adventures in other people's stories.

"I like waitressing," I admit. "It's hard work, and you certainly get some rude customers, but I enjoy being around people. It keeps things interesting. It's easy to get involved in your customers' lives. I actually met a girl this weekend and told her about the inn. She'd come down on the railroad and planned on traveling up here and visiting the camps. I wonder if she ever made it."

"The camps aren't any place for a young girl."

"I told her that, but she seemed pretty intent. Hopefully, Aunt Alice was able to help her out."

"Is your aunt your mother's sister or your father's?"

"My mother's. My mother and Alice didn't really get along," I confess, feeling guilty for talking about my family like this, as though my mother is sitting in the car with us, capable of overhearing my words. "Alice did as she pleased. Mama believed the highest duty a woman could serve was to God. The second highest to her husband.

"They loved each other, of course—I mean, they were sisters—but they couldn't have been more different. Alice owned the Sunrise Inn with her husband, and when he died young, she took it over. There were rumors about Alice during Prohibition. You get some smugglers in these parts, and I suppose Alice offered them lodging when they needed it, didn't report them to the authorities."

"I take it your mother didn't approve."

"Hardly. Alice doesn't care much whether anyone approves of her, though, which only bothered Mama more. Alice has this way about her—she's lived life on her own terms. I admire that about her."

"And you never thought about confiding in her?"

"It's complicated," I reply.

The truth is, I've considered coming to Alice a hundred, thousand times. Every time I found a reason not to.

But now there's the baby.

John slows the car, pointing up ahead. "That's it."

The Sunrise Inn is on the southern side of Islamorada, past the point where the highway crosses Mr. Flagler's railroad track. It's nothing fancy, and in her letters, my aunt has mentioned that many guests prefer the larger Matecumbe Hotel.

I have the vaguest memory of the building—my impressions of our visits here are more sounds and textures and the sensation of sand beneath my toes. It's a pretty enough structure—a bright white that suggests a recent coat of paint and cheerful blue shutters a few shades darker than the color of the ocean. The inn is two stories tall with an inviting front porch; chairs are arranged to give guests a place to sit and converse. There's no one sitting out there now, only two cars out front.

The baby is awake and kicking my belly as John parks the Plymouth and helps me out of the passenger seat.

I stop in front of the inn's entrance, doubt gnawing at me. "I haven't seen her since I was eighteen, since my mother's funeral. Now I show up like this. What will she think?"

"It sounds like she loves you from the way you talk of your time here with her. She'll want the best for you."

I stare up at him for a moment, overcome by emotion. "You know how to be a good friend. Don't ever think otherwise. Thank you for what you've done for me. For us. I will never forget it."

His cheeks flush. "It was nothing."

"It's not nothing."

I give him a shaky smile and we walk up the steps to the inn's entrance, John trailing behind me.

The inn's interior doesn't appear as new as the exterior, but it's neat and clean, the living area also doubling as a reception space. A man stands behind a desk near the staircase. I don't recognize him from my earlier visits, but he greets me as I walk toward him.

"Do you need a room this weekend?" he asks.

"Actually, I'm looking for my aunt. Alice Jones."

"You're Alice's niece? I can't believe it. You must be Helen, then. She told me all about you. I'm Matthew."

"It's nice to meet you. Is she here? She wasn't expecting me."

"She is. And she'll be so excited to see you. Alice!" he hollers in the direction of the staircase.

Moments later, a petite woman walks down the stairs.

Her blond hair is cut below her chin, her dress a shade of blue that reminds me of the color of the shutters. She holds a bundle of linens, her head bent as she fusses with an errant string, her free hand trailing down the banister.

"There's no need to yell, Matthew. I'm not so old that my hearing has gone."

Alice glances up as her foot hits the bottom step, and she stops in her tracks, her eyes widening at the sight of me. Despite the years since we've seen each other, I have enough of the look of my mother for my identity to be clear. While I shared my pregnancy in one of our most recent letters, no doubt the sheer size of my stomach and the realization that I am so close to my due date is alarming. Not to mention John standing beside me.

Her lips curve into a deep smile. "We have some catching up to do."

She opens her arms, and I walk into them, and I'm home.

JOHN AND I SAY A QUICK GOOD-BYE UNDER ALICE'S WATCHFUL EYES with the promise he'll return tomorrow to check on me. He walks away, his tall frame ambling out of the inn, the limp in his leg more pronounced now that the day has worn on, and Alice takes me back to her private apartments on the ground floor.

"You've left Tom, then," she says.

The sentiment is so matter-of-fact, and I am caught so off guard by the directness of it that I almost laugh despite the dire nature of the whole situation.

"I have."

"About time, I'd say."

I gesture toward my stomach. "Though, perhaps not the best time with the baby coming."

"I hate to tell you, but there's no such thing as a 'right time' in life. Things happen when they need to happen. The rest sort of falls into place." Her eyes narrow. "He knock you around?"

I nod, the familiar shame rushing back to me.

"Bastard. How much longer do you have?"

"A couple weeks."

"You scared?"

"Terrified."

"Of course you are. Nasty business what happens to women's bodies. You'll need a place to stay."

I blink, my muddled, tired brain struggling to keep up with her swift topic changes. "Yes. I do."

"You don't have any luggage with you." Her expression softens. "He didn't let you take anything with you?"

Tears well at the kindness in her voice, at the worry, the pity. "I didn't go back to the cottage. He'd gone out on a fishing trip, and the ferry was leaving. I was scared to go back. Afraid of what he'd do if I did."

"So he doesn't know you've left?"

"I don't know. He'll probably figure it out when I don't return from my shift this evening. If he hasn't already. That is, if he comes home tonight. Sometimes when he goes out on his fishing trips, he's gone for days, weeks, at a time. I never know when he'll be back."

"Were there other women as well?"

"Probably. There certainly could have been, but by the end I didn't care one way or another."

"So you mean to get a divorce, then?"

"I suppose so. To be honest, I hadn't really thought that far ahead."

"He knock you around while you were like this? Pregnant?"

"Yes."

"Have you had any pain? Any bleeding?"

"No. The baby is moving around. It seems to be fine. But there was this opportunity to leave, and I took it. It seems foolish now. If he comes after me, I—"

"Here's what we're going to do," Alice says. "You can't stay here. When Tom realizes you're gone he's going to come for you. How long before he looks here?"

"I thought of that. I—I don't have anywhere else to go. Nowhere he wouldn't know to find me, at least. I have my tips, and Ruby gave me an advance on my wages, plus a little extra, to be honest, but it's hardly enough to start over with." I take a deep breath, trying to ease the panic ripping through me. "I can work if there's a restaurant in town that needs help. I'm a good waitress. Or I could help out around here. I can clean the place, help serve the guests, I like working with people. I could—"

"There's no need to worry about that now. The most important thing is keeping you and that baby safe. I have a friend who owns some fishing cottages. You'd be nearby if you needed something, but Tom won't be able to find you. People here take care of their own. They'll help watch my niece. No one is going to tell him anything."

I'M BARELY AWAKE WHEN WE LEAVE THE SUNRISE INN AND DRIVE to Alice's friend's cottage. She chatters along the way, keeping up a steady stream of talk about the area that I can hardly follow in my tired state.

The fishing cottage is perfect—one clean room with a bed adorned with crisp white sheets. Alice packed a basket of food from the inn's dining service, threw some of her loose nightgowns together for me, as well as a few other essentials to tide me over.

"You must be exhausted," Alice says when I sink down on the edge of the bed. "Do you want me to fix you something to eat?"

I yawn. "I'd rather go to sleep if that's all right."

"Of course. I'll be back to check on you in the morning."

"Have you heard anything about the storm?" I ask her, my earlier conversation with John coming to mind again. I struggle to grasp what he said to me, but the words slip through my fingers like fine granules of sand. There's too much rolling around inside me right now: the baby, my fear that Tom will come after us, the uncertainty of the future.

"It should miss us entirely," Alice answers.

She leans down and presses her lips to my head in a move so reminiscent of my mother that a lump forms in my throat.

"There's no need to worry. You're safe now."

It's the last thing I hear before I fall asleep.

Fifteen

Mirta

In the end, our date on the boat is not meant to be. An afternoon thunderstorm hits as I return to the house from the beach, fat drops of rain falling on my head. I run the remaining several hundred yards to the house, arms and legs pumping, calves burning thanks to the uneven terrain beneath me. There's a flash of a memory—of me racing my brother as a child at our beach house in Varadero, our cousin Magdalena trailing behind us. He always beat me, but I never stopped trying to best him until one day my mother declared it unseemly for a girl my age to engage in such behaviors, and our beach races stopped for good.

As I near the house, through the blur of the rain, I spy Anthony standing on the front porch.

My cheeks burn as I approach the house, my bedraggled appearance keeping us from equal footing once more. Despite his upbringing, there's a sophistication to him—a worldliness—I doubt I could ever cultivate, and in this moment, my hair drenched, locks plastered to my skin, makeup likely mussed and running down my face, I have never felt decidedly less elegant.

Anthony doesn't move until I've climbed the steps and stopped a few feet away from him, the overhang of the wraparound porch providing some protection against the elements. Wordlessly, he hands me a white towel folded beside him on the railing.

He doesn't glance away as I dry myself off, his dark eyes following my ministrations, the lines and curves of my body. The whole thing is terribly intimate, and I am struck by the contradictions in the man I married. Last night, he eased me partway into marital communion and left me alone, but today, his bold gaze is a shock to my system like the rain on my skin.

"You should go inside and change. Get out of those wet clothes before you catch a cold."

His voice scrapes over me, his jaw clenched. The flashing in his dark eyes oscillates between what looks like desire and anger, and I instinctively take a step back, my body hitting the porch railing.

"You're upset."

"I sent people out searching for you," he says.

"I went for a walk. I suppose the afternoon got away from me."

"I was worried about you."

"It never occurred to me that you would worry." I try for a smile. "I'm still adjusting to being a wife."

Anthony takes a deep breath, running a hand through his hair where the faintest touch of gray resides at the temples. "No, I'm sorry. You're free to come and go as you please, of course. I didn't mean to suggest otherwise. But I did worry. I suppose you learn to see threats everywhere." His voice drops to nearly a whisper. "I don't know what I would do if something happened to you."

Surprise fills me.

"I'm sure I'm quite safe here," I tease, struggling to lighten the mood, to soften the intensity in his gaze and to tame the uncertainty churning inside me. "It's not as though there's anyone around to do me harm. We're practically alone here."

"In my line of work, it's hard to take that for granted." He hesitates. "I'm not an easy man."

Anthony wraps a strand of my hair around his finger, pulling me closer to him gently.

Something tumbles in my chest, his mouth inches from mine.

"I'm not an easy man," he continues. "But I am trying. I'm not used to being a husband. Or worrying about a wife. Be patient with me. Please," he amends.

"I will." Hesitantly, I reach between us and stroke my fingertips along the curve of his jaw.

A groan escapes Anthony, and he fists the damp fabric of my dress. He leans into my touch as my back scrapes against the railing, as his body resettles itself in the cradle of mine.

"Mirta."

My name sounds foreign falling from his lips, as though I have been remade into someone new.

He leans forward, and I wait expectantly for his kiss, only to be caught off guard when instead his forehead rests against mine.

"I missed you," he whispers.

The emotion in his words staggers me.

"I was worried about you," he repeats, the fervency in his voice enough to make me wonder if his life is truly as dangerous as he says. I thought I'd left my fears behind me in Cuba, and for a moment, I consider asking him if *I* should be worried, but we're on unfamiliar ground here, the budding intimacy between us too new, and I'm loath to shatter this fragile bond we're building with questions that can be put off for later.

My hand drifts higher, curving around his neck as my fingers thread through his hair, the desire in his gaze sending a flash of courage through me.

The muscles at the back of his neck are tense knots.

"Your meetings didn't go well?" I ask, hazarding a guess at his mood.

"No. They didn't. There's trouble back home in New York. I spent too much time in Havana, was away for too long. My enemies thought they could move in on my territory."

"You make it sound like things are dire."

"It's a different type of war than the one you're used to. Or maybe not. Maybe that's what we tell ourselves. Maybe all war is the same—a fight for power, for resources. On the streets, it's for territory. Respect. I protect what's mine. The people who work in my places, the families that live in my neighborhoods."

It sounds all too familiar. "And where do I fall in the hierarchy?"

"You are the most important thing for me to keep safe. You and our future children. My business will not touch you. I promise you that."

"Don't make me promises you can't keep."

My father promised us things back in Cuba—that he was smart to back Machado, that it would keep us protected, safe. Men behave as though the world is theirs to order and control, but life doesn't always work out like that. Often there's something around the corner you can't prepare for or muscle your way out of.

"You don't approve of my work, do you?" Anthony asks.

"Does it matter if I approve, really?"

"You'd be surprised."

"Then, no, I suppose I don't."

He releases me, taking a step back, his gaze on mine.

"You've heard the rumors about me. And yet, you married me anyway."

"I did. And yes, the rumors are fairly difficult to miss. Are they all true?"

"Enough are true."

So he is a criminal of sorts. That part doesn't bother me as much as it should—I've seen enough of Havana's prominent citizens dirty their hands in order to get ahead. I can't say I'm happy about the American Mafia's presence in Cuba, either, but my opinion matters little. They've made their claim on the island, so it seems better to ally ourselves.

"I'm scared," I admit. "When my father fell out of favor with the government, we lived with the threat of violence. I saw the toll it took on those I loved, lived with fear hanging over my head, death all around me. That's part of why I wanted to leave Cuba, why I wanted to give my family a chance for a better life."

"You married me because of my friendship with Batista."

"It wasn't only that. But yes, given the stakes at hand, I had to do what was best for my family. And you? Did you give my father money to marry me?"

"Why would you ask that?"

"I'm not stupid. It wasn't lost on me that suddenly my father's worries about money lessened after I accepted your proposal. That there was money for my wedding trousseau and new gowns when we'd been wearing the same old ones for two years. The day he presented your proposal, he told me my family desperately needed this. I assumed there was money involved."

"But you didn't ask him directly?"

"It wasn't my place."

Perhaps I overstep in discussing this with Anthony, but if he wants the "real" marriage he described earlier, then I want our marriage to be a partnership. I saw how my mother struggled during our family's troubles, my father shutting her out of all of it completely. Maybe he thought he was protecting her, but the end result of us losing everything was still the same. There is no power to be had in Anthony treating me as anything less than an equal.

"There was money," he confesses.

"A great deal?"

"Does it matter?"

"Maybe I want to know what I'm worth to you."

"Everything."

The way he says it—the conviction in his voice—I almost believe him.

"You sacrificed yourself to save your family. I don't want you to sacrifice yourself in this marriage, too."

"I wanted to be married. To have a family."

Even if I envisioned myself having a little more say in my choice of spouse.

"You wanted to escape," he says.

"Maybe I did."

All along, I saw myself being marched to this marriage, but truthfully, I wanted what Anthony represents—the potential for a family, a home of my own, security—even if the strings attached to him still give me pause.

"My business won't touch you. I promise you that. You are the most precious thing to me."

It seems like a serious statement to make for such a short acquaintance, and I don't trust his words entirely, but they fill me with pleasure, even if I can't discount the misgivings inside me.

This time, I'm the one who moves, who closes the distance between us. I wrap my arms around his neck once more, pulling his head down toward me, kissing him like he taught me last night, swallowing the sharp inhale of breath that escapes his lips as soon as we touch.

"I might like being married," I whisper.

He chuckles. "I'm glad to hear it. I know I will."

A flush spreads over my cheeks, and I shiver, goose bumps rising over my skin.

Anthony releases me with a sigh. "Why don't you change out of these wet clothes? I need to talk to Gus to see the latest update on the storm."

With another kiss, I leave him and go upstairs, undressing and getting into the bath one of the maids drew for me.

Outside, rain pounds the windows.

I slip deeper into the water, staring up at the ceiling, running the washcloth and soap over my body.

A knock sounds at the door. "Can I come in?" Anthony calls out.

"Yes."

The door opens, and he walks inside the small room.

Nerves fill me at this new intimacy between us, but Anthony says nothing of my current nude state.

He sits on the chair near the vanity, a few feet away from the edge of the bathtub. "I spoke with Gus. People are worried about the storm. It could be a bad one. We're going to bring the porch furniture inside. Start boarding up the windows. We should be able to finish before the storm hits."

"Does Gus think we're in danger?"

"I don't know. I figure you have more experience with these storms than I do. The locals seem concerned, so I'm inclined to take it seriously." He grimaces. "Some honeymoon. When we're back in New York, when things have settled down, I'll take you to Europe. Have you been to Paris?"

"I haven't."

There were those of our acquaintance back in Cuba who traveled there each season, purchasing the latest European fashions, but by the time I was old enough for us to do so, our fortunes were already far too precarious for such a frivolous thing.

"I want to make you happy," he says, the worry in his eyes suggesting such a thing is not as easy as one would like. "I want to give you the life you deserve."

Anthony leans over the edge of the bathtub, kissing my forehead, but there's little passion in the motion, and I can tell he's distracted by the weather update. "I'm going to get to work on the storm preparations. Make sure everything is done properly. The housekeeper left dinner out for you whenever you're ready to head downstairs. Don't worry about waiting for me to eat. This might take a while."

I finish bathing after he leaves and change into one of the few outfits I brought with me from my old life in Havana, a pale pink dress my mother and I bought together years ago at El Encanto. The fabric is soft from so many washings over the years, and there is a loose thread near the hem that I snip off with a pair of petite embroidery scissors from my sewing kit, but it smells like home.

I place a quick phone call to my family, exchanging a few words with my brother before he passes the phone to our father. They're unsure if the storm will hit Havana and are readying for potential landfall. Tears fill my eyes as we say good-bye, the sound of my father's voice bringing a fierce sensation of home and all I am missing.

I eat alone in the cavernous dining room, my gaze flicking to the seat Anthony occupied this morning. Outside, the sound of rain and men moving furniture around fills the night, the occasional shout or exclamation punctuating their efforts.

I gather some of the food the housekeeper prepared and left for us in the kitchen and take it with me to the front porch, setting it up on the tables they've yet to drag inside. The rain is coming down slanted now, some of it creeping inside the porch, but the overhang provides enough cover to keep the food safe from the elements.

I've learned how unpredictable storms can be—they can come in with a roar and peter out to nothing, or creep in slowly and catch you unaware—but if the weather tonight is any indication, it's an ominous harbinger of a nasty one indeed.

I search for Anthony near the front of the house, where some of the men are working on boarding up the windows, but he's nowhere to be found.

It takes a few trips to get the food all set out, but the house-keeper likely had the same idea I did and made enough to feed an army.

My gaze falls on the man I encountered earlier on my walk to the beach. He is standing apart from the crowd preparing for the storm, a cigarette hanging from his lips.

"There's food on the porch if you're hungry," I call out to him. He acknowledges my comment with a tip of his hat and a clipped nod before he pushes off from the house and disappears entirely.

A moment later, Anthony comes into view, his clothes sticking to his skin, his hair slicked back from the rain, sleeves rolled up on his dress shirt. His normally elegant appearance has been replaced by a rougher version of him, sweat and rain on his brow, dirt on his face and clothes. He hardly seems like the millionaire he is reported to be and more like the men with whom he shares a good-natured laugh before his gaze drifts to the porch and me.

He bounds the stairs in two quick steps.

The men hang back, as if awaiting his command.

"You didn't have to wait up," Anthony says. "Did you eat?"

"I did. I—I missed you at dinner. I wasn't sure how long you would be out here, but I figured you all would be hungry. My father and brother used to help out when a storm was coming, and—"

My words are cut off by his mouth against mine. Compared to the other kisses he's given me, this one is practically chaste, but there's an unmistakable sense of pride in the gesture, in the manner in which his hand tightens on my waist, holding me flush.

Anthony releases me as quickly as he embraced me.

"Thank you," he murmurs.

He waves the men up to the porch, telling them to get some food, and there's a knowing gleam in their eyes as they help them-selves to the food I set out, but I don't have it in me to be embar-rassed after a kiss like that.

I'M NEARLY ASLEEP WHEN ANTHONY COMES TO BED THAT EVENING, his hair wet from the bath, the smell of soap on his skin.

I reach for him in the dark, relief filling me when his arms wrap around me.

"How did it go?" I ask.

"We boarded up most of the downstairs windows, pulled the porch furniture inside. 'Course it was probably all for naught. As soon as we'd finished, the Weather Bureau released an update on the storm. It's going to miss us entirely. It'll hit up by Tampa most likely."

"I'm sorry you had to do all of that work."

"It was worth it for the look in your eyes when you saw me. I won't ever forget the sight of you standing up on the porch, wearing that dress, waiting for me to come home. I don't know that I've ever felt prouder."

My cheeks burn, and I bury my face in the pillow.

He chuckles. "I take it my wife likes when I get my hands dirty."

Admittedly, I'd never even considered such a thing, but the sight of him out there did do something to me.

I'm too embarrassed to reply.

"Don't worry," he whispers, his lips teasing the whorl of my ear. "I have the same sensation every time I see you."

His words are all it takes to coax me to face him once more, to wrap my limbs around him, and to let him show me exactly how he feels as the rain pounds outside.

Sixteen

꙳

Elizabeth

When I wake the next morning, Monday morning—Labor Day—
the weather fits the darkness of my mood.

Last night after the hurricane warning, Sam and I returned to
the inn. We didn't speak of the almost kiss between us, and we
retreated to our respective rooms. I was left with the embarrassed
sensation that I'd shared too much, let the mask fall for too long. I
haven't a clue where Sam's thoughts ran, and I spent a good portion
of the night sleepless because of it, not to mention my worry over
the situation with my brother, the conditions of the camps.

I dress quickly, bypassing Sam's room altogether, and walk
downstairs, the inn's lobby empty, the reception desk abandoned.
It's been raining on and off all morning, but there's a break in the
weather, and I desperately need the reprieve, so I head toward the
tiny stretch of beach I favored yesterday. As before, it's quiet and
abandoned, and I stare out at the water, the wind whipping around
me, kicking up sand in a mighty whirlwind. The waves churn too
violently for me to venture into the water, and truthfully, the im-
pulse was far more satisfactory than the reality, so I content myself

with watching the waves crest out over the reefs and break along the narrow stretch of shore, something soothing about that violent release of energy. There's a boat far off in the distance, fighting the waves as though it were little more than a child's toy.

What would inspire someone to venture out to sea in this weather?

"What are you doing out here?" a voice shouts behind me.

I pivot and watch Sam make his way through a gap in the mangroves, headed toward me, the expression on his face nearly as dark as the sky overhead.

"Not much of a day for sunning yourself, is it?" I call back.

"No, it isn't. What possessed you to come to the beach?"

I ignore his question. "Is this the hurricane?"

"I don't think so. Not yet, at least. I spoke with one of my friends at the Weather Bureau up in Jacksonville, and they're monitoring it, but they think it's still a couple days out if it hits us at all. The forecast keeps changing. It's moving slowly."

"A couple days?" I glance at the threatening sky. "They seemed worried yesterday at the camp that it was going to hit soon."

"These things are hard to predict. Everyone's doing the best they can, but with this one being so far out, we still have time."

"Will they evacuate the camps?" I ask.

"I don't know. Maybe if it's bad enough. It's too soon to tell."

"I thought we would visit another camp today. We still have the one down by the ferry, Camp Three. Unless you have work you need to do. Do you have any leads on the man you're searching for? I can always go by myself to the camps. Or if you'd like, later on I could help you. Maybe flirt with your quarry. Men have a way of opening up to a woman. It might work."

Better to do something, to make myself useful, than to stay here wringing my hands about the situation with my brother.

"Absolutely not. And I have enough leads, thank you very much. He's here, and he's not going anywhere. I told you I'd help you, and

I will, but it's not a good idea to go looking for your brother. Not in weather like this. Those camps can flood easily with how close they are to the water. You don't want to get caught up in that or add to the chaos when they're trying to take care of their people. Better to wait until it clears up and then we'll go."

"I thought you said the storm was days away from hitting us."

"Honestly, at the moment I don't know what to believe. You're right—that sky doesn't seem like it's days away. Maybe this is normal down here. An ugly summer storm. Who the hell knows? But it's not worth risking our safety. Smarter to go inside the inn and wait this thing out with the rest of the guests."

"And what about my brother?"

"I know you're worried about him, but he's probably safer than we are if a storm does hit. If there's a danger to the veterans, I'm sure they'll use the train to evacuate them. They'd be foolish to risk their safety after everything those men have been through. If we don't make it up there today, I'll call up to Jacksonville tomorrow when everyone's back to work after the holiday weekend and see if any of my contacts can put us in touch with someone at the camps to help track him down."

"I'm not good at waiting around for help. I didn't come here for a vacation; I came to bring my brother home. If I'm gone too long, people will start to notice."

"Your mother?"

"No, not my mother."

Sam's gaze drifts to my bare ring finger, the ring secure in my purse, and back to my face again.

"You're worried he'll come after you?"

What can I say? I'm engaged to a criminal who stokes fear in the hearts of many?

"Maybe. I didn't exactly tell him I was coming down here."

"He might be worried about you."

I snort. "Not likely."

"So you what? Agreed to marry a man for whom you have no affection? Why?"

"That's none of your business."

"I'm here helping you when he's not, so maybe it's a little my business. I can read between the lines. You're marrying some guy you aren't interested in, and you're hoping your brother can save you from it?"

"It's a little more complicated than that," I snap, even though the truth is, that pretty much was my plan.

"Then talk to me. What are you going to do if you can't locate your brother? Go back to New York and marry this man?"

"Who said I'm not interested in him?"

"You have. Every time we've talked."

"Because I flirt with you? I told you—you shouldn't take that personally."

"Fine. I won't take it personally. But, Elizabeth, you need to face the fact that your brother might not be here. He might not even be alive. So what's next for you?"

"Why do you keep saying my brother might be gone?"

"Because you don't understand what it's like down here. You keep acting like your brother is the same person you remember from your childhood, but none of these men are."

"None of us are," I shout. "Do you think I'm the same girl I was before the crash? Before we lost everything? Do you think I haven't changed? I am all that's left of my family. My father is gone, one of my brothers is gone, and my mother is all but lost to me. Maybe originally, I came here searching for my brother because I wanted him to fix things for me, but now, I need to know he's safe. He may not come back to New York with me, and no, I don't know what I'll do then. But I saw those camps, and I love him. I need to know he's alive."

"I can't make any promises, but I'll call Jacksonville and see if my friend at the Weather Bureau knows anything about the plans for the camps."

BACK AT THE INN, I WAIT IN THE SITTING ROOM WHILE SAM GOES into the front office to use their phone and call up to Jacksonville.

Outside, the weather has grown more ominous, rain falling down from the sky in thick sheets, gusts of wind blowing outside. The sky seems to be getting darker by the minute.

"Should we be worried about the storm?" I ask the woman at the front desk.

"I don't know. The weather folks say it's going to miss us, but I don't like the look of those waves. Better to take precautions than risk it. Hopefully, it'll pass by us quickly. You all should stay inside and keep away from the windows. This house has withstood a storm or two in its day, and it'll make it through this one."

Her words are accompanied by a clap of thunder, a crash somewhere in the distance.

Sam returns from his phone call.

"It's really getting bad out there," I warn. "What did you learn?"

"My friend can't help us. The camps are a mess today. Enough people on the ground here are worried about the coming storm that they're sending an evacuation train down to get the veterans out. The Weather Bureau's version doesn't line up with what people on the ground who are experienced in these matters believe. Haven't you noticed that the locals are starting to get nervous?"

"I have."

"We need to be prepared for the possibility that we're going to get some of the effects of the storm sooner than everyone anticipated."

"Should we evacuate?" I ask. "I talked to the woman at the front desk, and she said we should be fine here."

"You saw what those camps are like," Sam answers. "Half those tents couldn't survive a strong wind. The other half seem like they're about to drift into the water at a moment's notice. I'd be evacuating those men if I were in charge, too.

"The inn seems sturdy enough—built this close to the water, it has to have been designed to withstand the weather down here. And the hurricane still might miss us. Maybe this is the worst it's going to get. It's a lot harder moving hundreds of men than it would be for us to take shelter if we need it."

"Do you know where they're taking them?" I ask.

"My friend thought Miami, but he wasn't sure."

"If they're headed to Miami, maybe we should make our way up there."

"At most, they'll be gone a day or two. Better we stay here until they're back. Besides, you don't even know that your brother will evacuate. He might be down in Key West for the weekend. I know you want to find him. I'll do everything in my power to help you. You have my word. But you can't risk your life. We have to be smart about this. I'm not comfortable driving in this weather. The roads are going to start flooding soon. We don't know the area that well. Better we wait here than risk getting stranded somewhere without good shelter."

I stare out the window, the wind and rain blurring everything. The desire to go after my brother is inescapable, but knowing that someone is likely coming to rescue him makes it easier to do the thing I've always struggled with most—

To wait.

Seventeen

Mirta

When I wake the next morning, Anthony is already up and gone, a red rose lying on his pillow beside me.

I never would have thought Anthony would be such a romantic.

I stroke the soft petals, a smile spreading on my face. Last night was lovely, and while our marriage has yet to be fully consummated, I admit the intimacies between us thus far have made me more eager than afraid.

I rise, a new awareness of my body dawning. My mother told me there was power to be found in the marital bed, that my husband would be kinder to me if I pleased him, less likely to stray if I kept him satisfied. She never described it as anything other than a means to an end, never told me I could like it, that my husband could bring me pleasure.

I pick one of the prettier dresses from my trousseau, a lacy, frivolous confection that is wholly inappropriate for our current surroundings yet I'm sure Anthony will love.

When I peer out the window, though, the weather is hardly welcoming. When I went to sleep last night, it was calm and peaceful. Today, the wind rumbles outside the house, palm trees bending in the heavy breeze. A sinking feeling enters my stomach, the scene a familiar one. It looks like a hurricane is about to hit us, and suddenly, all thoughts of pretty dresses flee.

I hurry downstairs, searching for Anthony. It's difficult to appreciate how bad a storm can be if you haven't experienced one for yourself. It's like revolution—on the surface, it seems scary, but only those who have lived through it fully comprehend its true horrors.

Anthony stands at the bottom of the stairs, speaking to Gus in low, urgent tones. I'm too far away to make out everything they're saying, Anthony's back to me, but I hear enough of their conversation—

". . . barometer falling . . ."

". . . going to be an ugly one . . ."

Gus glances over Anthony's shoulder, and his gaze connects with mine. He tips his hat to me before scurrying out the front door, a grim look on his face.

Anthony turns, and his solemn expression tells me everything I need to know.

"The storm changed course?" I guess.

"The locals seem worried. The barometer's falling. I don't know exactly what that means," he admits, "but Gus seems concerned the storm will hit us."

"Should we evacuate?"

"I asked him, but he said there's nowhere to go. The storm's coming. Soon." Anthony grimaces. "We didn't get all of the hurricane preparations finished last night; they said the storm was going to miss us. It was so late, and everyone was tired, and I thought it was safe. I'm sorry."

"There's nothing to apologize for. Storms can be unpredictable. It might still miss us, and even if it doesn't, it might not be that bad. Often these storms are all bluster and trouble, but they peter out when they actually make landfall." I take a deep breath. "We have enough food and supplies. I suppose the best thing for us is to ride it out and see what happens."

"I'm going to help with any last preparations we can make before the weather gets really bad. I let the staff leave so they could go back to their homes and families. There are a couple men finishing up boarding the windows for us. Gus is assisting them and then they'll be on their way."

"Be careful."

Anthony leans into me, pressing his lips to mine in a movement that is already becoming familiar.

"I will."

OUTSIDE THE HOUSE, THE WEATHER KICKS UP WITH STARTLING intensity. Inside, the house creaks and moans, thuds and clanks sending a shiver down my spine. In Havana, I knew the home I grew up in, was assured the strong walls would protect us. But this house is wholly unfamiliar to me, and with each moment my unease grows.

After an hour has passed without an update from Anthony, I step out onto the front porch, surprised as the wind picks up the sand from the beach, stinging my eyes.

The screen door slaps against the frame angrily.

The storm isn't even here yet, and already the wind is this strong. I—

"Get inside," Anthony shouts, coming around the house, gripping the railing, his knuckles white.

My husband is by no means a small man, but at this moment, the wind blowing his body, it seems his grip on the railing is the only thing giving him the necessary purchase to keep from floating away.

He climbs the stairs up to the front porch quickly despite the wind pushing against him, panic in his eyes, his body tense like a bow.

I start to step back, but I can't make myself fully retreat inside the house until he's at the front door, his chest heaving from the effort. Behind him, something that appears to be a piece of a roof flies by.

The trees sway in the wind, bending as though they would snap and cleave into two at any moment.

Anthony hooks an arm around my waist, tugging me inside before releasing me and throwing his body against the front door to push it shut, turning the locks with force.

He pivots to face me. "It's going to hit us."

There's a vulnerability etched across Anthony's face I haven't seen in our short time married.

His gaze runs over my face, and he frowns. "You're bleeding."

"The sand," I reply after a beat, staring down at my hands, surprised to see he's right.

Angry drops of red cover my skin.

"You shouldn't have gone outside."

"I was worried about you."

"We were only able to board up a couple more windows. The wind is blowing so strong, it made it pretty much impossible. It's not safe to be outside anymore. People are blown around like they weigh nothing at all."

Not only people. I watch through the window, horrified, as the roof of one of the outbuildings peels up like paper, before waving in the wind and flapping back down again.

This storm isn't going to miss us, and it's going to be bad.

We walk into the kitchen, and Anthony cleans my wounds with soap and water, my raw skin stinging. He has a few cuts on his face and arms as well, and I locate a makeshift first aid kit in the kitchen and use some iodine to clean his injuries while the storm outside grows stronger, the unmistakable sound of debris flying around becoming louder and louder.

"How long will the storm last?" he asks me.

"I don't know. Sometimes they move quickly; other times they're slower. It seems like this one has to be close since it's so powerful."

"What do we do now?"

In this moment, for the first time in our relationship, I am the experienced one, the one being looked to for guidance.

"Now we wait."

Eighteen

Elizabeth

In a matter of hours, we have gone from ominous weather to a dangerous hurricane. We are surrounded by a cacophony of sounds—creaks and moans, groans and screeches, the heaving and sighing of metal and wood. It's as though the inn is saying, "Enough," the force of the storm coming on like a freight train, the strength of it simply too much for these old walls to bear.

The guests downstairs—an older married couple and a family of four—are arguing with Matthew, the man who works the reception desk, over whether we should stay here or evacuate.

Sam leaves me and joins the fray, his calm voice a balm compared to their panicked ones. The children cry, their parents valiantly trying to comfort them. The noise and fear grow to a crescendo, and I retreat to the small sitting room off the main reception area, desperate for a moment of quiet. There's an octave people reach in their most dire moments, the pitch of a wail that fills your ears, a resonance to terror that's unmistakable, and with which I am all too familiar.

Where is my brother? Is he sitting in one of those makeshift tents or canvas roof–covered shacks riding out the storm? Or is he somewhere else entirely, safe from all of this? I've already lost most of my family. I can't bear the thought of losing him, too.

I was never one for church save for Christmas and Easter, the times my mother insisted I go so we could be seen in the pews, but I revert to prayers I'd long since considered forgotten, the words sticking in my throat amid all the fear there.

Sam enters the room, his footsteps hard against the wood, causing the floor to shudder.

And then I realize that, of course, it isn't Sam at all. Something else entirely is making the house move.

The ground quivers beneath us.

"What's that?"

"The wind and the water," Sam replies, his voice grim. "The ocean is threatening the house. We need to get out of here. They're sending a rescue train to the station in Islamorada to get the veterans out. We need to get on it."

If my brother is indeed at one of the camps, at least he will be ferried to safety. And if he's going to be at the station in Islamorada, maybe I'll see him there.

"Evacuation might be our only prayer," Sam adds.

"How far is it to the station?"

"Not far. It's our best chance."

"Is that what everyone has decided?"

"No. No one else wants to leave. They're worried it's too dangerous out there, that we won't be able to make it to the station."

"And you want to go out in that? Maybe they're right to stay put."

"We don't have another option," Sam protests. "The inn isn't strong enough to withstand this kind of weather, and I don't think the worst of the storm is even here yet. There's not enough elevation between the ground and the sea—there is no higher place we can go to. The train is it. We have to try to outrun the storm. The water is already spilling out onto the road."

It was difficult enough driving back from the camps yesterday in a heavy rain. This is something else entirely. And at the same time, I've never been one for sitting around letting calamities befall me. If there's a chance of us surviving this, I'm going to take it.

"I'm with you. Let's catch the train."

"Good. I'm going to go back and see if I can convince anyone else to come with us. Why don't you throw some clothes in a suitcase in case we're gone for a few days?"

Sam leaves me, and I nearly run up the stairs, more debris hitting the house in loud thuds. I quicken my pace, making my way to my room first, wrenching open the armoire in the corner and throwing a few clothes and underclothes into my little satchel, adding a few toiletries. I take the old photo of my brother, the letter he wrote me postmarked from Key West, and add them to the bag.

A clap of thunder makes me jump.

The voices arguing downstairs mix with the roar of the storm as I walk next door to Sam's room.

Unlike me, Sam never bothered to fully unpack, some of his clothes still shoved in his black suitcase, others hanging haphazardly in the armoire that is nearly a twin to mine. It's strangely personal to go through his stuff in such a manner, but I pull out some of his shirts, pants, my cheeks burning as I add his underclothes and set them on the bed, making room in his bag for the essentials.

Papers fall from Sam's suitcase in my haste. I scoop them up quickly, my heart pounding, the storm breathing down my neck. I shove them back into the case.

"Are you ready?" Sam yells up to me from the stairs.

"Almost," I shout back.

I bend down and pick up the last piece of paper.

The image is familiar enough—my face, smiling, the night of my official presentation to society. A copy of it sat framed on my parents' mantel in our old apartment overlooking Central Park.

How did Sam end up with it?

I set down the picture on the stack of papers I disturbed earlier, lifting another one, heat rising as I scan the words written there.

"Elizabeth."

I whirl at the sound of Sam's voice.

He stands in the entryway of his room, his gaze on the papers in my hand. "I can explain—"

"Who are you, and why are you following me?"

Nineteen

Helen

I sleep restlessly, my dreams more of the same strange flashes and images that have accompanied me for most of my pregnancy; this time there is one important variation—I am the one on the boat, the seas swelling around me, water pouring over me in an image that is so realistic, I swear I can feel the ocean spray against my legs, my body rocking and swaying as it did on the ferry the day before.

When I wake, I am disoriented, a banging sound off in the distance. I roll onto my side to the area where Tom would normally lie, expecting to see his body beside me. Instead, there is merely empty space, and at once, I realize I am in Islamorada, at the cottage my aunt Alice found for me, Tom hopefully far away from here.

I rise from the bed, surprised my nightgown is damp, an ache in my back and belly, my body covered in a thin sheen of sweat. My muscles are sore, tension filling my limbs, and I grip the mattress for support as I attempt to get my bearings.

There's a damp spot on the mattress where I lay, and for a moment, my heart stops when I glance at it, expecting to see blood once more. So many of my earlier pregnancies ended like that—a spot of blood in the morning on the sheets when I woke that signaled another baby was not meant to be.

But this time, there's no blood, only clear liquid.

It seems like—

It seems like my water has broken.

It's too early. I'm not prepared, I—

The pain hits me, the dull ache that has plagued me for days sharpening to something far less bearable. I wince, gripping the mattress with one hand, the other wrapped around my stomach as my body bows forward to lessen the pain.

I ride the wave of the contraction, my legs sagging beneath me as I fall to the floor. The pain seems unending, but eventually it disappears, the sensation lessening until it subsides to the constant sense of discomfort I've felt for the last few days.

How much longer until Alice arrives?

The banging sound returns, louder than it was a moment ago, and I stumble over to the cottage's shutters, staring out to see what's making that noise. A wooden plank whizzes past me.

I slam the shutter closed.

Another contraction begins.

I clench my teeth through the pain, wishing I had something to bite down on, wishing—

I scream.

The baby is coming—quickly, if I had to guess.

Another contraction.

Another scream.

There's a pounding sound from the front of the cabin now, and the door flies open.

A man bursts into the room.

I almost think I'm hallucinating him from my position on the floor.

"I heard screaming," John says, rushing over to me. "Did you fall?"

Did I hit my head? I blink, but he's still there, inches away, concern in his gaze.

"No. I think I'm in labor." The pain is too great for me to muster up any embarrassment. "I woke and my water had broken." I take a deep breath, trying to steady the panic within me. "It's too early. The baby isn't due for a few weeks."

"Babies come when they're ready, unfortunately. How close are the contractions?"

I wince. "Close. What are you doing here? How did you find me?"

"I went by your aunt's inn searching for you. She asked me to check on you. She's coming over as soon as she can. She's making sure her guests are safe. The storm's coming; they're boarding up the inn."

The pain subsides slightly as the contraction recedes.

"I heard noises earlier, saw some debris go by the house. Is the wind really that bad?" I ask.

"The wind has kicked up considerably since I left the inn. Rain's coming down harder, too. Some of the roads will be washed out soon if they haven't been already."

"Everybody thought the hurricane was going to miss us."

"I don't know anything about predicting hurricanes, but someone got it wrong," he replies, his voice grim.

I can only focus on one crisis at a time. I've lived through my share of storms, so at the moment giving birth is the more fearsome thing. What if there's a complication? What if something's wrong with the baby? There's no doctor to call, no midwife to come to my aid, no female friends or family to have by my side. I'd always planned on having the baby at home, but I didn't envision being in such unfamiliar surroundings, in the middle of a hurricane.

"I told your aunt I'd take you back to the Sunrise Inn, but it's bad out there. If the baby is this close, the last thing you want is to be stranded on the road in the hurricane. It's best if we take shelter here until the storm passes." John glances around the cabin. "Let me get some hot water. Some towels. I'll clean off the sheets and we'll get you back in bed."

Another contraction hits, stronger than the last, the pain carrying me away. John kneels beside me, rubbing my back, his tone soothing, his words barely audible above the white noise rushing through my ears.

He sees me through the contraction, and the next, leaving me in the pauses between to gather supplies, to slip the soiled sheets from the bed. He moves with a surprising amount of calm, his movements quick and sure—confident, even.

Perhaps war prepares you for all manner of things.

In the time since John arrived, the weather has grown much worse. The shutters on the cottage are battened down, the sound of some unknown object hitting the house at random intervals.

Each time it does, John flinches.

"Are you all right?" I ask.

He nods, his lips in a tight line, his face pale.

John helps me lie back on the bed, a clean sheet he found in the cabin's armoire beneath me.

"Do you have much experience delivering babies?" I joke during the ever-narrowing space between contractions, trying to distract him from the growing storm outside.

"Much? No. I went to war right after I graduated medical school."

I blink. "You're a doctor?"

"I was a doctor."

Of all the answers I expected, that wasn't one of them.

"You're surprised by that?" he asks.

"Perhaps. Why didn't you mention it before?"

"Because I *was* a doctor. Before and during the war. I haven't been one for a long time. When I came home from France, I tried to resume my practice, but it was too difficult. The blood, the memories. I would freeze in the operating room, my hands shook—" He swallows. "I couldn't do it anymore."

"Is that why you went to the Sunrise Inn?" I ask. "Because you thought I might need help with the baby?"

"I was worried about you. They were talking about the hurricane in the camp today. They're going to run a special train to Islamorada to evacuate the men."

"You should have gone with them. Should have gotten on that train."

"I'm right where I'm supposed to be. How's the pain?"

"Not too bad," I lie.

"I'm here with you. I'm not going anywhere. You and the baby are going to be fine."

I'm too scared to voice the fears inside me. When you've experienced a loss, it's impossible to forget, to wholly ignore that little voice in your head that says that it can happen again. I'm not sure I'll relax until the baby is in my arms, and even then—

I take John's hand, squeezing as the next contraction hits, no longer able to talk through the pain. I am reduced to a haze around me, John beside me, holding on to me, his fingers trembling when the noises outside the cabin grow louder.

My body is no longer my own, and any embarrassment I might have over a near stranger, a man, seeing me in such a state is obliterated.

With each contraction, each passing moment, I change from the person I was to someone new, someone I barely recognize.

The delivery happens so quickly, the baby coming whether I am ready or not. The wind howls outside, the house quavers, and my surroundings simply disappear. John is somewhere down between my legs, his voice soothing, urgent, and then he vanishes, too, and I am alone, pushing, pushing—

A baby cries.

Twenty

Elizabeth

We face off in Sam's room at the inn, papers strewn on the ground, photographs of me—walking on the streets of New York, old pictures from newspaper clippings, photos that once graced frames in my parents' home.

"You've been lying to me all along," I accuse.

"No—I—not everything was a lie."

"Fine. Then start from the beginning. Who are you, really?"

"My name is Sam Watson. Just like I told you. I work for the government. None of that was a lie. The badge is real. I catch people. Criminals. Sometimes I infiltrate their organization, go undercover, make myself indispensable to them. It's the easiest way to get close to them, to get them to trust you."

This whole time I've been worried Frank would send someone after me. I failed to realize he already had.

"Like tailing an errant fiancée."

"Yes."

"So this all goes back to Frank, then."

"Yes."

"What did he tell you when he hired you? To what—follow me to Key West?"

"That his bride-to-be had run off. That she was young, spoiled, impetuous. Possibly in the company of another man. He said he was worried about her—you—and asked me to locate you. He knew you were headed down to the Keys and that you'd left on a Tuesday. He's had someone on you since the beginning. But it's a difficult time for Frank. There's trouble in New York, and he needed his most loyal men around him. So he sent me after you. He knew I was originally from Florida, that I was familiar with the area. It was just a matter of finding you on the train."

"So it wasn't a coincidence that we were seated by each other."

"No, it wasn't."

"When I flirted with you—" My eyes narrow. "If you were supposed to get close to me, why did you reject me on the train?"

"Because I saw you—the way you courted men and attention. I knew you would be bored if things were too easy for you. You would have collected me among your admirers and then cast me off. I needed to be a challenge for you." He gives me an apologetic look. "That's what I do in my job. I read people."

"Learn their weaknesses," I retort. "Did you even fight in the war? Or was that another lie you told, another way to get close to me, to prey on my feelings and my worry over my brother?"

"I didn't lie to you about that. I promise. Everything I said to you was true."

"But it wasn't. Bringing me to Matecumbe wasn't a matter of chivalry, but rather obligation."

And the friendship that I'd thought had sprung up between us wasn't real at all—the almost kiss on the beach—it was all a lie.

"Elizabeth." Sam steps forward.

"Stop. Just stop. Don't lie to me. You owe me the truth, at least. What did Frank want you to do with me?"

"He wanted me to follow you. To make sure you didn't get into trouble."

"Nice try. Frank isn't that altruistic."

"He wanted me to bring you home."

"And if I don't want to go home?"

"Do you really think I'd force you? That I'm the type of man who would be rough with a woman?"

"I don't know what type of man you are. I thought I did."

I foolishly viewed him as a white knight of sorts, the sort of man with whom a woman could be safe. It's that betrayal that cuts the deepest.

"I never meant to hurt you, Elizabeth."

"That's what everyone says, isn't it, after they hurt you?"

"We need to go," he pleads. "The storm is getting worse."

"Not until you answer me. I'm not going anywhere with you until you tell me the truth."

"Everything I told you was true."

"Everything except why you helped me in the first place."

"I helped you because it was the right thing to do. Because you needed my help."

"Frank can't want me to find my brother. He has to know that if I do, I won't marry him."

"I agreed to make sure you didn't get into any trouble," Sam replies.

"To make sure I didn't cause Frank any trouble," I correct.

"He said you were to be his wife."

"So that gives him a right to be what—my jailer? To spy on me?"

"I was doing my job. Making myself indispensable to him so he would let me into his inner circle. What about you? How did you end up with someone like Frank Morgan?"

"I did what I had to. Why didn't you tell me this from the beginning? That he was the man you were investigating?"

"Because I didn't know if I could trust you. We're building a case against him. It's been difficult, to say the least. The people he has working for him in his inner circle are loyal. I needed to know if you were. I didn't know why you were marrying Frank; if you were a love match, or—"

"Did you think we were a love match?"

"I try not to make too many speculative efforts in my line of work. I deal best with facts. My firsthand impressions of people. I wanted to see you. Get a sense of your motives for marrying Frank."

"Did I pass the test, then? When we nearly kissed on the beach yesterday—was that enough proof for you?"

His expression is pained. "I want to help you."

"So you trust me now," I say with a harsh laugh.

"I do. And I need you to trust me. The storm is coming. Fast. Right for us. We need to get out of here. If we miss that train, we're going to be stuck in the eye of the storm here."

He holds out his hand.

"Please, Elizabeth. Whatever anger you have, whatever mistrust exists between us, the most important thing right now is getting out of this storm. After that, I'll answer whatever questions you ask me. I promise."

OUTSIDE THE INN, THE CONDITIONS ARE EVEN MORE HAZARDOUS than I thought they'd be. We drive slowly, the water flooding the roadway. Sam grips the steering wheel, his knuckles white. The visibility is so bad, we can only see a foot or so ahead of us, the rest of the road obscured by the storm. The car appears featherlight as the wind blows it around, the struggle to keep it under control evident by the tension in Sam's face and body. There's no time for me to be angry at Sam; our sole focus is getting to the train, heading north, and escaping the hurricane's path.

I don't know how the forecasters got the trajectory or the timing so wrong, and at the moment, their oversight hardly matters. Survival is everything.

The storm makes the drive much longer than it should be, and it's late by the time we arrive at the train station. I fear we've missed our chance at escape, but when we approach the depot in Islamorada, we're confronted with a sea of men, women, and children.

Sam parks the car quickly, taking my hand and tugging me toward the station. The storm has already damaged the structure, and the hurricane is blowing even harder than before, debris flying past us. I use my free arm to shield my face from the sand and earth whizzing past us.

"Has the train already left?" Sam shouts to the man standing closest to us.

"No. It was delayed on its way down. We're still waiting for it."

I scan the crowd. There are many locals here, families pressed together, but also a fair share of men who look like the ones we saw in the camps.

Sam wraps his arm around me, bringing me against his side, sheltering me from the people pushing and shoving their way toward the train tracks. The chaotic nature of the scene is all too familiar, the desperation on people's faces reminding me of life after the crash when crowds gathered outside banks, angry, terrified—

"I've got you," Sam murmurs. I cling to him, grateful for his strength, for the fact that he hasn't left me alone in this madness. I don't trust him, but at the moment, I'd rather be with him than alone.

A rumble comes, building louder and louder, distinct from the sound of the storm.

The train surges into view, heaving its way down the tracks, a mighty beast.

"We made it," I shout, throwing my arms around Sam. I release him, gathering my bag sitting next to me on the ground, heading toward the train, joining the mass of people surging forward—

The train doesn't stop.

It keeps rolling down the track, car after car headed past us.

There's still Camp Three to the south of us. Is that where the train is headed? To get the veterans in that camp? Will it come back for us? Surely, it will be too late. The storm is too powerful, too close.

Beside me, people scream and cry, the terror settling over the crowd reaching a fever pitch as the train passes; our last shot at hope leaving us behind.

We are doomed.

The station has already sustained a considerable amount of damage from the storm. There's no way the structure will be able to shield all of us. How many people will die?

Hundreds.

"It's stopping," someone shouts.

Sure enough, the train has halted up ahead.

Around us, people are running now, babies scooped up in their mothers' arms, couples clinging to each other. We move in a blur, bodies clambering to get to the train, desperation moving us past the paralyzing sense of panic.

A woman brushes against me, a little girl clinging to her skirts. Her expression is grim, the little girl's cries barely audible over the din of the crowd.

On the other side of me, a man prays, reciting the same words over and over again, the pink color of his lips a stark contrast to the pallor of his face.

The crowd helps lift the children up onto the train, assisting the elderly, everyone scrambling for purchase. Sam grips my waist, hauling me up to an open car. Arms reach from above and pull me up. I stand on the edge, staring down, waiting while Sam climbs up with assistance.

Sam throws his arms around me, and I sag into his embrace, my earlier misgivings momentarily forgotten.

We're safe, and that's all that matters.

"They said the train is heading down to Camp Three to get the rest of the veterans out, and after that, we'll be out of here," a man near us shouts.

Camp Three is the camp we didn't get to visit earlier, and I hope my brother is waiting there for the train, that I'll see him shortly, that he'll be carried to safety, too.

Before the train can move forward, the railroad car shudders.

"Hold on," Sam shouts to me, as the impossible happens. The sturdy train car that moments ago seemed so imposing and *big* becomes as flimsy as a tin can.

I don't know how long the train wobbles and shakes, only that it's an eternity.

People scream around me, children crying.

As quickly as it began, it stops, and for a heartbeat, everything is still.

It's silent inside the car.

I leave Sam's embrace and lean toward one of the small windows in the train car, gazing out the water-soaked pane.

Surprisingly, the sky is clear.

The scene in front of me changes so abruptly I almost miss it. I blink, and the unnaturally bucolic landscape is gone. Instead of the ground and the sky, blue stares back at me.

A wall of blue.

It's the most gorgeous mix of blues—aqua, turquoise, and cerulean like the most perfect of stones.

My brain catches up with the image before me, and I see it—the water, like the hand of God, lifting itself up, up, until there is nothing else, rushing past us, curling over us in a massive wall with seemingly no end, Sam screaming—

It hits me then. As plain as day.

It is too soon. I am not ready. I do not want to die.

There is a righteous bellowing in the wind, debris floating past me as though I am in a dream, and a sharp pain hits the side of my head, a jolt, and I pitch forward, water engulfing me, and darkness envelops me.

Twenty-One

Mirta

The waves crash against the beach, water pounding the tin roof. The sound of the wind is deafening, a shriek like a never-ending whistle.

I stare out the window, trying to get my bearings.

I pull back the curtains—

Where I expected to see sand, I am greeted by the sea pushing against the white porch.

My heart pounds. "The water's rising. We need to get to higher ground. We should go upstairs."

I take Anthony's outstretched hand and follow him up the stairs.

My foot catches on one of the steps, and Anthony hoists me up, carrying me along. He doesn't let go of me until we reach the bedroom.

"How high has the water risen?" he asks me.

"Ten feet, maybe. We weren't that high above the ocean to begin with."

"Maybe it was a mistake to come upstairs," he says. "If the water continues to rise, where will we go?"

"We wouldn't have had a better chance out there. The water's too strong. It'll carry us away."

The sound of glass breaking somewhere in the house makes me jump.

"It's probably a window." Anthony strokes my back, unease threading through his voice.

Our surroundings have suddenly become hazardous, Mother Nature turning against us. It's not only the peril from the storm system you have to fear, it's anything the storm can sweep up in its path and use against you.

"The bathroom is probably the safest place for us to go," I say.

At least downstairs, most of the windows were boarded up. Now all that stands between us and death is the roof, and given the sounds of metal shearing, I don't have a lot of faith in the roof's sturdiness. But with the water rising—

There are no good options available to us.

We run to the bathroom and close the door, huddling together in the bathtub, Anthony's arms wrapped tightly around me, his breath hot on my neck.

"I hate this," he murmurs, his lips grazing my ear. "Hate being so helpless. We should have tried to leave. I should have taken you to safety."

"You had no way of knowing it would be this bad. I've never experienced a storm like this."

Anthony's grip on me tightens. "If we don't make it—"

"Don't say that."

"If we don't make it," he continues, "I want you to know that these past few days with you have been some of the happiest of my life."

I swallow, threading my fingers through his, lifting our joined hands, and pressing my lips to his knuckles.

We don't speak, the storm raging around us.

How many hours do we have left?

And then, the world stills.

Anthony releases me, and I follow him to the bedroom. He peers out at the ocean through one of the bedroom windows, one we never got around to boarding up.

The stars are out in the inky black sky, the breeze dormant, everything peaceful and calm.

"Is it over?" Anthony asks, and I am struck again by the sensation that we have switched places, that I am the experienced one as he looks to me for reassurance.

"No." Memories of my childhood in Cuba flash before me. "It's about to get worse. This happens with storms sometimes. There's a moment of calm before it kicks back up again, sometimes worse than it was to begin with."

A blistering curse falls from Anthony's lips. "Go back in the bathroom. I'm going downstairs to see if I can bring some food and supplies while the weather is calm. Who knows how long we'll be stuck up here, and I'd rather be prepared for the worst." He grimaces. "We certainly weren't ready for this."

"It's not your fault. No one could have predicted it."

"I made a vow to keep you safe." He gives me one of the Coleman lanterns, taking the other for himself. "I'll be back in a few minutes."

I grab his forearm. "Are you sure you want to go down there? The water was rising already. Who knows what it'll be like now? A few supplies aren't worth risking your life."

"They will be if we're stranded for days waiting to be rescued, and I don't want to chance the water and wind carrying everything away when the storm starts up again."

Anthony's right, of course, but I can't deny the fear that he will walk downstairs and never come back.

"I'll go with you, then. I'm a strong swimmer. I practically grew up in the ocean—"

"Mirta. No. I need you to stay here."

"Two of us can carry more items back."

"And there's a greater chance of something happening to both of us. Please. I'll be quick. I promise." He presses his lips to mine in a swift kiss that seems a lot like good-bye.

Tears sting my eyes, but I let him go.

The night is quiet, and I listen for the wind picking back up, the sea pummeling the house, for Anthony calling out for me if the waters get too deep below.

The wait seems interminable.

Finally, the sound of footsteps on the hardwood floor breaks up the quiet.

I leap from my position on the bathroom floor, lantern in hand, and go to greet Anthony.

"How bad are the conditions downstairs? Were you able to get supplies? I was so worried." I turn the doorknob, stepping out into the dark room. "Anthony?"

I grip the lantern, shining the light around the room.

It settles on a man.

He's dressed in a ratty pair of overalls, a threadbare shirt.

I recognize him instantly.

I've seen him lurking around the property, smoking a cigarette when everyone was boarding up the house yesterday, the one I thought might be one of the workers.

There's a knife in his hand, the metal gleaming in the ray of lantern light, desperation in his eyes.

"If you scream, I'll cut that pretty neck of yours."

My mouth goes dry, any noise I might make strangled in my

throat in a morass of terror. Perhaps he came here searching for refuge from the storm. Or maybe he came here for something else entirely.

"Give me the ring." He strides toward me with heavy footfalls. He stops inches away from me, his body towering over mine.

From a distance, he seemed physically imposing. Next to me, the knife in his hand, he's terrifying.

"Wh-What?"

"The ring. Give me the ring. The one I've seen you wearing."

I glance down at my finger, at the enormous diamond Anthony placed there back in Havana. Despite the reservations I felt wearing it, there's a sharp sense of loss as I slide it off.

The man grabs the ring from me with one hand, the knife inches away from my body.

Where is Anthony?

The noises downstairs could have been from the storm. Or the man in our bedroom could have an accomplice. Is Anthony hurt somewhere? Dead?

A loud thud hits the window, followed by the sound of breaking glass somewhere in the house. Outside, the wind rages and whines, a whistling sound filling my ears, the storm starting once more.

"Give me the rest of your jewelry," the man yells. "The cash, too."

Where is Anthony?

"Give me the jewelry," he repeats, the knife arcing closer to my body.

I don't argue, but instead walk over to the dresser, to the pretty wooden box I admired when I first explored the room. I lift the lid, scooping out the items Anthony has given me, a pang in my chest at the sight of the pieces I brought with me from Cuba, the necklace that belonged to generations of Perez women, that my father presented to me on my wedding day.

It's ridiculous, but it feels like I'm giving a piece of my family away as I hand the man the jewels, as he shoves them in his pockets.

I open my mouth to call for help, and he lunges toward me, the tip of the knife nearly grazing my side.

I gasp.

"Don't scream," the man commands.

Anthony walks into the bedroom.

He freezes, his gaze darting from me to the man holding the knife to my neck. He drops the supplies he gathered from downstairs to the ground.

He's no longer my husband, no longer someone I recognize. Instead, a mask slides over his face, and the warmth I usually see in his eyes is replaced with a cold and calculating stare. He looks fearsome, and for once, it is the most reassuring thing I have ever seen.

"Take your hand away from her neck. You don't want to hurt her. You want money. I'll give you all the cash you want."

Anthony steps forward, and the man jerks, his arm lashing out as Anthony sidesteps him, the blade barely missing his abdomen.

"Not you," the intruder snarls. "She can get it."

"There's cash in the nightstand," Anthony instructs me, his voice surprisingly calm. "Get the money and give it to him. Do you understand me?"

I nod.

"Drop the lantern," the man orders, and I set it down on the floor beside me.

I walk toward the nightstand, Anthony and the man squaring off behind me. I open the drawer, fumbling with the contents, my fingers curling around the crisp stack of bills.

The cool sensation of metal brushes my skin.

"She has the money," Anthony says behind me, his calm voice a sharp contrast to the panic beating in my chest. "It's enough for you to have a nice life somewhere."

The man is silent.

"What else do you want?" Anthony asks. "You didn't happen upon this house."

"No, no, he didn't," I say. "He's been lurking around."

I should have said something to Anthony. I should have warned him, asked more questions about why the man was always around the house but I never saw him working.

"I'm not just here for the money," the intruder replies.

"No, I didn't think you were. Who sent you? Carlo? Michael? Frank?" Anthony asks.

How many enemies does he have? How many enemies do *we* have?

"Mr. Morgan sends his regards," the man answers.

"I should have known Frank was behind this—it's his style to send his lackey after an innocent woman."

A loud bang hits the house from the storm outside, followed by a shrill whistle of wind, a shout piercing the night as Anthony moves, hurling his body at our attacker.

They tumble down, their limbs entangled, rolling around the bedroom floor.

It's an easy decision to make. Whatever Anthony's past, he's outmatched in this fight, the man far too large for him to have a chance in hand-to-hand combat. The knife glints in the lantern light.

I lift the gun I pulled from the nightstand—Anthony's revolver—and point it toward them. Their images blur as they move, fighting for the knife, everything too fast for me to get a clean shot. Our attacker is a bigger target to hit by virtue of his size, but the darkness makes it hard to tell the difference between them, the lantern giving off enough of a glow for me to make out one of their features before they roll away again, the sound of the storm mixing with the growing rumble of their struggle, until—

"Do it, Mirta," Anthony shouts from the fray, his voice pained.

My fingers shake as I pull the trigger.

There is a shout, and then—

All that is left is the wind bellowing outside, the storm pummeling the night.

Twenty-Two

Helen

I lean against the pillows, gazing at the baby sleeping in my arms, her tiny body wrapped in a blanket we found among the cabin's linens. In this moment, staring down at my daughter's face, her lips pursed, eyes closed, cheeks pink, I know there is nothing I would not do to protect her, that all the decisions I have made in my life were meant to bring me to this moment.

To her.

My daughter.

Lucy.

I never knew it was possible to love someone so much, to feel this sense of completeness.

She has my nose. Perhaps my mouth, too. I see little of Tom in her, or maybe that's my own prejudice. Whoever she favors, she is wholly and utterly perfect.

It's late in the day, and the storm has worsened considerably in the last hour or so. Concern is evident on John's face, his demeanor changing as he grows more silent with each passing moment. During the delivery and Lucy's first moments in the world, he was so intent on making sure she and I were doing well that he seemed unaware of the storm. But now that Lucy and I are stable and the noises from outside are louder, he's become tense, pacing back and forth.

"The noises remind you of the war, don't they?"

"They do."

"Does anything help?"

"Not much, unfortunately."

"It didn't seem to bother you as much earlier. When the baby came. Maybe the distraction helped."

"Maybe. I was worried. Like I said, it's been a long time since I practiced medicine, and these are hardly ideal conditions. You did well, though. You both did."

"I was terrified," I admit. "But you calmed me. It seemed as though you had it all under control. Thank you for that. For being here. For all you've done for us."

"I wouldn't want to be anywhere else. I'm glad you weren't alone. I've never seen the weather like this before."

"I haven't, either. Everyone thought it would miss us."

Is Tom out on the water caught up in this mess? Is the storm hitting Key West, too? Maybe he doesn't even know I've left yet; perhaps the hurricane is the perfect opportunity to disappear, to start over.

I can't go back to that life.

"I hope Aunt Alice stayed behind at the Sunrise Inn. I hope she never went out on the road."

"I'm sure she's fine. She probably realized she couldn't drive. The roads likely won't be passable for quite some time." He swallows as another crash sounds in the distance. "How long do storms like this normally last?"

"Hours. It depends on how big it is, how quickly it's moving, which parts of the storm we get."

John grimaces. "As soon as it clears, we should try to get you to a hospital. Just to make sure everything is all right. I checked the supplies in the kitchen while you were sleeping, and they won't last very long."

Another loud boom erupts, like the sound of something hitting the side of the cottage, and I grab John. His hand trembles in mine, and I offer a quick, reassuring squeeze.

Lucy stirs, her expression sleepy, and I shift her to my other arm. Her lips purse, and her eyes close again.

"She's beautiful," John whispers.

"She is."

"What are we going to do?" I ask him.

"There's nothing we can do. Hope for the best, I suppose."

I hold on to John, exhaustion taking over, my eyelids fluttering once more.

WHEN I WAKE, IT'S TO ANOTHER LOUD BOOM, A CRASH OF METAL, a terrible ripping sound, a sharp crack.

The baby cries.

Beside me on the bed, John's body quakes, his arms wrapped around me.

"What's happening?" I blink, trying to adjust to my surroundings. "How long was I asleep?"

"Not long. An hour at most," John replies, his voice grim. "The sea is rising. Quickly."

"Is it close to the house?"

"It is."

The bed is the highest point in the cottage, and there's no building close by that's higher in elevation. For the sea to overtake the cottage—

There's another ripping sound, like the top of a metal can being pulled off in one powerful motion, except much, much louder.

I glance up at the ceiling. "Is that—"

"We lost part of the roof," he confirms.

In the corner of the cottage, near the front door, rain begins falling through an open gap where the wind ripped the roof off. The floorboards are wet, and it takes a moment for me to realize that it's not the rain that caused it to accumulate—the water is coming into the cabin from the ground.

The sea is here. We have nowhere to go.

I'm so tired from giving birth that I feel as though I am in one of my dreams, as though none of this can be real. It's the dream with the boat again, and I'm rocking back and forth, swaying from side to side.

Lucy cries once more, the noise piercing the haze, and I pull the neck of the nightgown Alice lent me aside, letting the baby nurse. It's taken a few tries for us to get the hang of it, but now her mouth latches on hungrily.

I stare down at the bundle in my arms, another wave of tiredness filling me. Maybe the exhaustion is a blessing, a way to numb the reality of the situation before us.

But we're still swaying. It's almost like the cottage is moving, carrying on like a boat on the sea, the bed rocking, sliding.

I try to move, but my body is so weak and I sag against the bed. Water splashes my leg, wetting the hem of my nightgown. The sea is rising, nearing the bed, moving on a steady current.

"Is the house—" I can't finish the thought, can't accept what I'm seeing as true.

"It's floating," John answers, his voice grim.

I swallow. "Floating?"

"The storm must have carried the house away. Ripped it off its stilts."

"We're going to die, aren't we?"

He doesn't answer me.

Is this it? All the years I spent hoping for a child, the months with the baby inside me, those first kicks, the tiny flutters that became all-consuming, my body changing, the child inside of me becoming a part of me until we were inseparable. The pain of a few hours ago, the dull ache in my back sharpening to something more unbearable, the sensation and emotion stealing my breath. All of the hopes and dreams for this baby, the stories I conjured up in my mind, the adventures we'd have, the simplicity of daily domesticity no longer me alone, but with a bright-haired child beside me, filling the spaces of our days with cheerful words and laughter. That first sight of my daughter's eyes meeting mine, her little face scrunched up, her weight settled in the crook of my arms as though she belonged there.

We can't die.

I hold on to Lucy as tightly as I can, John's arm wrapped around both of us as the cottage floats along the sea, the storm battering the structure.

How will we survive this night?

Twenty-Three

Mirta

My limbs are frozen, an ache in my chest, my breaths coming in ragged spurts. The eye of the hurricane passed us, and the wind is back again, the water hammering the house, and as I feared, it is worse than before. It's as though the world is ending, the fabric of it being ripped apart at the seams. And, of course, there is the dead body lying a few feet away from me.

We covered the intruder's body with one of the bedsheets, wrapping it around his bulk. We briefly contemplated dumping the body outside, allowing the storm to carry it away, but the weather was too dangerous, too unpredictable to risk it. A red stain grows over the white fabric, spreading larger and larger, until I can't look away from it, the stain on me as well as the body.

What have I done?

"Mirta." Anthony shakes me—once—twice. "Mirta."

My gaze jerks away from the dead man and up to my husband. Every action is a tremendous effort, my legs heavy as though they are trudging through the sand, my arms weighed down by the sea.

"You're in shock," Anthony murmurs, rubbing my bare arms.

There's a splatter of red on the sleeve of my dress from where the man's blood—

I shudder.

"You're safe," Anthony croons in my ear. "Everything is going to be fine."

I brush him off, a spark of anger breaking through all that cold. "I killed a man. How will everything be fine?"

"He would have killed you if you didn't kill him first."

"I killed him," I repeat, scarcely able to believe it.

"You did what you had to do." He takes my hand. "You'll get no judgment here."

No, I wouldn't, would I? What sort of world am I entering into? And despite what my mother implored me, all of her earnestly imparted marital advice, I cannot resist the urge to speak my mind. What's the point in pretending anymore if we're only going to die anyway?

"He came after us because of your job. Because of your enemies. As what, retaliation for the times you pointed a gun at a man and his family?"

"I have never targeted anyone's family. You can choose to believe whatever you'd like about me, but there is a measure of honor among the men of my acquaintance, some lines you don't cross. Frank Morgan has no honor. To send a man like that to the home where I am spending my honeymoon, to have a man like that confront my wife—"

"Why didn't you warn me? You told me you had a bad business meeting, but I had no idea what that meant, that I should be on guard for someone trying to kill me. If I'd known, I would have told you when I first noticed him hanging around the house. I assumed he was one of the men who worked for you, and I didn't want to cause problems. I wanted them to like me."

"You're right. This is entirely my fault. I met with some of Frank's local representatives down here to orchestrate a truce between us. It didn't go as well as I'd hoped, but I didn't anticipate him moving against me like this."

"Was he hiding here the entire time?" I ask.

"Maybe he didn't intend to strike this early, but the house was probably too good of a shelter to pass up. He was as trapped as we are."

"Do you think he came alone?"

"I don't know, but at least we're prepared now," Anthony replies, the gun in his free hand.

There is nothing to do but wait, nowhere to go. Our fate is resigned to whether or not we can outlast the weather, and so we stay together in the corner, hoping the unknown men who built this house long ago did their job well.

Minutes pass, an hour, more.

I'm nearly asleep when Anthony nudges me awake. "It sounds like it's over."

He's right—it's quieted down considerably.

I take hold of his free hand, the gun in his other one, the lantern in mine, and we walk out of the bedroom, past the dead man, into the hall. I shine the lantern at the staircase below. Water fills the ground floor. It's not as deep as I feared, certainly passable, but enough to cause serious damage.

Anthony grimaces. "So much for the rest of the supplies."

"Something might be salvageable."

After the loudness of the storm, it's eerie how quiet and still everything is.

"Did you hear that noise?" Anthony asks.

I strain to listen, the sound distant but audible—a soft swishing. My heart pounds.

He walks down the rest of the stairs, his foot sinking into the water on the ground floor. It comes up to his knees. "It sounds like it's coming from the front porch."

"Please don't go out there," I say, closing the distance between us. "The storm might not be over. It could be dangerous."

"I'm not going outside. I'm going to see if someone's out there."

I grab Anthony's arm to stop him, and he tenses, the expression on his face the one I imagine his enemies see in their final moments. Here is the man they whispered about in Havana, the ruthless criminal who won his fortune through force and cunning. It is both a little frightening and a little comforting to see this other side of the man I married.

"I'll be cautious," he replies. "I promise."

I release him, and he walks over to the window.

I hand him the lantern, and he shines the light in front of the pane.

"The water's—gone," he says. "There's sand where the ocean was."

I've seen this before, know exactly what will happen next.

"It's going to come back."

THE DEAD MAN IS UPSTAIRS IN OUR BEDROOM, HIS BLOOD STAINING the wood floor, the window of time before the ocean rushes back toward the house narrowing.

"I need to get rid of the body," Anthony says.

"How?"

He gives me a look that suggests he isn't a novice at such things.

"What if someone finds him?" I ask.

"We have to make sure they don't. The storm will help. If we move quickly, hopefully, he'll disappear. It's going to be a mess out there."

"He was shot."

"And if they never discover the body, that won't matter," he replies.

"And if they do?"

"I doubt they're going to be overly concerned with one more dead body. Especially a man like that. And even if they do investigate his death, there's nothing tying him to us."

"Will it be like this everywhere we go?" I ask. "Enemies in every corner? If we're to be partners in this marriage, then you should trust me in this. I don't want secrets between us. How many threats are there?"

"There aren't supposed to be any."

"But this Frank Morgan person—now we've killed someone who worked for him. What will he do to retaliate?"

"He'll never know. The storm is the perfect cover. Besides, this man was hardly a valuable member of Frank's organization. More likely a local who could be bought cheaply and was expendable should he fail.

"Which is why we need to act quickly. I'd rather get rid of him now than wait until tomorrow, when it's light out and there's a chance of someone finding him," Anthony says. "Burying him would take too long even if we could locate something to use to dig in the ground, which I doubt we can in this mess. Plus there's always the risk of an animal unearthing him later."

He sounds far too familiar with the particulars of concealing a body.

"The sea is unpredictable, and without a boat to row him out in, not ideal, but the storm has likely messed up the tide," Anthony continues. "Who knows where he'll end up? And even if it is here, the best we can hope for is that someone will think he was blown off course by the hurricane. When the sun comes up, nothing will appear the way it did before. If only we had a knife or a saw . . ."

My stomach rebels against the image his words conjure up.

Anthony's gaze darts to the kerosene. "We could use the kerosene, but the last thing we need is a fire taking down our remaining shelter, and with the winds as unpredictable as they are this evening—"

"The sea will have to do," I say decisively.

I don't know what marriage and this place have done to me, but I'm behaving as though it is the most natural thing in the world to dispose of a body.

IT TAKES LONGER THAN I EXPECTED FOR ANTHONY TO PULL THE dead man down the stairs in a series of awkward thuds and drag him out the front door to the beach. There's no way to know when the water will wash back onto the beach, but this is our last, best chance to get rid of him.

"He's a heavy bastard," Anthony grunts, leaning against the broken front porch railing. The exterior is in shambles, half the roof torn off the house. Windows are broken, shutters gone, trees pulled from the earth, their massive trunks and roots exposed. It's too dark to make out the full extent of the damage, but the hint of it illuminated by the lantern and the moon is ominous enough, indeed. Rain lashes the ground, the wind strong even though the storm has moved past us.

"Stay back on the porch," Anthony calls to me. "It's windier out here than it seems. Hold on to the railing."

I grip the wood, my heart sinking at how flimsy it is—parts of it have broken off and disappeared completely. The whole structure appears ready to blow away entirely, the railing wobbling with each gust of breeze.

"Are we safe to stay in the house tonight?" I ask Anthony.

"It's probably the best shelter we can hope for considering the circumstances. The car's gone, and I wouldn't want to venture out in this weather anyway."

Anthony drags the body toward the water, wading into the sea as I watch from my perch near the porch. There's some wrestling and some cursing, Anthony disappearing into the dark night as my heart pounds, waiting for his safe return.

What seems like an age passes before I spy him walking back to the house.

"It's bad out there," he says, his voice grim.

"What did you do with him?"

"He's tangled up in some mangroves now. Hopefully when the tide comes back, it'll carry him off somewhere else. Either way, with how strong this storm was, people will likely turn up all over the place."

I shiver at the macabre thought, at the image it presents, and Anthony wraps his arm around me, leading me back toward the house.

It isn't until much later, when we are nearly asleep, Anthony's fingers entwined with mine, that I glance down at my hand and realize my engagement ring is gone.

Twenty-Four

TUESDAY, SEPTEMBER 3, 1935

Helen

When I wake, there is light. Not the bright sunlight I'm used to, but a muted shade that signifies day has broken, albeit reluctantly.

John stands near one of the cottage windows, the shutters ripped off long ago in the storm, Lucy in his arms.

"Is it over?" I ask.

"You're awake." He walks over, handing Lucy to me. He looks away as I adjust her so she can nurse.

Half the roof is gone, the remnants of the rising water in the cabin still visible, but we're no longer moving.

"It's over, but I'm not entirely sure where we are," John answers. "Up by Windley Key, maybe? It appears like we were swept north, but the landscape isn't like anything I remember seeing. All the trees are gone. Everything is gone. There are holes where you can tell there used to be *something*, but I don't know what."

"I can't believe I fell asleep. That I didn't wake up."

"Your body went through a huge shock between the delivery and the storm. You needed the rest. The worst part was already over when you started dozing off. We've been beached here for hours."

My senses are dulled, sluggish. There is Lucy—piercing through the haze—but everything else seems as though it's happening to someone else, as though I am someone else. There's Tom out there somewhere, but at this moment, we are truly alone in the world, and I haven't come to terms with all that has happened or how much we have endured.

I have no idea what comes next.

I gaze down at the baby nursing comfortably on my breast. "Is she doing all right? She seems healthy."

He smiles. "I'd say she's a fighter. Her mother, too."

"I didn't do anything—just rode out the storm."

"I couldn't have gotten through it without you. You helped me keep it together. Stayed strong for me, for her, too. Now we have to get out of here. There's some canned supplies over in the kitchen area, but water's going to be a problem eventually, and you really should be checked out by a doctor. Same with Lucy.

"The cabin seems to be fine on this stretch of beach," he adds. "It's not going anywhere. I wouldn't recommend taking Lucy out in this until we know what the conditions are like. I don't want to leave you, but it's best for you two to stay here. Lie in bed and get some rest. I'll see if there's someone nearby to help."

John leans down, and his lips ghost across my forehead. "I'll be back. I promise."

Twenty-Five

Mirta

We huddle together on the settee in the living room, our limbs intertwined, Anthony's long legs hanging off the edge. It's hardly comfortable, and we're unable to piece together more than a few hours of sleep, but considering how bad the storm was, it's a miracle we made it through the night.

When the sun comes up, its rays are dimmed considerably.

"I need to go out and see how bad this is. Try to get help." Anthony hesitates. "I don't want to leave you here."

"I'll go with you."

"Mirta."

"You said it yourself—you don't want to leave me. The aftermath of a storm can be difficult. Looters and the like. We've experienced the same thing in Havana. Not to mention this Frank Morgan situation—you don't know who's out there, and I don't want to worry that there are more men coming after us."

Anthony picks up the gun and tucks it into the waistband of his pants. "Let's go, then."

My hand tightly clasped in his, we set out of the house in search of assistance. Our feet hit the top step of the porch before we freeze. The view we've grown accustomed to these past few days is completely gone. The trees that framed the entrance to the house—towering palms with fat coconuts hanging from them—are nowhere to be found. Nor are the coconuts. The sand has been swept all over the porch, the steps from the house to the beach another casualty of the storm. An icebox rests on its side, and I'm fairly certain it's not the house's icebox.

The roof is gone from large sections of the house, windows blown out, walls ragged and lilting like a bomb has exploded. The porch sags in places where it appears as though the railings were ripped away by the wind.

There is all manner of debris strewn about—foliage from the mangroves, palm fronds, clothes I don't recognize as ours.

My gaze sweeps over the beach and rests on a white wooden object sitting on curved legs.

Pink painted ribbons adorn the side, and I can barely make out a name—

Ruth.

It's a cradle.

I run toward it, my heart in my throat, listening for the sound of a baby's cries—

It's empty.

"Mirta."

Anthony wraps his arms around me from behind and holds me tight against him.

I can't tear my eyes away from the sight of that name painstakingly painted on the wood. "Do you think the baby is safe? There's no sign of a body, but the nearest house must be at least a mile away. How could—"

"I'm sure the baby's fine," Anthony replies, his tone belying the certainty in his words. "The cradle probably blew away in the storm."

We move forward, and as hard as I try to forget the sight of the cradle, of *Ruth*, it follows me like a chill that settles in my bones.

How many others haven't been as lucky as we are? How many perished last night?

We continue on, heading toward the main road. The farther we walk, the more obvious the scope of the destruction becomes.

I stumble, nearly losing my balance. I open my mouth to cry out, but no sound escapes.

A body hangs from the limbs of a tree, mangled beyond recognition.

For a moment, I think it's the man I shot, come back to haunt me, but it's a woman, I realize, stepping closer as the breeze blows a lock of long red hair like a ribbon fluttering in the wind.

It could be the girl from New York I met earlier on the beach.

Elizabeth.

It could be anyone.

Beside me, Anthony swears.

I have seen the aftermath of many storms.

I have never seen anything like this.

"Should we—"

The words "help her" stick in my throat.

"She's beyond any help we could give her now," Anthony replies, his voice achingly gentle as though I might unravel at any moment.

We walk on, and there are more bodies. On the ground, wrapped in whatever trees survived the wind's fury, bodies poking through rubble of homes that were obliterated by the storm. A few times, Anthony rushes over to the body as though the person can be saved, as if there is some assistance to be given, but it quickly becomes apparent that there is no point.

We are surrounded by death.

In the distance, I spot two figures walking toward us. I grip Anthony's arm, and he tenses beside me as we assess the new arrivals—two men, their clothes tattered, cuts all over their faces and arms, their faces slack with shock.

They're brothers, and their house was destroyed in the storm. Their eyes well with tears discussing it. I cannot fathom how devastating it must be to see your home laid to waste, your family and friends gone.

We walk on with the men, and others join us, more survivors of the storm wearing the shocked expressions that no doubt must mirror our own, their bodies in various stages of undress, their clothing blown away by the elements, their shoes gone, feet scraped by the rocks as they wander aimlessly, as they search for their loved ones.

Some of the locals stop every once in a while to pick up something of theirs that was blown away by the storm. My heart clenches at the pain in their eyes, their scattered possessions clutched in their arms, at the losses they've suffered. Homes are destroyed. Lives are lost. The entire island has effectively been wiped away.

These people were already struggling. What will they do now?

Bodies litter the beach. Around us, the locals cry as they recognize one of their own, but just as frequently, the appearance of the body is left with more questions than answers.

Could it be Nancy Thompson?

Perhaps.

No, it's too tall to be Nancy.

It's the Miller girl, isn't it?

A pause. A wiping of brows.

It might be the Miller girl.

And on and on it goes. There are women and men. There are children. Babies.

No one should see the things we see today.

More than once, Anthony urges me to return to the house, but I stay as I am, my hand clutched in his.

Each step we take reveals another fantastical, horrific thing:

Mr. Flagler's mighty railroad lies in ruins, stretches of track destroyed, cars broken and twisted. An enormous freighter marooned near a beach rather than far off in the ocean where it should be, the storm's strength and power ominous, indeed. The Matecumbe Hotel is severely damaged, yet intact enough to provide shelter to some of the survivors. So many dead that I begin to lose count, the violence of their deaths becoming less shocking with each mile we traverse, the storm's indiscriminate cruelty numbing me.

It's the worst by the railroad station. Bodies are tangled in the mangroves, the stench unbearable. They litter the ground like discarded trash.

"They didn't even have a chance," the woman beside me whispers, crossing herself.

The strangest thing is that in the midst of all this destruction, there are items that are untouched, blown far away from their owners yet perfectly preserved. A dress on the ground. A shoe. A bed. These things defy logic, explanation.

Anthony gestures toward a group of men up ahead he's been talking to. "They're going to try to ferry some of the people who need medical assistance out. The most vulnerable need to be taken to safety. Most of the food and supplies have been swept away. Things are going to get bad for everyone stuck here. Water, in particular, will be a problem.

"I'm going to help them. You should head back to the house. Get some rest. It's late. You don't want to be out after dark in this. Please. I don't want to be worried about you the whole time." Anthony pulls the gun out of his pocket. "Take this. Keep it on you. There could be looters. People trying to take advantage of the situation."

A grim look passes between us—there could be more enemies of his.

"I don't want to leave you, but they need men who can help carry the injured, and—"

I press my lips to his, cutting off his words.

When the kiss ends, I lean back and gaze into his eyes.

"Come home to me."

Twenty-Six

Helen

It's late in the afternoon when John returns to the cabin, Lucy sleeping peacefully. I've made the most of the canned goods, but he wasn't wrong—water is already in short supply. We can't stay here much longer.

"What's it like out there?" I ask. I've done little more than peek out the windows at the unfamiliar landscape since he left.

"We're definitely near Windley Key. It's a mess. The telephone lines aren't working. Same with the telegraph lines. The roads are blocked. The bridges are gone."

"The hospital?"

"That's gone, too."

My heart sinks.

"Everything is gone," John adds. "A boat came down from Miami; they're helping get the injured out and taking them to safety, ferrying them up to the hospital on the mainland. You and Lucy should go."

"What about you?"

"I'll join you later, stay behind until there's a chance for the rest of us to get out. Right now, the most important thing is that you're both safe."

With everything we've been through together, his presence has been a comfort, and I'm hesitant to separate now.

John must see the indecision and fear in my eyes, because he sits down beside me on the bed and wraps his arm around me.

"I'll be up there as soon as I can get out of here. I promise. You'll be in good hands."

THE MEN COME TO THE CABIN AN HOUR LATER WITH A BOAT LIKE John said. My legs are weak from the delivery as I walk from the structure to the water's edge where the boat waits, and John scoops me up, Lucy cradled in my arms, carrying me the rest of the way, my worn nightgown trailing behind me, my head resting in the curve where his neck and shoulder meet, the scent of sweat and man filling my nostrils. I grip his neck, clinging to him.

We walk past a group of men standing near the shore, looking worse for the wear. One of them seems familiar, and I struggle to place where I have seen him before.

John carries me through the water, his pants growing wet as he wades deeper, until we reach the boat bobbing in the sea.

Neither one of us speaks.

The owner of the vessel has come down from Miami and is the only one who is not sporting visible injuries from the storm, his clothes in far better condition than those of the rest of the survivors.

John sets us down gently, and I clutch Lucy to my breast, the rocking of the waves jostling us.

I want to hold on to John, to the security I have known these past few days, but I force myself to release him.

"I'll find you as soon as I can get out of here," he vows.

What happens next? Where will we go? And what awaits us when we get there?

John turns to the man with the boat, and they exchange a few words before we cast off.

I bat at the tears running down my face, crooning to Lucy as she fusses at the pitching of the waves.

It is only once we are out to sea that I recognize the man on the shore—he is the man from Ruby's, the one with the young, pretty Cuban wife, Mirta. He appears nothing like he did days ago, his clothes dirty and torn, his face haunted.

What happened to his wife?

I hope she is somewhere safe.

I keep my eyes trained to the shore, on John, until the Keys are behind us and he is little more than a speck on the beach, the ocean surrounding us, and we're alone once more.

Twenty-Seven

Mirta

As exhausted as I am from the night before, I cannot sleep. I wait for Anthony, the gun clasped tightly in my hand, my heart racing at every creak of the house, every noise outside.

The communications are still down—given the destruction caused by the storm they likely will be gone for a very long time—and considering we are cut off from the rest of the world, it's easy to feel both alone and entirely too cramped on this tiny island. Are there people out there in the night scavenging for whatever they can find? Anthony was right to be concerned earlier—depending on how long it takes for us to be rescued, food and water shortages will likely be a problem.

A noise breaks through the relative silence of the night—a rustling, followed by the fall of footsteps over the floorboards on the front porch.

Gun in hand, I walk from the sitting room to the front door, my heart hammering in my breast.

"It's me," a familiar voice shouts, and I open the door in time to see Anthony make his way up the porch.

I close the distance between us, meeting him halfway, and he sags against my body, his arms around my waist.

We stand there holding each other, no words between us. What is left to say? We have lived what seems like a lifetime in the past twenty-four hours, and I am hollowed out and strung tight. At the moment, I only want to forget everything that has happened.

I want Anthony.

I press my lips to his, my body taking over.

I sense the same desperation that lives in me in him as the kiss changes, his body shifting from pliant to possessive. From the moment our lips meet, it's clear this embrace is different from all the ones we've shared up to this point; maybe he's been holding back from me, and now I'm seeing a new side of him.

Or maybe he's as broken up by what we've seen today as I am.

We move apart, and I look at him, and suddenly, it's like something has been unlocked inside me.

"Why did you want to marry me?" I demand.

I hear my mother's voice in my ear, admonishing me for my forwardness, and I don't have the energy to care.

"Because I wanted you."

His words send a thrill through me.

"And you always get what you want?" I ask.

"Almost always."

"And you want what exactly? From me?"

"Everything."

My heart pounds.

"I want you to respect me. I don't want you to regret this." He takes a deep breath. "I want you to love me."

"I want that, too," I acknowledge, surprising myself with how much I mean it. "But you can't tell me you want those things and not give me more of yourself. Why did you want me? What about *me* specifically? Was it merely that you'd heard through the grapevine that my father was in dire straits and I was pretty enough to suit your needs?"

"No. You sell yourself too short."

"I've learned to be pragmatic."

"You don't have to worry about such things anymore."

"Does anyone really stop worrying about them?"

"No, I suppose they don't. And I did know you. In a manner of speaking, at least."

"That day in the library—"

"That day in the library was the first time we talked, but it wasn't the first time I saw you. The first time I saw you was outside my hotel. You were walking with friends. In this dress I won't ever forget." He pauses as though the memory deserves a moment of reflection.

"What color was the dress?" I ask, wanting to be a part of this history he has that I was unaware of until now.

"Blue."

The moment is hazy, a night of innocence and splendor in a long string of them like a rope of pearls around my neck.

Anthony's hands drift down to my waist. "It was fitted here, and when I saw you, I thought I could span the width of you." I stare down at his hands encircling me. "Just so," he adds with a swallow.

"The skirt fell away from you—" His hands drift lower, skimming my hips, cupping, caressing.

"I remember the dress," I reply, a little faint.

"I thought you were the most beautiful thing I'd ever seen."

"You didn't approach me."

"No, I didn't. It would have hardly been appropriate with my reputation. I never thought our paths would cross again, but then there you were. Turning up when I least expected it, flashes of you around Havana—an elbow here, the curve of your neck there, the whirl of your skirts passing me by—the idea of you getting stuck in my head like a tune I couldn't shake."

"More romance," I tease, even as my heart thuds in my chest, because it *is* starting to sound romantic, and the idea of this man watching me dash around Cuba sends a thrill inside me even though I realize that such things are not enough of a foundation for a happy marriage, for a partnership.

"You want romance, I'll give you enough romance to make you blush."

I want more.

"One day, your father sat down across from me at a poker table."

This is the part of the story I didn't get. The whispers I heard— *Mirta Perez's father sold her over a card game.*

"Did you know when he sat down what you intended to do?"

"No. I don't believe in much, but something kept throwing you in my path, and I've never been one to miss a shot at what I wanted."

"So you struck a deal for me."

"I offered to marry you, yes. It seemed a solution to everyone's problems. Your family needed help—extra funds and favor with Batista—and I wanted, needed—"

He doesn't say it aloud, but I can finish his thought anyway.

You.

Has anyone ever needed me in all my life until him?

Anthony's grip on me tightens. "That night in your father's library, the first night we talked . . ." His eyes gleam. "I wanted to do this . . ."

It's all I can do to remain still, my throat thick with some emotion I cannot name.

The family I want, the marriage I crave, is within my grasp.

We could be happy together. I could be happy with him.

Now I am the one who is greedy. He speaks of my beauty, my body, but I want all of him.

I want his heart.

Anthony's cologne fills my nostrils, his body hard in all the places I am soft, evidence of a man who has gotten through life using brute force and brawn.

His lips catch mine as I tilt my head toward him, his tongue parting the seam of my mouth, and I open to him, easing into the kiss.

Nothing in my life so far has prepared me for this. For him.

"Breathe," he murmurs against my lips, stroking my hair.

I take a deep breath, his ministrations unspooling something tightly wound within me as I grasp my future.

My nightgown drops to the floor, and the look in his eyes sends a thrill through me, my name escaping his lips on a strangled breath as I move toward him.

By the end of the night, I'm officially a wife in every way.

Twenty-Eight

WEDNESDAY, SEPTEMBER 4, 1935

Elizabeth

I used to be utterly consumed by the thought of death. My mother said it was unnatural for a girl of my position to be so preoccupied with such things, but given my family's history, I couldn't help but wonder what my father's and brother's final moments were like, whether they knew they were going to die, if there was an instant when they wished they could undo the decision they made, a flash of regret. In my more fanciful moments, I expected warmth, and white light, and angels heralding them to their final destination.

When I died, I felt cold. And darkness.

One moment, I was in the train, holding on to Sam, and the next, I was gone, one thought flitting through my mind before everything went dark—

I don't want to die.

When I wake, a woman leans over me, her outfit a bright white, a light shining in my eyes. Her voice rings in my ear over and over again.

"Elizabeth—Elizabeth—"

There's a dull ache in my head, my throat scratchy and dry. My body throbs, an ugly bruise on my hand. Another one on my wrist. I try to lift my arms, but I can't move, I—

Panic fills me.

"Elizabeth."

I swallow, blinking, gazing beyond the nurse to a spot over her shoulder, a now familiar voice.

Sam.

He takes my hand.

The nurse speaks, but it sounds like she's far away, as though I am submerged in water.

The train—

"Water—"

"Do you want some water?" she asks.

I shake my head, trying again, the words a jumble in my mind. "Water. There was water."

"The storm carried us away," Sam interjects. "A wave came. It flooded the train car. You were tossed around when the wave crashed over us, and you hit your head against the side of the car. You were unconscious."

"I was underwater."

"You nearly drowned."

"Where am I?"

"A hospital in Miami," Sam answers. "A Coast Guard cutter brought us up here. They've been evacuating people from Mate-cumbe Key to the mainland. They took you out as soon as possible because you're injured."

"I'll give you a few moments," the nurse says, her heels clipping against the floor until the door shuts gently behind her and we are alone.

"It happened so quickly." He squeezes my hand. "The storm

surge overtook the train, and the cars filled with water. I held on as best as I could, tried to hold on to you. All around me people were doing the same thing. One minute you were with me, and then you were gone. The current was too strong. It ripped me away. It's a miracle we didn't drown."

"I don't remember any of it."

"I've never been so scared in my life. The evacuation train . . ." His jaw twitches. "It was swept off the tracks. Some people made it out through the windows, some held on to the tracks and the train, but many were swept up by the ocean and drowned."

"All those people—the children."

"No one knows yet how many died. They're still trying to locate survivors, uncover bodies." He pauses. "It's bad out there. The recovery is going to be a long and arduous process. It seems like the storm swept in and took everything with it. It's a wasteland.

"I found your body lying on the ground a few hundred yards away from the station. I don't know how you got there, but when I discovered you I thought you were dead. You wouldn't open your eyes, and I couldn't feel a pulse at first."

"The veterans—" *My brother.*

"I don't know. The camps are gone. Destroyed by the storm. Not everyone evacuated, and the ones who did—"

The expression on his face, the sheer horror there—

"What about the guests who stayed at the Sunrise Inn and didn't evacuate with us?"

"Most of the structures are gone. I'm not sure if any are still standing. I don't know what happened to everyone else."

Tears fill my eyes, running down my cheeks.

"You have a concussion," Sam tells me. "They want to monitor you for a few days to make sure you're fine. You were pretty banged up. Maybe your body got tangled up in something that kept you in place. That'd explain the bruises, at least."

"How were you hurt?" I ask, gesturing in the direction of his face. There's a nasty laceration near his eye.

"Flying debris, I think. It's all a blur, pieces of it I don't remember, but at least I only have some cuts and bruises. Nothing too bad."

"Have you seen a doctor?"

"They checked me out when we first came up here. They had far worse injuries to tend to than mine. I'm fine."

"How long have we been in Miami?"

"A day. Some people came down with boats to get the injured out. There are still rescue efforts to help the rest of the survivors."

"Is there a list of names somewhere? I need to locate my brother."

"I'll talk to some of the officials. See what I can learn. Right now, you worry about getting better. The doctors said the most important thing is for you to relax." He swallows. "I thought you were dead."

The emotion in his voice surprises me.

"Things are complicated," I say. "What you told me at the inn, the papers I found, I don't know how I feel about it."

"I know."

"I'm grateful to you for what you've done for me, for coming here with me, but I deserve more answers than what you've given me so far."

"I'll tell you everything I can, whenever you're ready."

I want to believe him, want to think there's loyalty between us after everything we've been through, but something holds me back. I've been burned by other people enough times to learn that my trust shouldn't be so easily won.

My gaze drifts to the table next to my bed, a fat red bouquet of roses perched on top.

"They're beautiful. But you didn't have to send me flowers."

"I didn't."

A white card sticks out from the overabundance of red, and Sam plucks it from the bouquet and hands it to me wordlessly.

A chill slides down my spine as I read the words scrawled in black ink.

The card slips from my hand, fluttering to the hospital room floor.

I was very sorry to hear of your accident. Frank.

Twenty-Nine

Helen

The rescue boat takes us to Riverside Hospital in Miami. The doctors examine Lucy and proclaim her healthy, clearing me as well, and tuck us into one of the empty rooms. I try to answer their questions as best I can, fill out the paperwork they put in front of me, but before I realize it, my eyes are drooping, the lack of sleep from the baby and the hurricane catching up to me.

When I wake, a nurse mills around the room, John seated in the corner in a rocking chair, Lucy in his arms. A lump forms in my throat at the sight of them, at the sound of him singing softly to the baby, a hint of a melody I remember from my own childhood, his voice surprisingly pleasant.

John glances over her head, and our gazes meet.

I smile, relief filling me. "You're back."

"I got a boat out this morning. I wanted to come check on you. How are you?"

"Tired," I admit, already reaching for the baby as he settles her in my arms.

Lucy searches for my breast, nuzzling my skin, and I don't have it in me to be embarrassed by sharing this moment with him, not after all the other intimacies we've experienced. Facing death has a way of bonding you with another.

"I read your chart," he says. "Everything seems good. You're healing nicely. They said you should be able to go home in a day or so. Lucy is doing well, too."

Home.

I don't even know where that is anymore. I've given the hospital staff Aunt Alice's information to see if she's been admitted, but so far she hasn't turned up.

"Do you know if the storm hit Key West?" I ask.

"We bore the brunt of it. They're saying Key West is mostly fine. But power is out, communication lines down, people missing, taken to various locations to get help. They've evacuated all injured who wished to leave the Keys. The National Guard has been called in."

"I can't help wondering about Tom. Did he head south to Cuba to go fishing? Or did he head north? Was he caught in the storm? Is he even alive? I keep waiting for him to walk through the door. If he is searching for us, the hospital has to be a logical place he'd look."

"There are police officers here. The nurses will keep an eye on you. He's not going to hurt you again."

"I'll be better when we can leave." When we can disappear. "Have you heard anything about my aunt?"

"No, I haven't. I'll keep asking. If she wasn't injured too badly in the storm, they probably wouldn't have evacuated her until later. Hopefully, she'll show up here soon."

"And the men in the camps? Did the train get them out safely?"

I've been ensconced with Lucy in this hotel room, cut off from the rest of the world. I keep thinking about the people who came

to dine at Ruby's passing on to their next destination, everyone who
called this stretch of the Keys home.

John is silent for a few moments, his gaze fixated on some point
on the wall behind me.

"They tried to evacuate the men from the camps. Sent a train to
get them out, but it ran into problems on the way down and was
delayed. It didn't even make it to the camp where I worked. It
hardly mattered. It was too late for most of them by the time the
train arrived at the other camps. The tidal surge got them. They say
the train cars are littered across the ground, the railroad destroyed.
They're still unearthing the bodies."

I gasp. "How many—"

"Hundreds, maybe. That's what they're saying, at least. It's a
shame. A damn shame. They were good men. They deserved better
than what they got." He clears his throat, tears swimming in his
eyes. "They're mounting rescue efforts to go down and treat people.
To help with the bodies. There's a real risk of disease spreading and
becoming an issue with that many corpses."

"Your medical training will be useful."

"It will be. I don't want to leave you and Lucy, not when you
don't know where your husband is, or your aunt, when you're afraid,
but you saw what it was like down there. I worked beside so many
of those men. I have a duty to them. If there are people to be treated,
rescued, they're going to need all the help they can get."

"Of course."

Worry fills me, but my fear hardly seems reasonable in the face
of all everyone else has lost.

"I'll be back in a day or two." John leans forward, and his lips
brush my forehead, the scent of his soap filling my nostrils.

There's so much I wish to say, but words seem inadequate,
and as I try to conjure the right ones, they slip away from me. I
never realized giving birth would be such exhausting work, but

I'm drained, my limbs heavy, gait sluggish, brain foggy. The nurses say it's my body's response to the two shocks—the storm and labor—but I can't help but wonder if I'll ever feel like myself again.

"I'll come back to you soon," he promises.

Thirty

FRIDAY, SEPTEMBER 6, 1935

Mirta

The smell of death surrounds us, the decay of flesh unbearable. What was an island paradise now feels unmistakably like hell.

There's a lawlessness down here, a sense of fear that has settled among the survivors. Looters scavenge the beaches, stealing from empty, damaged houses.

I am someone I no longer recognize, a feral creature who has lost all sense of niceness and politeness, who is concerned with one thing and one thing only:

Survival.

"There's a boat," Anthony shouts, and I follow him out the front door, to the space where our dock used to be before the storm hit, and there's a boat waiting for us.

The Coast Guard.

It's finally our turn to leave.

THEY'VE SET UP ASSISTANCE FOR THE STORM SURVIVORS AT THE First Baptist Church in Homestead, Florida, and people trickle in all day long after we arrive, the seriously injured heading north to the hospital in Miami.

One of Anthony's local friends and business partners greets us at the church, dropping off a car and some fresh clothes for us, a few essentials.

We arrive at the Biltmore Hotel in Coral Gables in the early evening, checking into a sumptuous suite.

Anthony leaves me alone to make some phone calls and meet with his business associates. I undress, sinking into a warm bath and washing away the grime of the past few days. Anthony sends up food with a note not to wait for him, and after my bath and a quick phone call to my family in Havana to let them know I'm fine, I dine on steak paired with a fine vintage of red wine, devouring the thick, juicy cut of meat with a hunger I've never experienced before.

After I've finished, chocolate mousse for dessert, the hotel room door opens, and Anthony crosses the threshold. He seems exhausted, the suit he changed into earlier rumpled, his hair mussed.

"How did your meetings go?" I ask, rising to greet him with a kiss.

"Things seem to be in order. I got us tickets for the railroad to take us back to New York. With everything that happened, it seems best to go home as soon as possible. If Frank Morgan is going to move against me, I need to be prepared. I'm too exposed here." He pours himself a drink from the wine bottle sitting on the table. "We should have done this all along. We should have stayed in some elegant hotel rather than roughing it like we did. I'm sorry I took you down there, that I put you in danger. I wanted us to get to know each other, away from everyone else and all the stories of my past." He gives a bitter laugh. "I wanted you to get to know me without seeing me as some gangster who wasn't worth your time. I know we're an unusual match. I know if things were different, you could have married someone far better than me. But I wanted to make you happy."

I wrap my arms around him, resting my head against his chest, making a space for myself in the curve of his embrace.

"I keep seeing that man holding a knife to your neck," he whispers.

"I keep seeing his eyes in the moments before he died," I confess.

"You shouldn't feel guilty about that."

"You keep saying that, but it doesn't make it easier. Will there be other men who come after us? Is this what our future will look like?" I take a deep breath. "One day, will a man hold a knife to one of our children's necks?"

"I will never let that happen."

"How will you stop it? You told me your enemies want what you have, that power is a target on your back."

"What would you have me do? Get out of the business altogether? There are those who will view me abandoning my less legitimate interests as a sign of weakness, who will be emboldened by it and will strike against me because they believe they can."

"Then make it impossible for them to see you as weak. But this life—how will we raise a family like this? How will we be happy if we are constantly glancing over our shoulders, fearing the next attack?"

"Is that what you want from me? A family? After what you've seen of my life?"

"What else is there?"

"I don't know." He rakes a hand through his hair. "You could go back to Cuba. Buy a house close to your family. You'd be safer there. I would understand if that's what you wanted. This marriage—I was wrong to think I could bring a wife into this life. To go about things as I did. I'm so sorry."

His apology isn't enough.

Once, I would have been grateful for it, taken the scraps he tossed my way as an encouraging sign that he was a good man, that he respected me.

It's not enough.

I want it all—a partnership, his love, and I want the safety and security of a future where I don't have to worry that I will be collateral damage for another man's whims.

I demand it.

"I'm not going back to Cuba. I am your wife. My place is by your side. Those promises we made when we married each other—I want them. But we can't have that life if we're constantly in danger. And what's the alternative? We go into hiding somewhere?

"I'm tired. Tired of making myself small so no one will strike against me or my family. We did that in Cuba when my father's decisions led to our ruin, and I won't do it again. I'm tired of always being afraid, of my life being dictated by others' decisions. You want me, you want to have a family with me, then you fix this."

"What would you have me do?"

I meet his gaze. "Whatever it takes."

"You'll stay beside me?"

It's a chance for a fresh start to our relationship; despite how we began, in this moment, for our future, I am choosing him.

"I will."

He pulls a small black box out of his jacket pocket. "I didn't do this properly the first time; I hope this makes up for it."

Anthony kneels down before me and opens the jewelry box.

The diamond is smaller than the one he gave me back in Havana, the ring that could be somewhere with a dead man. The new ring sports a round stone, encircled by more diamonds, the thin band studded with them.

It's beautiful, and unmistakably something I would have chosen for myself.

"I love it."

I extend my hand to Anthony, and he slides the engagement ring on my finger beside the simple band he gave me during our marriage ceremony in Cuba.

We come together in a frenzy, the depth of my desire staggering me.

For as long as I remember, I was told not to want more than I could have, to be pleasing, and pliant, and subordinate my wants to the needs of my family, taught that the greatest height I could hope to achieve was to belong to another. No longer. Let him belong to me. Let him work to earn my affections.

I'm done settling for anything less.

Thirty-One

Helen

They've printed a list of the dead and missing in the *Miami Herald*, and I scan the names, my heart in my throat, searching for Tom.

His name isn't there.

Is Tom scanning the lists for *my* name, or is he up here looking for me himself, wondering if I'm one of the nameless victims whose bodies have been found but not yet identified?

The fear of the unknown haunts me.

In the hurricane's aftermath, we exist in a state of waiting for news, the recovery process slowed by how many are still unable to find answers about what happened on September 2. I can't fathom learning a loved one has died from reading their name in a newspaper. How do you go on after a thing like that? How do you wish to?

For as much as I hope to see Tom's name printed in black and white among the dead and missing, I worry equally that I will see my aunt Alice's there.

But her name isn't, either.

In John's absence, I turn to the newspapers, to the nurses for updates. They say the National Guard is preventing people from going home. That there are so many dead bodies that it's unsafe to return. They're searching for victims on land, by boat.

What sort of horrors is John seeing as he helps with the recovery efforts?

People are still dying from their injuries; others simply disappeared, their bodies unaccounted for, their families desperately searching for them.

I'm not sure what would be harder, the finality of death, or the uncertainty of it all, the absence of a body, the inability to achieve a sense of closure. Then again, how do you get closure after a thing like this?

There are some who never will.

It's as though the hand of God has come down and reordered the world as we know it. Entire families are gone, swept away by the water and winds, and the living are left with the question:

Why were we spared when so many others weren't?

With each day that passes without Tom, Lucy and I become more and more of a family, and I settle into the idea of raising her on my own, allowing myself to slip into the dream of a life without him. Sometimes it's easy to forget that he was ever here at all, the sight of my daughter so all-consuming, as though little else mattered before she came into the world. My life is divided into "before" and "after," and I have come out of the experience of motherhood reborn as someone new.

But other times, I can't forget him, the memory of his body pressing me into the mattress, his hot breath on my neck, his hands—

I jolt awake, my heart pounding, my body covered in sweat. I turn toward the crib where the nurses have allowed Lucy to sleep in my room.

It's empty.

I lurch up from the bed, pulling back the sheets.

"Helen. I have the baby. She's right here."

John walks toward the bed from his corner of the room, Lucy bundled up in his arms, and hands her to me.

"I didn't mean to scare you. I came back tonight and I wanted to check on you. You were sleeping, but Lucy was awake and I wanted you to get some rest."

I help the baby latch on to nurse, my heartbeat still erratic.

"No, it's fine, I just had a bad dream. When I woke up, and she was gone, I thought Tom might have taken her."

John strokes my hair. "You're safe."

Will I ever be safe? Or will I always need to glance over my shoulder as long as my husband is in this world?

"I'm glad you're back safely. How bad was it?"

"I thought I'd seen the worst that could happen to a man when I went to war. But nothing prepared me for this. You expect to see death on the battlefield. But these weren't soldiers. There were women, children. People trapped in their homes who had nowhere to go when the storm hit."

"Are you all right?"

"I am. As bad as it was, it helped to do something. There was this little girl who'd hurt her shoulder. Had to set it. She was so brave. She'd lost her father and her brother, and we pulled her out from beneath an icebox. It wasn't even their icebox. Some neighbor's that blew for miles. When we found her body, it seemed like her death was a foregone conclusion. But then I realized she was breathing. It took a few of us to pull the icebox off her. It was a miracle she survived. She's going to make it, though. We brought her up to the hospital here."

"I'm glad you were able to help her. You're good at that—taking care of people."

"It felt good. Even in the midst of all that horribleness, there was hope. I don't know. I guess I missed practicing medicine more than I realized.

"In the war, there was so little to be done for so many. It was difficult to face a man and know he likely wouldn't survive his injuries, that for all my training and experience, there wasn't much I could do. I forgot how good it feels to give someone a chance."

"You could go back to practicing medicine, couldn't you?"

"Maybe."

"Would you want to?"

"I don't know. When I came home from France, I didn't understand why my life was saved when so many others weren't. A part of me wanted to die, too, because living with their voices in my head, their final moments playing over and over again, was infinitely harder. But now, it seems like there should be something more than death. Like maybe there is something else I am meant to do while I am on this earth."

"You saved us."

"No. You saved yourself. You would have done what you had to do to protect Lucy. I happened to be there at the right time."

"I'll kill him." The words come out louder than I intended in the quiet, dark night, but I have never meant anything more. "God help me, if he comes after me and Lucy, if he tries to hurt her, to take her, I will kill him."

John is silent for a beat, and I wonder if I've horrified him with my honesty, if he's not equipped to handle the fury inside me burning bright and sharp.

He leans forward and kisses my forehead, his voice in my ear.

"He's never going to hurt you again."

WHEN I WAKE THE NEXT MORNING, JOHN IS GONE, AND THE NURSE tells me he went to get some food and will be back shortly.

"You're healing well," she informs me. "That baby of yours is doing fine, too. They'll let you all go home soon."

I've been so focused on recovering, on what will happen if Tom finds us; I've thought little of what happens next, of where we will go when we are released from the hospital. I've still heard nothing of Aunt Alice, and based on the scene John described and the pictures of the hurricane's destruction that fill the newspaper, I can't imagine returning to Islamorada.

At the same time, Key West isn't home anymore, either, especially if Tom is alive.

"You have a visitor," one of the nurses announces. Her eyes widen slightly. "A new one. A man."

My heart pounds. "Did he tell you his name?"

"He said his name was Matthew."

She returns with a man dressed in a pair of overalls and a white shirt.

I recognize him instantly from the Sunrise Inn—he worked behind the front desk for my aunt.

The expression on his face, his hat in hand, tells me everything I need to know.

"She's gone," I say.

"Yes." His voice cracks over the word.

Tears well in my eyes, spilling onto my cheeks.

"What happened?" I ask.

"We were hit hard. The inn wasn't strong enough to hold up against the wind, the water. She ran out to check on you, to make sure you were safe. The roads were already washed out when she set out, and she had to turn back. We waited out the storm in the inn; there wasn't anyplace to go." His eyes swim with tears. "Only two of us made it. The rest—"

He wipes at his brow.

"I loved that woman. Your aunt. Worked for her for almost a

decade, when your uncle was still alive, and after. I always thought there would be time to tell her. To get her used to the idea. I knew she cared for me, but I didn't know if she felt the same way, if—" His voice breaks off. "I would have traded places with her in a heartbeat."

"I'm so sorry."

"She loved you," he says. "Used to show me all those letters you sent her. She was so proud of you."

I can't speak through the knot of unshed tears clogging my throat.

"There's some money," he says. "A life insurance policy. Five thousand dollars. You're the beneficiary on the policy."

My jaw drops. It is an unimaginable sum.

"She paid it faithfully every week. Knew she wanted it to go to you. She was proud of you, but she also worried about you. She didn't like Tom, and with your parents gone, you wouldn't have anyone if something happened to her. She wanted you to have options."

"I can't—"

"She told me what you were running from the night you came to see her, the night before she died. That you wanted a fresh start for yourself and the baby.

"That inn was her life. No one would blame you if you wanted to take the insurance money and go, least of all your aunt. But if you don't, if you wish to stay and rebuild, I'm happy to do whatever I can to help out. She owned the land the inn was on, and it'll be yours, too. People around these parts loved her. That inn she built meant something, gave people jobs, gave them a chance. It would be a shame to see her legacy wiped out by the storm."

Tears spill down my cheeks. It's hard to envision a world without Alice in it, the letters we sent back and forth a constant in my life. If I am to be comforted by anything, it is the knowledge that she is surely with her beloved husband now, that she is in a better place. And still—it seems wrong that she is not here.

"I'm staying up at my sister's in Miami while we wait for them to let us go home," Matthew adds. "I'll leave you the address in case you need anything."

"Aunt Alice—are there plans for a funeral? I'd like to be there when she's laid to rest."

"She lived her whole life in Islamorada. She shouldn't be buried anywhere else." He swallows. "Her husband was buried on the edge of the property. She'd like to be buried with him."

WHEN I LOST MY PARENTS, I FELT A PROFOUND SENSE OF SADNESS, but it was still early enough in my marriage that having Tom beside me was a balm. I don't remember him being particularly kind, but I remember taking comfort in the notion that I belonged to someone. I was no longer a daughter, but I was a wife, and in that, I wasn't alone.

But now Alice is gone, and I have no living family save my daughter. I have left my husband. I belong to no one.

Is this how Alice felt after her husband died? Her letters to me were filled with stories of the life she'd built in Islamorada, and I always admired that she'd forged her own path rather than following in the expectations others had for her.

Sometimes I can't understand the way this world works, why good people like Alice are taken while others are saved in spite of their wicked ways.

All of the emotions of the past few days flood me, and once I start crying, I can't seem to stop, as though a valve has been turned on inside of me.

"What happened?"

I glance up as John crosses the threshold into my hospital room, concern on his face.

"Your aunt?"

I nod.

He sits beside me on the bed, wrapping his arms around me, and holds me while I cry, my tears wetting his shirtfront.

I pull back and meet his gaze, struggling to get my breathing under control.

"The man who worked at the front desk at the inn came to tell me what happened," I say. "There were only two survivors. Everyone else perished. They want to bury her there."

He holds me tightly while I cry some more, the sobs racking my body, until I fall asleep.

When I wake in the middle of the night after another nightmare, the tears wrung from my body, John is asleep beside me in the hospital bed, half his body hanging off the edge, his feet dangling over.

In the darkness, while he sleeps, I allow myself to watch him. He spoke of how the loud noises unsettled him after the war, but I wonder if he's plagued with nightmares as I am, if the horrors of the war haunt him in sleep.

I lay my head against his shoulder, listening to the sound of his breathing, and when I fall back asleep the nightmares are gone.

WHEN THEY PRINT THE NAMES OF THE MISSING AND THE DEAD IN the newspaper the next day, there is one notable addition to the list of the missing:

Thomas Berner

Thirty-Two

Elizabeth

I wake in the dark with a jolt, the sight of Sam sleeping in a chair near my hospital bed, the soft sound of his rhythmic snores, doing little to calm my racing heart.

In the dark, in sleep, I'm back in the train car, in a coffin filled with water. I relive those final moments, the hope that was snatched so swiftly away from us. It's the ones who suffered through all of it, who died slowly, that haunt me most. For me, it was an instantaneous sense of darkness that overtook me, but what about the others? Those who came so close, who saw escape within their grasp, only to have it snatched away from them as they descended into despair, as they likely realized their death was unavoidable, as they watched their loved ones pass away in front of them.

Why do some suffer, and why are others spared?

The stories trickling out of the Keys are truly horrific. Bodies are showing up far from the storm's path, blown miles and miles away, some dead from their injuries, others too weak to be expected to survive. It seems that it's not enough to have lived through the storm itself; others have survived the immediate aftermath only to languish and ultimately succumb to their injuries.

I'm not sure I'll ever sleep through the night again.

I have no news of my brother.

Now that the government offices are open, Sam was able to confirm that my brother was indeed working at the camps—the one by the ferry landing that we never made it to.

What happened after that is anyone's guess. So many are missing, unaccounted for.

Dead.

My physical injuries are mending, the bump on my head lessening, the pain subsiding, the mottled bruising transforming to an ugly color the nurses assure me is a sign I am "healing." I wish I could say the same about the rest of me, wish it was easy to put the awful things out of my mind.

I take Sam's hand, his arm resting near my blanket-covered leg in the hospital bed. I roll onto my side, lacing our fingers together.

The flowers are gone, removed by one of the nurses when I asked her if she could get rid of them. If only I could erase the memory of Frank's words with such ease.

There's so much Sam and I have yet to speak of, his lies I have not begun to fully unravel, but right now it doesn't matter. The things I worried over before pale in comparison to the losses so many have suffered, and at the moment, all I care about is that I am alive and I am safe.

I close my eyes and drift back to sleep, Sam's hand in mine.

BY FRIDAY, THE DOCTORS ARE READY TO RELEASE ME, AND SAM helps me secure a room in Miami at a hotel where he's been staying when he's not by my side at the hospital. I wait in the hospital sitting area while Sam goes to make a phone call for work.

A woman sits down next to me, a baby curled in her arms.

"She's beautiful," I say.

She beams. "Thank you. Her name is Lucy."

"That's a lovely name."

Something about the woman—

"We met before, didn't we?" I ask, recognition dawning. "When you were still pregnant. In Key West at Ruby's Café. You're Helen. You gave me the pie."

Her eyes widen. "We did. Elizabeth, right? You were searching for your boyfriend. Did you locate him?"

"Not my boyfriend. My brother, actually. And no, I haven't. We found out he was working at one of the camps, but no one knows what happened to him. So many of the men are missing."

"You were caught in the storm?" Helen asks.

"Yes. We tried to take the evacuation train in Islamorada. The storm surge swept it off the tracks."

Helen's eyes widen. "That must have been terrifying."

"It was. I hit my head, and they kept me here for observation. I'm finally leaving today, though. I've had enough of hospitals to last a lifetime." And then I remember why she recommended the Sunrise Inn, and what Sam told me about the rest of the people who stayed behind. "I heard about your aunt. I'm sorry for your loss."

Her eyes well with tears. "Thank you."

"I didn't spend much time with her while I was at the inn, but from what I saw, she seemed like a wonderful woman. It was a welcoming place."

"She was."

"Were you caught in the storm? Is that how you ended up here?" I ask.

"Yes. I left Key West right before the storm hit. Bad timing, I suppose."

I gesture toward the babe in her arms. "Was she born before the storm?"

"During."

My jaw drops. After everything we experienced, I can't fathom giving birth in such conditions. "How did you survive?"

"I'm not entirely sure," Helen answers. "We were fortunate." She smiles. "And we had a guardian angel of sorts who helped us."

"What will you do now?" Helen asks me.

"I haven't decided. I'd like to know what happened to my brother. I came down here hoping he could help me, but now I want to know he's all right."

"I have a friend who was at one of the camps," Helen replies. "He might know your brother or be able to help point you in the right direction. I'm happy to ask him." Her expression changes, a smile lighting up her face, as she glances past me to someone over my shoulder. "Here he is now."

I turn in time to see a big man walk toward us, his clothes worn, his eyes on Helen and her child.

I grip the arm of the chair.

"The nurses told me you were getting some fresh air," he says to her. "How do you feel?"

It's his voice I recognize first, the sound of it unchanged despite time, distance, and the war between us. He sounds like our father.

"John."

He turns away from Helen and faces me. He blinks. "You look like someone—" His face goes slack with shock. "Elizabeth?"

I burst into tears.

A FEW DAYS AGO, I MIGHT HAVE HUGGED HIM. NOW I UNDERSTAND a little more what he's been through, now I am more cautious, ready to give him space.

Helen excuses herself, returning to her hospital room with the baby so that John and I can catch up.

"You're alive," I say. "I feared you were dead."

"What are you doing here? Why aren't you in New York?" he asks.

I take a deep breath, steadying myself. "I came down here searching for you. But I didn't know where you were, so I ended up in Key West, since your last letter was postmarked there, and I went to this café—Ruby's—and a waitress—your friend Helen—told me the veterans lived up north. So I traveled to Islamorada. And then the storm came. We tried to get out, but it was too late. We were on the rescue train when the hurricane hit."

Horror fills his eyes. "Thank God you're alive," John says, stepping forward and wrapping his arms around me. "I can't believe you're here." He pulls back, his gaze running over me. "It's been so long since I saw you. You were just a girl, then."

"Not anymore."

"No. Not anymore." He frowns. "Did you come down here by yourself? From New York?"

"On Mr. Flagler's railroad."

"I should be surprised, but somehow I'm not. You always were the bravest one of all of us."

"I don't know about brave. Desperate, more like. And it's not like there's anyone else. You left us without a way to get in touch with you."

Something that seems a lot like shame flashes across his face. "I didn't think you'd need me. You're right, I should have kept in touch."

"Why didn't you?"

His expression is pained. "I don't know. I wish I could give you a better explanation, wish I could explain it to myself. I felt like I was drowning in New York, like it was choking me, and I needed to get away, needed to get lost somewhere where people didn't know me from before, didn't expect me to be the same person they knew before I went away to war. I told myself you were all better without me."

"We weren't. We *aren't*. Things are bad. My mother isn't well. With George and our father gone, the money went, too."

A curse falls from John's lips. "I'm sorry, Elizabeth. I had no idea about the money. Not the full extent of it, at least. I figured their finances took a hit after the crash, but I didn't think they'd lose all that money."

"But you knew they were gone. You knew we were alone."

"I thought they would have made sure you were taken care of."

"They didn't. We weren't." I laugh bitterly. "Business was bad. Father tried to save it as best he could, but in doing so he borrowed a lot of money from the kind of people you don't want to owe money to."

"Who?" John asks.

"No one you would know. Trust me, no one you would want to know."

"Is this man threatening you? Trying to collect on the money?"

"In a manner of speaking. There was no way we could repay the debt, so he agreed to renegotiate for something other than money. We're to be married."

"You're joking."

"I'm not." I pull the gaudy diamond from my purse.

He winces. "That's some ring." He sighs. "You shouldn't have to marry someone you don't love. How could our father be so reckless?"

"He was probably just desperate. It's expensive to live the way we do—the way we did. He likely didn't want to disappoint us."

"And in doing so, he all but sold you to a gangster."

"I thought it would help—kill two birds, so to speak—clear the debt and ensure we had enough money to survive." I shudder. "I can't marry him, though."

"No, you can't. What will you do?"

"I don't know."

As hard as I try, I can't figure a way out of this mess.

"Do you think of them?" I ask. "Father and George?"

"Sometimes."

"Me too." I take a deep breath. "There was this moment before the wave hit the train when I knew I was going to die. And it hit me then that I didn't want to. Do you think it was like that for them before they killed themselves?"

"I don't know. God, I hope not."

"I was angry with them for a long time. Angry they left everyone here to clean up their mess. I was angry with you for a long time," I admit. "Upset with you for leaving, for not being stronger, I guess." Shame fills me. "I didn't know what it must have been like for you."

"No one does. Not until you live it."

"I have nightmares," I whisper. "The screams. The crying. The bodies. The dark. It was so cold, and I felt my body being pulled away—"

"The nightmares will stay with you. I wish I could tell you they won't, but they'll become a part of you."

I take a deep breath, asking the question I came down here to ask him, even if I already know the answer, even if I've already worked out for myself somewhere along the way that John isn't the solution I'm looking for.

"Will you ever come home?" I ask.

I understand now—the boy who went off to war has been replaced by the man before me. A man I no longer recognize, but one I'd like to get to know just the same.

"I don't know," John replies.

WE SPEND THE REST OF THE DAY TOGETHER, AND I INTRODUCE him to Sam. After we've spent hours talking in the hospital waiting room, it's time to go, and I give John the name and address of the hotel where Sam secured us two rooms.

"Are you sure you don't want to stay with me?" he asks me.

"That's kind of you, but I'll be fine. I want to get out of this hospital and sleep in a normal bed, wear regular clothes, feel like myself again."

"I have some money," he offers. "It's not much, but I saved most of what I made working."

I lift the diamond engagement ring Frank gave me out of my pocket. "Don't worry. If I get into trouble, this will help."

I was too afraid to pawn it before, but it could be the start to a whole new life.

"That guy—" John jerks his head toward the front door, where Sam left to get his car. "He seems like a good one."

"I hope he is. I'm not sure I'm much of a judge of character anymore, but when you've been through something like this—"

"You see people at their best and worst, and from there you can take the measure of a man," John finishes for me.

I nod. "What about you?" I ask.

"What about me?"

"The woman here in the hospital. Helen. With the baby. Is that my niece?"

"No."

Surprise fills me. "And the father?"

He doesn't answer me.

"What are you going to do?" I ask.

"What do you mean?"

"With the woman? The child? You care for them."

"I don't know. It's not—I'm not anyone to them. I just helped her when she was having a hard time."

"She called you her friend. She looked at you like you were maybe more than that."

A flash of something that sure seems a whole lot like hope mixed with pain crosses his face.

"She has a husband."

"She isn't with him, though, is she? Does she love him?"

"I don't know. How could I ask her something like that?"

"Are they separated?" I ask.

Somehow I can't fathom my big brother, my war hero of a big brother, stealing someone's wife. Then again, who knows how much has changed.

"She left him," John answers.

"So not wholly married, then."

"No, not entirely. He's on the missing list after the storm. But it's so crazy down there; that could mean anything. He could be missing, he could be dead, he could be on his way up to Miami."

"Then you still have a chance. Worry about one problem at a time. He's not here right now. You are. The way I see it, if she'd wanted to stay with him, she would have. She chose to leave and make her own way. You should take your shot."

His lips curve. "You haven't changed, have you?"

"I have, actually. I'm not a girl anymore. And it's time I fixed my own problems."

Thirty-Three

Sam and I check into the hotel in Miami under false names, as a brother and sister traveling from Connecticut. It's not the most plausible of disguises considering our meager bags and injuries—we appear exactly as we are, people who have fled a natural disaster and are still stunned by the whole experience, but hopefully, it will be enough to momentarily draw Frank's people away from our trail if they are looking for us.

Surely, Frank himself is too important to come down here, too disinterested in our relationship to do more than send a few lackeys down to inquire about my whereabouts. Perhaps he is content with the knowledge that Sam is with me and the flowers were a mere formality.

The not knowing is the worst part.

We shuffle to our rooms in silence. There is so much unresolved with Sam, so much we were unable to discuss. If Frank came for me now, would Sam protect me? Can I trust him?

We stop in front of a pair of rooms.

"This is us," Sam says, opening the door to my room first. "Do you want me to check it for you?"

"Please."

He pulls a gun from the waistband of his trousers.

I follow him into the room and close the door behind us, leaning back against the wall. Sam sets down our bags on the ground and flicks on the light. He goes through the room with military precision, his body tense, weapon in hand. When he's finished checking the bathroom, the closet, he lowers the weapon.

"You should be safe here for the night. I'll be next door if you need me."

"You're worried Frank is coming after me, aren't you?"

"I don't know. The flowers—"

"They scared me," I admit, even as much as it pains me. I've always prided myself on my ability to survive, on my strength, and I hate that Frank Morgan has taken a piece of that away from me.

"I know. We don't have enough to arrest him," Sam says. "Frank isn't a stupid man. He's spent years cultivating the right connections within the government. There are rumors that he has contacts within the Bureau, which wouldn't surprise me. Other agents have tried to build cases against him and found nothing but trouble and death for their efforts."

"Do you think he's figured out that you're working for the government? That you're with the FBI?"

"I don't know. Part of the reason I was chosen for this mission is because I wasn't known in New York circles. I've spent most of my career in Florida, a bit in Cuba. But Frank doesn't strike me as a particularly trusting man, so I wouldn't be surprised if he's done some digging."

"There has to be something to get me out of this. Something he's done that will put him behind bars."

"He's very careful about the people closest to him. He buys their loyalty through a combination of fear and greed. The lower-level grunts are too unreliable. They don't have any proof, any real connection to him."

"I'm one of the people closest to him. Who is more privy to personal information than a wife?"

"You are not marrying Frank Morgan."

"Because he's a criminal?" I ask, my heart pounding.

Tell me I'm not alone in this. Tell me you want me, too, that this was never only a job to you, that you wanted me when we first met on the train, that—

A muscle tics in his jaw. "No, not just because he's a criminal."

"Why?"

"You know why."

"You've never said it," I reply. "How could I know?"

"Because you're mine."

It's no louder than a whisper, but in this quiet hotel room, against the hammering of my heart, it might as well be a shout.

"I don't want to be alone tonight," I say, taking an unsteady step toward him.

I stop when I'm close enough to wrap my arms around his neck, pulling his head down toward me until our mouths are a hairbreadth apart.

"Do you trust me?" he asks.

I do.

"As much as I trust anyone. Are you going to kiss me? Properly?"

Sam's answer is the brush of his lips against mine, his arms around my waist, holding me tightly against his hard frame. He kisses with a gentleness that's wholly unexpected, as though we are learning each other, easing into the embrace.

"I've done this before," I say against his mouth.

I think I know him well enough by this point to not worry about his reaction, to not expect judgment. But at the same time, men are so funny about these things that the truth is, I don't know what he'll say.

"Me too," he replies with a wry grin, moving his hands up my back until he arrives at the top of my dress. "This is going to complicate everything," he warns, undoing the first button.

"I'm not afraid of complicated," I murmur, kissing his neck.

"That makes one of us, then." He removes another button. And another.

My dress falls to the floor.

The thing that surprised me most about the lazy afternoons lounging naked on the couch with Billy while his parents were off somewhere else, those stolen afternoons, was how it was possible to learn a part of someone—to know a sliver of them—the expanse of freckles on their back, the sound of their sighs, the shudder of their body against yours—but for so much else to be a mystery. I thought the physical intimacy we shared all those years ago was like a key that would help me gain admittance to a locked room where all the interesting stuff was held, when in reality, it was a different room altogether—uninteresting and drab with a lumpy couch and a poor view of the road.

I am not ready to share every part of myself with Sam, and in this moment, I am grateful for the separation between sex and intimacy, the ability to choose the parts I give of myself to another, the freedom of it.

We tumble into bed together, hands fumbling, our remaining articles of clothing falling to the floor, limbs entangled, my laughter filling the air.

"You're stunning," Sam whispers up at me.

I smile, shifting so I straddle him. "I'm happy," I reply as my mouth finds his.

It's different than it was before with Billy. Maybe there is something to be said for being with an older man, a man who has seen the world and knows himself. Or perhaps, it's because I'm different this time.

Despite this madness with Frank, for the first time in my life, I'm in control of my future. For the first time in as long as I can remember, I feel strong.

"WHAT I SAID EARLIER—ABOUT BEING CLOSE TO FRANK." I GAZE UP at the ceiling, my head resting in the crook of Sam's arm. "What if we used that to our advantage? I could gather information for you. I could—"

"Absolutely not. I meant what I said earlier. I'm not going to let you get close to Frank Morgan to help me put him behind bars. It's too dangerous. He's too dangerous."

I prop myself up on my elbow, peering down at Sam lying on his back in bed.

"'Let' me?"

"You know what I mean."

"I don't, actually. Frank Morgan is my problem. My father borrowed money from him. A man like him isn't going to go away. It's my responsibility to see he isn't a threat to my family."

"This isn't a game. He isn't some college boy you can manage with a hint of your cleavage and some blushes. He's a monster. Anyone who gets in his way, he eliminates. When he threatens them, he goes after their families. Their children. Maybe you haven't seen that side of him yet, but that just means you haven't seen it *yet*, because if you get in his way, if you interfere with his business, if you threaten him, he will kill you."

"And what will he do to you, then? If he's as powerful as you say, then he won't be above going after a federal agent. Especially after that federal agent double-crossed him and ended up in bed with his fiancée."

"I mentioned it would be complicated."

"But do you regret it?" I ask him.

"Not at all."

Thirty-Four

SUNDAY, SEPTEMBER 8, 1935

Helen

In the two days after his visit, I consider Matthew's suggestion that I rebuild the Sunrise Inn, turning the notion around and around in my mind long after my tears have dried.

The area will likely be uninhabitable for a while. Even with the insurance money and Matthew's help, the task of rebuilding the inn will be great indeed. I watched Aunt Alice run the business when I visited her over the summer as a young girl, but she had a manner of making it appear easy when I've no doubt it was anything but.

I know nothing of running a business, nothing of bringing in lodgers. The prudent thing would be to use the insurance money to get a fresh start elsewhere; after all, if Tom is still alive, he'll eventually make his way to Islamorada to look for us.

But in spite of all of my reservations, my mind keeps drifting to what I would do if it were mine, the color I'd paint the shutters, how I'd sit with Lucy on the front porch and gaze out at the sea, telling her all about her great-aunt Alice; the inn is Lucy's birthright, too. And perhaps, it's not just the two of us sitting on that wide porch. Maybe if I'm being completely honest with myself, as much as it terrifies me, I see John there, too.

Impossible dreams.

There are moments when I see a hint of emotion in his eyes, when I hear the affection in his voice, and I wonder if it's possible that I'm not the only one who could picture us as more than friends.

But I am another man's wife, and there are so many things John and I have never spoken of, so many things I'm not ready to face.

On Sunday, they finally release me and Lucy from the hospital, and we accompany John to a ceremony for the veterans who died in the storm. His sister Elizabeth and her friend Sam come with us.

The closer we get to the park where the memorial service is to be held, the quieter John becomes, and I take his hand, lacing my fingers through his, trying to pass some of my strength on to him. It seems supremely unfair that these were the survivors of the Great War, the men who came home and should have lived out their remaining days lauded as heroes. Instead, they went from one tragedy to the next.

How much can people withstand until they break?

We don't speak as we approach the crowd standing near the entrances to Bayfront Park. There are veterans lined up together, but John doesn't move to join them. Instead, his grip on me tightens, as though he's afraid I'll let go, as if he doesn't belong with them.

Sam and Elizabeth stand behind us, giving John his space, and when I turn around, I spy their fingers linked.

Military planes fly overhead, dropping hundreds of roses from the sky. There are speeches, and prayers, and the whole thing is terribly formal. With each moment that passes, John tenses more and more, tugging at his clothes, shifting from side to side, his body practically vibrating with barely contained energy, as though he would bolt at any moment if he could.

When it's all over, he turns without a word to anyone else, striding quickly toward the park's exit, past his sister and Sam. I follow behind him, Lucy tucked in my arms.

John stops before the street, his jaw clenched.

"I shouldn't have asked you to come today. I thought I could handle it, thought it was the right thing to do, but that spectacle—" A blistering curse falls from his lips. "They should have evacuated them earlier. Why didn't they? They didn't even give them a chance. What's the point of honoring their death when you threw them away in life? You should have seen the condition those camps were in, the way we lived. This is all a big farce, and it doesn't mean a damned thing." He grimaces, tugging at the collar of his shirt. "I couldn't breathe back there. I kept seeing the faces of all of those men, imagining what their final moments must have been like, how they were given hope, thinking help was coming, only to be disappointed once again."

I shift Lucy to my side and step forward, wrapping my arm around John.

He stiffens for an instant, and then he relaxes into the hug, some of the tension leaving his body. We stay like that for a long time, the breeze blowing around us, the mourners come to pay their respects walking past us.

When Lucy begins to fuss, I pull back from the embrace.

John lets out a deep breath, and another, his cheeks pink. There's a gleam in his eyes when he looks down at me, emotions swimming there, and once again I imagine I see the same emotions that I feel inside: confusion, fear, want.

It's too soon. I am a married woman. There's Lucy, and the whole world has been upended, and most importantly, I have already been disappointed by a man once. How can I survive another disappointment?

I take another step back, cradling Lucy against my chest.

John grimaces. "I shouldn't have—"

"No, I was the one who—" I take a deep breath. It's ridiculous to be embarrassed in front of this man, considering how many intimacies we've shared over the past week, but I *am* embarrassed. What if he thinks I'm searching for a man to take care of me now that I have left Tom? Who would want to be saddled with another man's wife? Another man's child?

I swallow. "What will you do now?"

"I don't know. There's talk they're going to ship the vets left at the camps on the Keys up here. Have them join the Civilian Conservation Corps. Send them to one of those camps now."

My mouth goes dry, a tingle starting at the base of my spine, heat wafting over me. I knew, of course, that his presence was temporary.

"So you'll go with them, then?"

"I hadn't—No—No, I don't want to join the CCC. I'm done with the government. With the military. I can't stay after all of this." He's silent for a moment. "Where will you go?"

I try for a shaky smile. "There's some insurance money from Aunt Alice. Matthew—the man who worked at the inn—told me about it. There's the land around the inn, too. She owned that. He wants me to rebuild. The inn was her whole life. It seems like a way to honor her memory, but at the same time, I don't know anything about running an inn. Probably smarter to take the money and get a fresh start somewhere."

"You sell yourself too short. You're good at welcoming people. Making them feel at home. You had that way about you at Ruby's, always putting people at ease. You would be wonderful at it."

I flush. "Thank you."

"Are you worried about your husband finding you?" he asks. "Is that holding you back?"

"He's still listed as missing," I reply. "I talked to Ruby—no one's seen him in Key West since Labor Day weekend. Maybe he's safe somewhere; maybe he's gone. I suppose all I can do is hope he'll never turn up."

"If not the camps, where will you go?" I ask John.

"Home. New York."

"Your family needs you."

"I've been gone too long. Seeing Elizabeth reminded me of that. My father and brother left a mess behind when they died, and it isn't fair that she should shoulder that burden alone."

"Will you stay there permanently?"

"I don't know," he replies.

I take a deep, shaky breath, tears threatening.

"I suppose this is good-bye, then."

He nods, his jaw clenched, his gaze fixed on some point over my shoulder. "Are you going to stay in a hotel tonight?"

"Yes. Tomorrow, I'll visit Matthew at his sister's house in Miami to see about rebuilding."

"Do you need anything?"

"No, you've done enough. It's time Lucy and I took care of ourselves. Will you be all right?"

"I will," he replies. "Thank you. This past week has been—"

His voice breaks off.

I cannot cry.

I extend my hand to him. "I will never be able to thank you enough for all you've done for us. The kindness you've shown us."

He doesn't take my hand, but instead leans forward, his lips brushing my cheek.

I still.

It's his words, though, that unravel me.

"You asked me once what I did when I came down to Key West so often. I came to Ruby's. I came to see you."

And then, the last confession—

"I don't even like key lime pie."

He leans down and kisses the top of Lucy's head, caressing her blond hair, and when he stares back up at me, tears swim in his eyes.

The instinct is there to reach for him, but I can't trust it. I can't trust myself. There is too much between us, my life is too complicated, and more than anything, I am afraid.

And then he's gone.

Thirty-Five

MONDAY, SEPTEMBER 9, 1935

Elizabeth

I wake the next morning to an empty bed, a pair of train tickets set on the nightstand next to me, Sam nowhere to be seen.

Our train leaves in a few hours, our meager belongings packed in a bag by the door. The notion of being in such a tight space is hardly appealing, nor is the prospect of hours in a train car after what we've experienced, but it's time to face the music and go home.

Sam returns to the room as I finish dressing.

"Frank Morgan is dead," he announces.

My jaw drops. "What are you talking about?"

Sam hands me a folded-up newspaper.

Mobster Frank Morgan Gunned Down in Front of Home

"How? When?"

"Last night. No one got a good look at the gunman, or if they did, they aren't talking. I called the Bureau to try to see if I could get more details, but it's too early for them to know much."

"But he's dead. He's really dead?"

"He is."

I sink down to the edge of the bed, my heart pounding.

"He won't ever harm you," Sam says.

And I don't have to marry a man I don't love.

"What about the debts my father owed him?" I ask. "Will they die with Frank? Or will whoever takes over his organization simply come after us down the road?"

"Whoever takes over for Frank will have their hands full for some time. There's a power struggle going on amid New York's criminal element at the moment, and this was the first shot across the bow."

"Do you think that's why someone killed him?"

"It's the most likely explanation. There have been rumors that Anthony Cordero is making moves back in New York. If I had to guess, this is one of his moves."

My eyes narrow. "Anthony Cordero?"

"Yes, he was one of Frank's biggest threats."

"I know who he is. He isn't in New York. He's here. On his honeymoon. I met his new wife."

"The one he met in Havana?"

"Yes."

"How did you meet her? What was she like?" Sam asks. "We haven't been able to learn much about her."

"We met walking on the beach in Islamorada. I liked her. She reminded me of myself actually, before everything fell apart. She invited me over to their house to visit, but with the storm, I never made it."

"You got an invitation to Anthony Cordero's house?"

"I did." I shrug. "What can I say? People like me."

"I would have paid good money to see the expression on his face when Frank Morgan's fiancée walked through his front door."

"You think he knows who I am?"

"I'm sure he's made it his business to know what Frank Morgan is up to, whatever weaknesses he could exploit."

"And what does this mean for us?" I ask. "Frank's gone now. In the beginning, I was, what—a chance for you to get close to him? There's no need for that anymore. Is this where we part ways?"

"Is that what you want?" Sam asks. "To part ways?"

I'm not entirely sure what I want. As horrible as it sounds, Frank Morgan's death seems like a gift that was dropped in my lap, the solution to a problem I was still working my way around.

"I don't know," I reply. "I hadn't thought that far ahead, to be honest. I was still trying to figure out how to get myself out of this mess with Frank, and it seems like Anthony Cordero took care of that for me."

"Then what do you want? Now that you can go back to New York and not worry about your father's debt, about marrying a man you don't love. What do you want from your life?"

"I want the space to figure it out. I would like a job, something I enjoy, that enables me to support myself and to help take care of my mother. Something I'm good at. I'd like friends. Real friends, not ones who pretend to be there for me because it's fashionable. Interesting friends. And I'd like you."

He swallows. "Me?"

"Yes. You."

ON THE JOURNEY FROM MIAMI TO NEW YORK, WE SIT BESIDE EACH other on the train, my hand clutched in Sam's, my head resting on his shoulder. We've made each other no promises, and I like him better for it, for the unspoken understanding between us that I am not interested in tying myself to another for the time being.

I've had my fair share of alcoholic drinks along the journey, the rolling of the train cars sending flashes back to that night. Sam is tense beside me, declining my offer to join me drinking, opting instead to keep his back to the wall, his gaze on the other occupants of the car.

Sam is to return to his job at the Bureau, cracking down on organized crime in New York City, and I hope to establish a new life for myself in the city now that I am really and truly free. For as hard as times are and as much as has been lost, there is a strength that comes from surviving, from enduring, that I draw from now.

"I had an idea," I say. "These investigations you do—"

"No. Absolutely not."

"You didn't even let me finish," I retort.

"Whatever you were going to say is a bad idea. A terrible one."

"You can't know that for sure unless you give me a shot."

"Fine. What is this brilliant plan?"

"These criminals you catch—well, they can't be all that different from most men. I bet they'd open up more to a woman. Men like to brag about their conquests and those sorts of things."

"I'm not using you as bait to catch criminals. You're not a federal agent."

"I'm not a federal agent—*yet*."

"Chasing criminals is not the perfect job for you if that's what you're thinking."

They certainly have female detectives and private investigators. Why shouldn't I join their ranks? The engagement ring I pawned back in Miami will go a long way to helping out financially, but it's hardly enough.

I smile, no point in arguing with him. He'll learn eventually that it's easier to agree with me than to bother protesting. I am nothing if not tenacious. After all, I made it all the way down here by myself.

"Tell me the truth—if you hadn't been on the train looking for me, if you weren't working for Frank, would you have noticed me?" I ask Sam, changing tack. "Would you have approached me?"

"The truth? I noticed you the moment I boarded the train. I could have sat anywhere in the car, but I sat across from you because you were the most beautiful thing I'd ever seen. The most interesting, too. And I thought I'd be close by in case that poor boy had heart troubles with the way you were flirting."

"I was trying to get you to notice me," I confess. "You were staring at your folder like it was the most important thing in the world."

"I was staring at my folder because I'd realized who you were a few minutes after I realized you were fascinating."

"And trouble."

He smiles. "It turns out I like a bit of trouble. More than a bit," he amends.

"It's a long trip to New York."

"It is. Are you going to practice some of those infamous flirting skills on me?"

I laugh. "You might be too easy of a conquest—after all, you're already smitten with me."

"Confident, aren't you?"

"Always." I lean forward, my lips brushing his.

"I might be falling in love with you, Elizabeth Preston," he murmurs against my mouth, his words sending a thrill through me.

The funny thing is, I was just thinking the same thing about him.

For the first time in a long time, the future is bright.

Thirty-Six

Mirta

I shudder as I scan the cover of Sunday's edition of the Miami Beach *Daily Tribune*.

The headline screams of an estimated death toll of one thousand people, and the photos are more gruesome than the headline. By the images of the hurricane's mighty impact, it seems impossible to believe we survived. It's as though it happened to someone else, and I suppose, in a manner it did. We are safely ensconced in the plush surroundings of the Florida East Coast Railway car, headed home to Anthony's apartment in New York. For the locals, their homes have been utterly destroyed, the island they called home likely uninhabitable for some time.

"Interesting reading?"

I glance up at a man dressed in a suit standing over me. His clothes lack the flashiness of Anthony's, the suit more serviceable than extravagant, the tailoring not quite so fine. After the attack during the hurricane, I'm more cautious than I was, and I glance around the train car for Anthony, who left to fetch me a drink.

"I prefer the New York papers, myself," the man adds, his tone friendly, conversational, but for the knowing gleam in his eyes, his focus wholly upon me.

He slides a newspaper toward me, folded to a story on the front page.

Mob Boss Frank Morgan Gunned Down

A picture of the infamous Mr. Morgan stares back at me, his expression unsmiling. He appears considerably older than Anthony, his eyes dark and cold. I recognize the name instantly, of course. A thing like that tends to stick with you when a man tries to have you killed.

I glance up at the man, handing him the newspaper. "Who are you?"

"My apologies. I should have introduced myself earlier." He pulls a badge out of his jacket pocket. "Sam Watson. Federal Bureau of Investigation."

I swallow, lifting my chin a notch, injecting a thread of steel in my voice. I am my mother, I am my aunts, all of the women of my acquaintance who can set a man down with a shift in the tone of their voice.

"And what are you investigating, Mr. Watson?"

"Mr. Morgan had many enemies."

I glance down at the headline once more, heart pounding.

"That probably comes with the territory in his line of work," I reply, careful to keep my voice neutral.

"I bet you're right. Morgan wanted to carve out more of New York for his own territory, but someone stood in his way. Can you guess who that someone was, Mrs. Cordero?"

"Are you bothering my wife, Agent?"

Anthony stands behind the agent, his dark eyes flashing with anger, an unmistakable threat contained in the words "my wife."

"He wasn't," I say, rising from my seat. I move beside my husband, linking my arm with his. Anthony doesn't seem the sort of man given to fits of temper, but there is entirely too much male aggression in the car for my liking.

Agent Watson's gaze darts from me to Anthony and back again.

"Congratulations on your marriage, Mr. Cordero. I confess we were surprised at the Bureau to hear you'd decided to marry, but seeing how lovely she is, I can't say I blame you."

Anthony stiffens beside me, his hand resting protectively on my waist. "Is that all?"

It takes a great deal of restraint to refrain from jabbing Anthony in the side. Male ego notwithstanding, it seems foolish to goad a federal agent investigating a murder you're likely responsible for.

Agent Watson smiles. "No, it isn't, actually. There will be a void in New York now that Morgan's gone. Makes a man wonder who will step in to fill it."

"I confess, I hadn't given it much thought."

"I heard rumors about more than your marriage. There were those in the Bureau who speculated you were going legitimate. That you'd scheduled a meeting with some of Mr. Morgan's representatives to smooth over the transition. Strange that he should turn up dead shortly after this proposed meeting was scheduled."

"Life is full of unusual coincidences," Anthony replies. "Not that I know anything about any meeting, of course. I came down here on my honeymoon. Nothing more."

"Of course," Agent Watson replies, his tone of voice as smooth as Anthony's. "You can't predict what men will do when they're greedy and reckless. But you wouldn't know a thing about that, would you? You're a family man now. I bet you'd do anything to keep that lovely wife of yours safe."

"I would."

Something passes between them, an unspoken conversation occurring between the pauses and the words they say aloud.

Whatever it is, Agent Watson nods. "Best of luck to you both."

He snaps up the newspaper, folding it under his arm and leaving us alone.

"I'm sorry," Anthony whispers, his lips brushing my ear. "He never should have approached you."

"It's fine. It surprised me—that's all."

I move away from Anthony, returning to my seat. He sits next to me, shifting so that his back is toward the rest of the train, his gaze on me.

"Are you going to ask me if I'm responsible?" he asks, his voice low.

"No. I'm not."

I've learned enough about the man I've married to have the answer to my own question without having to ask it. And for better or worse, I've learned enough about myself to know that whatever answer he would give me is not as important as the reason behind his actions.

"You're upset," Anthony says.

"No. I wish we didn't have to worry about such things, wish they weren't part of our lives, but I understand why you did what you did. I know a thing or two about protecting the people you love. After all, I can't say I didn't do the same thing back in Islamorada. Or that I regret it."

It's the first time the word "love" has come up between us, but in this, it's another question I think I know the answer to.

Anthony takes my hand, the diamond glinting in the afternoon sun coming through the windows of the train car. "I meant what I said when we married. I'm going to protect you. That side of my life is over. No one is coming after us now, and if they do, I'll handle it."

What sort of man have I married?

Now I know.

I lean forward and kiss him, my lips curving at his sharp inhale as our mouths touch, a thrill running through me as his arms move to my waist, his palms pressing into my back, pulling me closer to him.

The motion of the train departing the station jolts us apart, and he wraps his arm around me once more, holding me close against his side as we journey north to New York City—as we head home.

I sleep for several hours, using Anthony's shoulder as my pillow. When I wake, it is to the sight of him watching me, his expression softer than any I have seen him wear before.

Perhaps we will be safe now that Frank Morgan is out of the picture. Or maybe this safety is little more than an illusion and there will always be another threat lurking around the corner. Who can say for certain? If I have learned anything in this life, it is that you cannot prepare for the unexpected that sneaks up on you and turns your world upside down.

My husband is happy. My family is safe in Cuba, the revolution over, the storm having missed them entirely. We are alive. I am falling in love.

In this moment, that seems a great many things to be grateful for indeed.

That evening, we make our way to the dining car. Anthony orders us a bottle of champagne, and we dine on a gourmet meal, the conversation around us filled with other passengers discussing the hurricane, guessing at what it must have been like to survive such an ordeal.

Agent Watson sits alone at a table, a drink in front of him, his gaze on the entrance to the dining car, his body tense as though he is anticipating a potential threat to emerge at any moment.

There's a commotion, a low buzz that has me turning my head to see what has caught everyone's attention.

A woman walks into the train car, her red hair gleaming, her beauty eye-catching.

I recognize her instantly from that day on the beach.

Elizabeth.

She walks toward Agent Watson's table, a smile on her lips. There's no question that she's aware of the attention she's drawn or that she enjoys it.

Anthony watches her sit across from Agent Watson, a sharp laugh escaping from his mouth.

"What?"

"I don't think we have anything to worry about with Agent Watson," he answers.

At the moment, the man hardly seems threatening, the obvious affection for the redhead shining in his eyes.

"I met her before the hurricane hit. She said she'd come down from New York by herself."

"She was Frank Morgan's fiancée," Anthony drawls.

I gape at him.

He shrugs. "I make it my business to know everything about my enemies. She was a society girl whose father made a bad deal with Morgan. Can't guess how she got involved with a federal agent, but by the expression on Watson's face, I'd wager he's not too broken up about Morgan's death."

No, he doesn't appear upset at all. He looks like a man in love, and Elizabeth hardly seems to be in mourning.

She's incandescent.

Our gazes meet across the train car, and she inclines her head in a silent nod of recognition.

She smiles.

The train rumbles on, carrying us north, out of Florida, carrying us home.

Thirty-Seven

APRIL 1936

Helen

When the winds cease, and the waters recede, the sand settling back to some semblance of what it once was, palms scattered about the ground, roofs torn off homes—mansions and shacks alike, Mr. Flagler's magical railroad in twisted metal pieces, we are left with the storm's aftermath.

There are funeral pyres everywhere, the bodies of the dead heaped upon one another. There was talk of giving them a proper burial, but those plans were swiftly abandoned in the name of expediency and concern over the potential spread of disease from the decay.

Aunt Alice's body burned in one of those pyres, the desire to bury her on the land she loved taken out of our hands. Instead, we erected a small memorial between the inn and the ocean, a place where I carry flowers and share the thoughts I would have once put in my letters to her.

I hope she would have been proud of the new Sunrise Inn. It is much like the original, with a room for Lucy and me in the back that overlooks the water, a porch where I like to sit and drink my coffee in the early-morning hours.

All around us, people are rebuilding, attempting to recover from the hurricane's aftermath.

The physical structures are the easiest to replace, the rest of it much more difficult.

More than two hundred fifty of the veterans—over half—have perished. The work camps have been obliterated. We now know at least four hundred people are dead throughout the Keys. So many more are missing, unaccounted for, families unable to grieve, to mourn, left without answers.

We will likely never be the same.

Nature has destroyed the railroad that Man spent decades building, the lifeline that was going to bring more tourists, increase opportunities for residents. Nature has destroyed that which so many men sacrificed for.

Ironically, it is those once forgotten men—the heroes who were sent down here so Washington wouldn't have to deal with them—that have brought the most attention to our plight. Their deaths have led the charge for someone to be responsible for what was lost.

There are those who point fingers at the Weather Bureau for the insufficient warnings, for mistakes that were made. There are some who blame the men running the camps. Others, the government itself for once again letting its people down. And there are those who shake their fists at the Almighty, as if it was his hand that scooped up the sand and sea and shook it around, turning our world upside down. There have been investigations, and congressional hearings, and men fired, and to some perhaps that is its own form of justice. There is anger and there will be more; there is grief and there will be more.

They say it is the strongest storm to ever hit the United States, and for those of us who have lived through it, that fact is indisputable. People talk about wind speed, and hurricane categories, and I remember the bodies strewn upon the ground, and see the wreckage of the lives so many attempted to build here. This was an act of

God, and despite the missteps the papers speak of, the mistakes that caused an even greater loss of life than expected, there is an inevitability to all of this. There is nothing we could have done to save ourselves in the face of the storm that battered our shores.

We are a blank slate now, as though the storm came in and re-ordered everything.

The inn isn't ready for guests yet, but Lucy and I share the property with Matthew, who lives in a caretaker's cottage set away from the main building. It's nothing fancy, and there is still much work to be done, but it's clean enough, and most importantly, it is ours.

In the evenings, Lucy and I sit on the porch and gaze out at the water, as I tell her stories of my day, as she coos in response. Each day I marvel at the changes in her, the rapid rate at which she grows. She is a sturdy, healthy child, and while there are moments when I recognize myself in her eyes, her mouth, her nose, her features are her own.

For the first time in as long as I can remember, I have a semblance of peace.

In the months that have passed since the storm, the nightmares have lessened, the fear that Tom will find us a low-level hum in the back of my mind as I go about my days building a life for us near Islamorada. It's always with me, and I don't know that I'll ever forget what I lived through with him, only that each day I'm working on myself, too, growing stronger, forging a new future.

Tom's name is still listed among the missing.

I often wonder if he came up to Islamorada searching for me and was caught in the hurricane's path, or if it was simply an ill-timed fishing trip, his belief that the storm would miss us entirely his downfall, or if he is alive and well, down in Cuba somewhere drinking his life away.

One evening, as I've finished clearing the plates from our dinner, there's a knock at the door.

I cradle Lucy in my arms and walk to the front of the inn, shifting her to the side as I open the door.

A man in a gray suit stands on the porch, his hat in hand, a gold wedding band on his ring finger. And behind him—

My knees buckle in surprise, and I grab the doorframe to steady myself with my free hand.

"John."

He steps forward, standing next to the man in the gray suit.

John is dressed in a suit himself, his skin paler than I remembered, his body less imposing than when he worked on the highway. He looks like a different man, his appearance better suited to the city than life down here, and I run a hand through my hair, belatedly realizing there is a spot of paint on the hem of my dress, the fabric not particularly fine, the flowers faded.

"Helen."

He doesn't say my name as much as breathe it, and the emotion in his eyes—

He is the man I remember.

"You are well?" he asks.

"I am."

He searches my face, and I flush under his perusal.

"I wasn't prepared for guests. We've been painting the inn all day, trying to get it ready to open."

"You're lovely," he replies. "Just as I remembered."

The man in the gray suit beside John—the man I realize I met at the memorial service when John and I said good-bye—Sam—coughs, a smile on his face.

John's gaze drops from me to Lucy.

"She's gotten so big," he says, his voice filled with wonder.

"She has." I fight to keep the tremor from mine, to meet his gaze. "Would you like to hold her?"

He swallows. "I would."

I step back, allowing John and the other man to cross the threshold.

Lucy squirms as I set her in John's arms, the lump in my throat growing at the sight of them together.

"Ma'am—"

I turn toward Sam.

"Is there somewhere we could sit and talk?" he asks. He flashes an official-looking badge proclaiming him to be a federal agent. "Since John's my brother-in-law, and he wanted to come with me today, I said it was fine for him to accompany me, but I'm here on official business."

"Of course."

"It'll be all right, Helen," John murmurs to me, Lucy's little fist wrapped around his finger.

Something tightens around my heart.

I shut the front door behind them, leading them to the main seating area where we will one day welcome guests. There are only two couches in the room now, and I take one, John sitting down beside me, Lucy in his arms.

"You've done a good job with the inn. It's amazing," John says.

I smile. "Thank you. Matthew has been a great help, and we've hired some locals who needed work. Everyone's trying to get their life back after the storm."

Sam takes the opposite couch, his gaze intent on me.

"Would you prefer to have this conversation in private?" Sam asks, his voice surprisingly gentle.

"No, of course not. John can stay."

"I thought it might help to have him here. I'm sorry to tell you, but we found your husband, Tom."

There's a rushing noise in my ears, my heart pounding.

"It looks like there was a dispute of some kind," Sam adds. "We don't know when it happened or who was involved. He was shot. We found this in his pocket."

Sam pulls out a ring, holding it out to me.

The diamond sparkles in the late-afternoon light, the sheer size of it awe-inspiring sitting atop such a delicate band.

Who could afford a ring like this around here? How would Tom's path have crossed with someone who owned such a stone? It must have been a tourist, or—

I blink.

Something about the ring is familiar. Or perhaps, it's that I've seen a similar one before.

"Do you recognize it?" Sam asks, his gaze narrowing.

I do.

The girl on her honeymoon—Mirta.

The one who didn't know how her husband took his coffee.

A lifetime ago at Ruby's.

How did Tom end up with her engagement ring on him? And why was he shot?

"He might have stolen it," Sam adds. "Pardon me, but it's the likeliest assumption we've come up with. Was your husband worried about money? Did he run with a rough crowd?"

I can't do more than nod, because who isn't worried about money in times like these?

Who isn't a little desperate?

I square my shoulders, handing the diamond back to Sam.

I know enough of my husband's nature to wish Mirta well wherever she is.

"No," I lie. "I don't recognize the ring."

Lucy stirs in John's arms, a soft sigh falling from her lips, and he passes her to me wordlessly, as though it is the most natural thing in the world.

"I'm sorry to disturb you, ma'am; I have a few more questions and then I'll go," Sam replies. "I'll be honest with you; I work on an organized crime task force. Rum-running was a real big industry in these parts during Prohibition, and some of these fisherman got involved with some nefarious creatures—smuggling and the like. Some of them didn't break those ties when Prohibition ended. Was your husband involved in anything like that?"

"I don't know. He didn't talk to me about what he did."

"Is there anyone who might have had a grudge against your husband?" Sam asks. "Who might have had a reason to shoot him?"

I meet his gaze, and I no longer see the agent in front of me in his natty little suit, but the girl from Ruby's in her elegant dress, the fear and hopelessness in her eyes, and then that flash of fire.

"No one I can think of."

The agent takes a deep breath, bracing himself to deliver an invisible blow, like a man's fist in that moment right before impact.

The prayer runs through my mind again over and over again, the dream of the little boat bobbing in the water, of my husband tipping over the side.

And then—

"Your husband is dead."

AFTER SAM IS GONE, AFTER I'VE FED LUCY AND PUT HER DOWN FOR a nap, I stand on the front porch of the Sunrise Inn and stare out at that blue expanse of sea that months ago brought such destruction. Today, the ocean is calm, the sun glittering off the water as far as the eye can see.

In this moment, it's beautiful.

I remember the boy I married who loved the sea, the boy I fell in love with when I was little more than a child myself. Maybe Tom was never a good man and I couldn't see it. Maybe he did the best he could and life knocked him down until he became someone unrecognizable. And maybe the truth is somewhere in between. I don't know. I hope wherever he is, he is in a better place.

I know I am.

Footsteps sound behind me, and then John's hand is at my waist, resting there lightly, a question in the gesture.

John stayed behind after Sam left, citing his need to return to his new wife and their honeymoon down in Key West.

I take a deep breath, praying for courage now. "How is New York?" I ask.

"The same as it always was. Too big, too noisy, too hectic. It was good that I went back, though. Elizabeth's married now. She and Sam are happy together. Her mother is settled with a nurse. Things are as they should be."

"And you?"

"I've missed you," he says.

The words knock the wind out of me.

"Missed Lucy. Missed this place, if you can believe it. When Sam told me he was coming down here, that they'd found your husband, I insisted on coming with him.

"You've built a life for yourself and for Lucy," he continues, "and I understand if you need time, but if you could ever see yourself having a life with me, I would like nothing more. I want to spend the rest of my days making you happy, building a future with you and Lucy. I would like a family. I would like you both to be my family."

I move into his embrace, hesitantly at first, leaning up on my tiptoes and pressing my lips to his. John freezes, and then it's as though he comes to life, his arms wrapping around my waist gently, returning the kiss.

It's strange how your life can change so quickly, how one moment you can barely eke by, desperation filling your days, and suddenly, out of the unimaginably horrific, a glimmer of something beautiful can appear like a bud pushing through the hard-formed earth.

There's so much broken around us; maybe all we can do is try to fix each other, do what we can to preserve these precious moments in a world where there is so much sadness and loss.

The dream I used to have when I lived in a cramped cottage, in a strangling marriage, disappears, and another takes its place. I'm filled with an emotion I haven't felt in such a long time that I almost don't recognize it, the taste of it sweet and tangy in my mouth—

Hope.

A little house somewhere quiet. A child's laughter. An arm wrapped around my waist at night, a hand holding mine. A future I dreamed of years ago that I thought I'd lost somewhere along the way.

Maybe some would say my dreams are too small. Perhaps they would dream of railroads that go over the sea, great, wonderful things. Maybe others want riches and jewels, a chance to travel the globe.

For me, this is enough:

A corner of paradise in this wretched world that I am able to call my own.

Author's Note

In the late summer of 2017, I was nearly finished drafting *When We Left Cuba*, and I was beginning to brainstorm my next project. It was hurricane season, and as a Florida native, I was all too familiar with the sense of uncertainty and fear nature can conjure. In the hurricane coverage, there was a story of a hurricane I was unfamiliar with—the 1935 Labor Day hurricane, one of the strongest and deadliest storms to strike the United States. It wasn't the hurricane itself that caught my eye, though; it was the story of World War I veterans who had been sent down to work on the highway and whose lives were tragically lost. The more I researched the story, the more it called to me, and I soon began to envision the women who would populate the book and how their lives would intersect.

In my research, *Storm of the Century* by Willie Drye, *Category 5: The 1935 Labor Day Hurricane* by Thomas Neil Knowles, *Hemingway's Hurricane: The Great Florida Keys Storm of 1935* by Phil Scott, and *Last Train to Paradise* by Les Standiford were all invaluable resources, and I highly recommend them if you'd like to learn more about the Labor Day hurricane.

The hurricane of 1935 that struck the Florida Keys is one of the strongest Atlantic hurricanes in history. While the death toll is disputed, numbers range between approximately four hundred and eight hundred lost souls. More than a third of the veterans who were living on Windley and Matecumbe Keys were killed by the storm, and it is generally accepted that more than half of the residents and workers caught in the hurricane lost their lives.

The Overseas Extension of the Florida East Coast Railway— once referred to as "Flagler's Folly"—was destroyed and never rebuilt, and in 1938, the new Overseas Highway was opened using stretches of the destroyed Overseas Railroad. After World War II, Key West became a thriving tourist destination, and remnants of "Flagler's Folly" can still be seen off in the distance.

Acknowledgments

The past few years have been a dream beyond anything I could have imagined, and I am *so* grateful to all of the booksellers, bloggers, librarians, readers, and reviewers who have embarked on this adventure with me. Thanks for embracing my characters and their stories.

Thank you to Reese Witherspoon and the amazing team at Hello Sunshine for all of your support for my books and for sharing my work with your fabulous book club family.

To my editor Kate Seaver and agent Kevan Lyon—I couldn't do any of this without you, and I definitely wouldn't want to. Thanks for championing my work and for making this dream come true.

I am so fortunate to work with an incredibly talented group of people who make my job possible. Thanks to my publicist Diana Franco and marketing representative Fareeda Bullert for working so hard on my behalf. Thank you to the extraordinary team at Berkley: Madeline McIntosh, Allison Dobson, Ivan Held, Christine Ball, Claire Zion, Jeanne-Marie Hudson, Craig Burke, Tawanna Sullivan, Sarah Blumenstock, Mary Geren, and Stephanie Felty, as well as the subrights department and the Berkley art department, and all of the others who support my books. Thanks to Patricia Nelson and Marsal Lyon Literary Agency for your work on my behalf and to the team at Frolic Media.

To my friends and family—thanks for all of your love and encouragement. You're the best.

The
Last Train
to
Key West

CHANEL CLEETON

Questions for Discussion

1. At the beginning of the novel, Helen says, "People are what circumstances make them." Do you agree with her statement? Why or why not? Are there places in the book where this sentiment seems to be true? How do the characters demonstrate this?

2. The hurricane hits Key West in 1935, during the Great Depression. What effect does the Depression have on the characters, on the setting? How do larger world events shape characters' lives in the book?

3. What parallels do you see between the effects the hurricane has on the characters and that of fighting in the Great War?

4. How is the treatment of the veterans of the Great War similar to the problems faced by society during the Great Depression? Were you surprised to hear about the veterans' lives after they came home from the war and some of the challenges they faced?

5. Helen and John have both experienced trauma. How does it shape them? What similarities do you see between their experiences and the way they cope with them? What differences?

6. Mirta and Elizabeth both come from wealthy families that have fallen on hard times. What similarities do you see in their personali-

ties? What differences? How do those similarities and differences influence the choices they make throughout the novel?

7. *The Last Train to Key West* alternates between Helen's, Mirta's, and
Elizabeth's perspectives. Which character did you identify with most?
How do they grow and change throughout the novel?

8. Elizabeth tells Sam that the Depression has been particularly hard
on women. What examples do you see throughout the book where
women's lives are influenced by society's expectations for them? How
do they react to these expectations?

9. During the Depression, marriage rates dropped significantly. At the
same time, marriage plays an important role in the characters' lives.
How do the heroines' views on marriage change throughout the
novel? Do the women find power in their relationships?

10. Mirta and Anthony's marriage changes throughout the novel.
What shifts do you see in their relationship? What roles do they take
on, and how do they evolve in those roles?

11. All of the main characters are searching for something at the start
of the novel. Do you they ultimately find what they were looking for?
How does the journey change them? What were they really searching
for to begin with?

12. The characters' lives are largely shaped by the hurricane and its
aftermath. Have you ever experienced a natural disaster? How did the
experience influence you?

CHANEL CLEETON is the *New York Times* and *USA Today* bestselling author of *When We Left Cuba* and the Reese Book Club pick *Next Year in Havana*. Originally from Florida, she grew up on stories of her family's exodus from Cuba following the events of the Cuban Revolution. Her passion for politics and history continued during her years spent studying in England, where she earned a bachelor's degree in international relations from Richmond, the American International University in London, and a master's degree in global politics from the London School of Economics and Political Science. Chanel also received her Juris Doctor from the University of South Carolina School of Law. She loves to travel and has lived in the Caribbean, Europe, and Asia.

Ready to find
your next great read?

Let us help.

Visit prh.com/nextread